"She punched Alex Thompson today."

"And if you show up tomorrow in one of these outfits, your social standing is going to skyrocket," Corey enthused. "Just don't forget about us when you're hobnobbing with the Notables."

I snorted. "*Hobnobbing?* Yeah, right. Chelsea Halloway and I are going to become lunch buddies. Get real."

"Well, my work here is done." He flapped a hand in the direction of the mirror. "Go admire yourself some more."

It was strange feeling like I was at the part in a movie when the camera zooms in to capture the expression that says it all: a mixture of doe-eyed innocence, confusion, amazement, and nerves on the plucky heroine's face. That's kind of how I looked—a little panicky, but pretty nonetheless. And "pretty" is not a word that ever gets applied to me. Unless I put a lot of work into it and hit "cute," I usually land squarely in the "all right" category.

But the girl staring back at me in the mirror looked more like the leading lady instead of the trusty sidekick.

One thing was obvious: I wasn't going to be Invisible anymore.

More by Marni Bates

AWKWARD

DECKED WITH HOLLY

Published by Kensington Publishing Corp.

INVISIBLE

Marni Bates

KENSINGTON PUBLISHING CORP.

www.kensingtonbooks.com

K TEEN BOOKS are published by

Kensington Publishing Corp.
119 West 40th Street
New York, NY 10018

All Kensington titles, imprints, and distributed lines are available at special quantity discounts for bulk purchases for sales promotion, premiums, fund-raising, and educational or institutional use.

Special book excerpts or customized printings can also be created to fit specific needs. For details, write or phone the office of the Kensington Special Sales Manager: Kensington Publishing Corp., 119 West 40th Street, New York, NY 10018. Attn. Special Sales Department. Phone: 1-800-221-2647.

Kensington and K Teen Reg. U.S. Pat. & TM Off.

ISBN-13: 978-0-7582-6938-6
ISBN-10: 0-7582-6938-2
First Kensington Trade Paperback Printing: July 2013

eISBN-13: 978-0-7582-8913-1
eISBN-10: 0-7582-8913-8
First Kensington Electronic Edition: July 2013

10 9 8 7 6 5 4 3 2 1

Printed in the United States of America

This book is for everyone who feels like they've been cast
as the sidekick in someone else's story.
It's never too late to be your own main character.

Acknowledgments

No author is an island. At the very least, we're ships that bounce around a heavily populated archipelago that includes best friends and bloggers, reviewers and readers, and friendly neighborhood baristas who keep the coffee coming.

I love you all so freaking much.

I'm especially grateful to have superagent Laurie McLean captaining my ship. She has nobly prevented me from going overboard on multiple occasions. You're the best, Laurie!

A big thank-you to my KTeen editors extraordinaire: Megan Records and Alicia Condon. Without these ladies . . . well, I'd be tied to the mast by people who appreciate it when a story actually, y'know, *ends*.

Karen Bates, Abigail Dock, and Marina Adair have all saved my ship on multiple occasions. They've helped me bail out water when I was sinking faster than the *Titanic*'s twenty-five-mile-per-hour descent to the ocean floor.

Lastly, I'd like to thank my big sister, Shayna. I know it's not always easy to have an author in the family, especially when everyone assumes she's recounting more fact than fiction. So for the record, I'd like to state that this particular ship quite likes having an anchor in her life. I'd be lost without you.

INVISIBLE

Chapter 1

Nobody notices the best friend of an overnight Internet sensation.

Which in a lot of ways is a *really* good thing. Thousands of people around the world don't rate the hotness of *my* every outfit. No magazines pass judgment about what Smith High School nobody Jane Smith wears on a daily basis. At most, I get a handful of puns tossed my way because of the unfortunate coincidence that leaves me sharing a last name with my school. Best of all, I don't have to deal with unfounded rumors that I'm cheating on my hockey-captain boyfriend.

Not that I have a boyfriend.

But that's why I was perfectly happy leaving the title of America's Most Awkward Girl to Mackenzie Wellesley, aka my best friend since elementary school.

And I was thrilled that my other best friend, Corey O'Neal, was now dating the lead singer from the rock band ReadySet. Sure, I had my doubts about how long his secret long-distance relationship with Timothy Goff would last . . . but I was still excited for Corey.

Psyched for them both.

Really.

But even though I was happy for them, that didn't mean it wasn't a huge adjustment for me—one that came with absolutely no warning. After all, *nobody* at Smith High School could have anticipated my two geeky best friends going from Invisible to *famous* in under a week. They had somehow managed to even out-Notable the Notables—the effortlessly popular kids that every school has but which every guidance counselor assures incoming students don't really exist. You know the type: girls with short skirts and big, erm, *pom-poms,* and athletic guys who drool over the aforementioned girls' skirts.

Kenzie's overnight-sensation status skyrocketed her well beyond their level of popularity, making her a regular geek superhero: going where no Invisible had gone before.

Which was great for her. But for me?

Not so much.

The whole time Kenzie and Corey were going to parties and traveling with rock stars and appearing on *The Ellen De-Generes Show*—I was doing my homework. It's not that my two best friends ditched me . . . though it was hard not to see it that way—it's just that they were busier now. That's why they had less time for me. Correction: why they had *no* time for me. Because their new relationships required both care and attention.

Which left me . . . alone.

That's when my Invisibility started to annoy me. Back when we were a band of geeks, everything was fine. I didn't care if nobody at Smith High School could pick me out of a lineup, because my best friends were in the exact same position. That's what made it fun. We could revel in our geekdom, secure in the knowledge that no matter what high school threw at us, our friendship would remain intact.

Until Mackenzie became famous for attempting some seriously unnecessary CPR on a football player who just wanted the crazy girl to stop trying to jump-start his heart. And I was left as the last nerd standing.

That's why I decided to try getting a little attention for a change.

Only . . . well, I never expected it to happen the way that it did.

To be fair: Nobody warned me about how easy it is to get in over your head when your best friends have backstage passes and unrestricted access to all things Hollywood. Probably because . . . well, almost nobody has that problem. And I really should have figured it out myself. *Of course,* when you piss off (even accidentally) the rich, powerful, and famous, they'll come at you with everything in their arsenal.

I just didn't consider that part of the equation until it was too late.

Not until I experienced firsthand just how easy it was to go from a newspaper byline to a headline . . . and how fully one story could blast my well-ordered, well-regulated, well-planned life to hell.

Chapter 2

"Are you sure you're ready for this, Jane?"

"Um . . . yes?"

"But you don't confront people. Ever. So maybe telling Mr. Elliot your idea for changing the school paper isn't such a good plan."

I sat up straighter against the vinyl seat coverings of the school bus. "Gee, thanks for that vote of confidence, Isobel. I feel so much better."

My friend Isobel, who had been nervously pushing her glasses higher up on her nose, paused mid-gesture.

"I'm sorry, Jane. I didn't mean—"

Great, not only was I almost trembling with nerves, but I had managed to upset my only friend who *hadn't* recently become famous. I wished Kenzie were still riding the bus with me. She would have instantly recognized my sarcasm as poorly disguised panic talking. But ever since she'd started dating the captain of Smith High School's hockey team, Logan Beckett, he picked her up in his car. I tried not to take this change personally, but I still missed her. Don't get me wrong: Isobel's great. It's just that we didn't have a shared history. No inside jokes. No meaningful glances that communicate everything we're thinking.

And that meant I had to apologize.

"No, I'm sorry. I don't mean to sound snippy. It's just . . . nerves," I explained. "This *really* matters to me so . . . please tell me this isn't a huge mistake."

Isobel looked at me owlishly, her natural expression behind thick horn-rimmed glasses that she probably thought helped her blend with the hipster crowd. They didn't. "It *might* not be a disaster," she hedged.

"So you think I can get Mr. Elliot to add a fiction page to the school newspaper?"

She paused thoughtfully, and I knew that she would thoroughly analyze the situation before shelling out advice. That's why she was the first person I told about my plan to be more involved with *The Smithsonian*. Plus, I trusted her to be painfully honest with me—even if I didn't want to hear it. Isobel couldn't lie convincingly unless her life depended on it . . . and maybe not even then.

She sighed and looked up at me, concern evident in her eyes. "We're talking about *Mr. Elliot,* here! He chews out people all the time. Didn't you tell me he made a girl cry last week? How are *you* going to persuade him to do anything? Bad idea. Really bad."

She was absolutely right. Unfortunately, it was also my only plan. Well, my only feasible one, unless time travel became possible. In which case, I would just rewind about a month and prevent Kenzie from ever becoming an overnight YouTube sensation.

That would have solved everything.

I let my head fall forward and land with a low *whump* against the vinyl-covered bus seat in front of me.

"Sorry, Jane. You know I love you, but . . . you're the biggest pushover Smith High School has ever seen."

"Hey!"

"Well, it's true. Take that group project for your English

class you were complaining about last week. You practically wrote and researched all of Shake's section as well as your own."

I stared at her—not because she had botched one of the nicknames for the Notable Evil Trio: Chelsea, Fake, and Bake—but because I'd never heard Isobel call me a pushover before. I didn't think she was in the best position to criticize me, given the way she quivers in terror whenever a Notable comes within fifteen feet of her, but apparently that didn't stop her.

"Fake. Not Shake," I corrected, mentally conceding that Isobel's nickname worked too. The girl definitely puts some shimmy into her, ahem, *assets* whenever she's around a Notable guy. But since everything about Steffani Larson, from the tips of her plastic fingernails to the roots of her blond hair, is capital-letter FAKE, I wanted her original nickname to stick. I had no doubt, given the frequency with which Ashley visited tanning salons, that "Bake" would describe her perfectly for years to come. Especially because nothing rhymes with "orange."

Not that I would ever use either nickname around anyone but my closest friends.

"And what was I supposed to do?" I continued defensively. "If I hadn't researched her part, the grade for our whole presentation would've tanked."

"Maybe if she hadn't expected you to pick up the slack, she would've done it herself."

I rolled my eyes. Fake would do her part of an assignment on the same day zombies descended upon our high school and ate everyone's brains. Even then, she'd probably find a way to flirt a zombie into eating the geeks first. But at that particular moment what I needed wasn't an in-depth analysis of Fake; I needed a partner in crime. But I no longer knew who to ask for good advice. Logan, Kenzie, and Corey would all tell me that there was no reason for me to worry about being entirely alone. That I was making a big deal out of nothing. Then again, it's easy for the hockey player, the Internet sensation, and the boyfriend of a rock star to shrug and say *No big deal.* I was the only one most commonly referred to as *Mackenzie's little friend.*

I'd had enough of that to last a lifetime.

Especially since I'd only just started to emerge from under my sister's shadow. Okay, maybe that's a bit of an exaggeration, because it's not like I'd done anything to separate myself from former Notable queen Elle Smith's legacy—except avoid everything that she listed on her college application sheets. And since my sister was involved in *everything,* my options for social expansion were pretty limited. Not unless I wanted to go back to being known as *Elle Smith's dorky kid sister,* and that held absolutely no appeal for me.

None at all.

So I couldn't go anywhere near the dance squad. Or the cheerleaders. Or the drama club. Or the yearbook committee. And I was going to stay far, far away from the Miss Portland Pageant. Which left me with only a handful of viable options if my newspaper plan didn't work out: Speech and Debate (which would require public speaking . . . yeah, not in this lifetime) or the chess club (which would probably only further cement my geeky reputation).

If I wasn't careful, I could easily slip into some kind of nerd vortex and disappear right in plain sight.

And then I really would be Invisible.

So I kept sorting through potential plans. Maybe I should wait for the next issue to be released before I asked about including a fiction page. Maybe I should discuss it with Mr. Elliot outside of class. Maybe I should follow the chain of command and ask our editor-in-charge-of-everything, Lisa Anne. Maybe . . . I couldn't decide on anything.

Even making eye contact with Mr. Elliot seemed risky.

"So what do you suggest, Isobel? That I just keep correcting grammar on the paper forever?"

Isobel pushed up her glasses again. She could have gotten them fixed so that they wouldn't slide down her nose, but I doubt the idea had ever occurred to her.

"I think you *should* discuss it with him. I just don't think you will." The bus lurched to a stop at Smith High School, but that didn't slow Isobel down. "Are you honestly going to assert yourself this time?"

Well, when she put it *that* way. "I . . . hope so."

"Good luck, then. Put your game face on. Show no mercy. All that good stuff."

I stared at her and then burst out laughing. "You sound completely insane."

Isobel smiled. "I don't do pep talks. So . . . just, go get 'em or something."

"Will do, chief."

Isobel swung her backpack, bulging to the point of explosion, across her shoulders. Then she tugged at her mousy brown hair until long strands dislodged from her ponytail and swung down to frame her round face.

"Don't wimp out then."

For someone who hated pep talks, Isobel wasn't doing half bad. She also had a point. As much as I didn't want to admit it, I've got a tendency to postpone important conversations. But nothing would ever change if I continued silently adding semicolons to other people's newspaper stories instead of writing my own.

My days of being a pushover were over.

Except when I entered the journalism classroom to find Mr. Elliot already mid-rant . . . I kept my mouth firmly shut.

The yelling wasn't exactly an infrequent occurrence, since even on his best days Mr. Elliot was unpredictable. He believed that his yelling would prove to us that he cared. And according to that rationale, he successfully demonstrated that he cared. A lot.

It's always best to let him get the ranting out of his system before doing anything controversial—you know, like *breathing* too loudly.

Although I sincerely doubted that any of his long-winded speeches about "stepping up our game" had ever made a difference. Our class was split between the kids who were using their work on the school paper to impress colleges and the ones who thought it would be easy to ditch and go smoke behind the gym. The handful of us who actually cared about the quality of *The Smithsonian* fell under the jurisdiction of Lisa Anne Montgomery: senior editor of the school paper, future Yale or Harvard graduate, and all-around Most Likely to Succeed shoe-in. I had no trouble imagining her golden future, which would probably include hosting an Emmy-winning political talk show.

Good morning! You're live with Lisa Anne! It's time to welcome our first guest, former vice president Al Gore. So tell me, Al, what projects are you working on now?

She'd be a media darling. I predicted that within the next ten years, Smith High School would start begging for Lisa Anne to give the convocation speech at graduation . . . which she'd probably have to decline in order to interview wounded soldiers or angry jihadists or something.

Not that I'm jealous of her.

Much.

"Smith!" My head jerked up from my notebook, where I had been doodling little gravestones with my name on them. I'm not overly superstitious, but that didn't seem like a good omen. Although as far as evil portents go, being singled out in the middle of a Mr. Elliot tirade was significantly more damning than a series of morbid scribbles.

I just hoped that nobody noticed the way my hand instantly started trembling.

"Um . . . yes?"

Mr. Elliot waved his arms in a brilliant imitation of a windmill. "For the past year, Smith has done a great job with the copyediting and . . . other things like, erm, layout. That side of journalism is important too! More of you should get involved. *It's time to step up your game!*"

It's possible I would've felt honored if he hadn't been completely off base. And if he had taken the time to address me by my first name, which I wasn't entirely sure he knew. I really hated the way he called everyone (except Lisa Anne) solely by their last names, as if we were soldiers in the military waiting for our marching orders.

It always made me hyperaware of the fact that I'm the geekier of the two Smith girls.

So I took a deep breath and said, "Uh, actually, Mr. Elliot—" before I lost the ability to speak. Formulating a complete sentence seemed impossible with all eyes in my journalism class staring at me.

"What, Smith?" he snapped impatiently. I definitely should have kept my mouth shut.

Too late now.

"It's just . . . this is my *third* year copyediting. And I was wondering if maybe I could . . . well, do something else?"

A frown furrowed his brow, and my stomach clenched. He was going to say no. He was going to insist that my copyediting was a vital part of the paper. I would graduate from Smith High School next year having contributed nothing more to *The Smithsonian* than a handful of punctuation marks.

And I'd continue being universally ignored while my two best friends flitted off to Hollywood without me.

"Listen up, everyone," Mr. Elliot barked, panning the room. "This is what I'm talking about! Smith is *finally* stepping up to the plate, and we're going to run with it." He skewered me with one of his intense looks. "You've got the front page, Smith. Talk to Lisa Anne."

My mouth fell open in shock, but before I could say, *I don't want the front page! I want to write fiction,* he held up a hand to stop me.

"Make it work, Smith. Now where was I? Right, we really need to improve our advertising. . . ."

He went off on an entirely different tirade, leaving me reeling in his wake.

The front page? I had never wanted the front page. If my fiction plan didn't work out, I had been hoping he might promote me to the cafeteria beat. Maybe let me write an article about the chocolate chip muffins—something small so that I could get my bearings on the actual writing side of things. I never meant for Mr. Elliot to send me from copy editor to front-page reporter overnight. It sounded like a Cinderella, rags-to-riches type deal, only this particular pauper didn't know how to dance at a grand ball.

And she wanted time to learn the steps so that she wouldn't trip over her stilettos and land flat on her face.

I had no ideas. I had no plans. I had no experience.

What I did have was an impulsive order given by an unstable teacher—and an irate Lisa Anne, who marched over as soon as Mr. Elliot finished ranting.

"What the hell is this?" she demanded. "Amateur hour! Okay, let me put this simply, Grammar Girl: Mr. Elliot might be the teacher, but you answer to me. Now, if you don't deliver the steamiest, sexiest, most groundbreaking cover story I've ever seen, I will personally ensure that proofreading will be the closest you ever get to journalism. Are we clear?"

Oh yeah. She'd be a media darling . . . and a complete terror to work with when she wasn't broadcasting. I could imagine a never-ending rotation of interns burning out under the strain of her demands.

I gulped. "Yeah, we're clear."

"Excellent." Lisa Anne straightened the collar of her button-down shirt. She was the only senior who always appeared ready for a Harvard admissions interview. I thought just the number of preppy argyle sweaters she wore on a regular basis ought to qualify her for admittance: After all, she already looked the part.

"Obviously, you aren't ready to take on this challenge alone," Lisa Anne continued. Even though I had been thinking the exact same thing, hearing the words drip disdainfully from her perfectly glossed lips put me on the defensive.

"I can wri—"

"If I thought the matter was subjective, I would have refrained from using the word 'obviously.' This is *not* up for discussion."

I didn't like it, but I couldn't contradict her. She held the power and we both knew it. Then again, Lisa Anne never doubted her abilities: She pushed until she got what she wanted. And even when she shut me down with a single sentence, I couldn't stop myself from envying Lisa Anne's extreme self-confidence.

Nobody would ever dismiss Lisa Anne Montgomery as the unimportant best friend.

"Scott!"

My head snapped up.

"What are you doing?" I hissed. "I'll be fine. I don't need him. I'm good. The story will practically write itself."

Lisa Anne raised a single eyebrow, waiting for the rest of my lies to fade out.

"Really, that's not necessary. Please. Don't."

"Grammar Girl, I don't care whether you think it's necessary. My priority is the paper. Front-page stories require front-page photographs." She paused and together we watched my nemesis, Scott Fraser, walk over. All five feet eleven inches of rumpled hotness in black Converse sneakers, dark blue jeans, a slightly wrinkled black T-shirt, and a gray jacket, with his ever-present Nikon in hand. "Scott, Jane is your new assignment."

His green eyes were speckled with brown, and he made no attempt to hide his derision.

"Lucky me."

He went heavy on the sarcasm.

Lisa Anne shrugged. "Well, you're in charge of making sure she doesn't bomb, since I don't have time to babysit. The issue goes out on Tuesday. So do whatever is necessary to make this work." She turned back to me. "Don't forget, Grammar Girl, screw this up and you'll never write for *The Smithsonian* again." She smiled. "No pressure."

I was so dead.

Chapter 3

"**S**o what's your angle?"

I couldn't get over the weirdness of sitting across from Scott Fraser, as if nothing had happened between us. As if I hadn't tried to befriend him when he transferred from some private school in Los Angeles . . . only to be stabbed in the back when he told Lisa Anne, "Jane? She doesn't have what it takes to become a reporter."

Direct quote.

I guess if you're an attractive seventeen-year-old guy with a talent for photography you can blow off the geeks as soon as you get settled in. That's probably how Scott viewed the situation, anyway. Not that I called him out on the whole "she doesn't have what it takes" thing. Isobel was right: I'm not good with confrontation.

So I didn't stalk over and yell: *How do you know I can't hack it as a reporter? I haven't written so much as a muffin review! Thanks a lot for trashing me, jerk!*

Instead, I did a silent 180-degree turn and headed straight to the library without saying a word. The worst part was that I had honestly thought we were becoming friends. That's why I had arrived early to our journalism class, to see if he wanted to hang out with Corey, Kenzie, and me in Portland. I thought he might enjoy a brief respite from the boredom that is life in

Forest Grove. I was just about to invite him when I over-heard him talking to Lisa Anne. I fled without being noticed at all, because even in the midst of a verbal trashing, I was still a freaking master at the art of invisibility.

Too bad I felt like crap.

Still, I had wanted to give him the benefit of the doubt. Even though the likelihood that Scott would apologize and explain that it was all just one big misunderstanding . . . not exactly good betting odds. I mean, part of me knew that was never going to happen. Not in this lifetime.

I just hadn't wanted to accept it.

At the time, Kenzie's fame was skyrocketing, and it was just starting to sink in that no matter how her newfound no-toriety worked out, nothing would be the same again. The American public would either love her or mock her merci-lessly, but in either scenario, the spotlight would follow her every move.

Relegating me back into the shadows.

That's why I had hoped that the whole thing with Scott had been blown out of proportion in my head. I didn't want to believe anything bad about my one new friend—someone who hadn't known me since elementary school, who didn't care about my sister's popularity, who never treated me like the pathetic sidekick.

I couldn't have been more wrong about the creep.

Turns out the reason he spent his first week at Smith High School fiddling on Photoshop next to me had nothing to do with my wit, my personality, or my dimpled grin. He had only *pretended* to like me because he wanted access to Kenzie.

I should've guessed as much from the very beginning.

Instead, I was blindsided when Lisa Anne congratulated him publicly on his amazing photo of *my* best friend, frozen in fear, as the media mobbed her. The one he must have snapped the day I attempted to introduce them to each other.

In the end he hadn't even needed my help to capture his front-page-worthy photo—rendering me even more obsolete than before. Unbeknownst to me, that must have been the day he completed his metamorphosis from The New Kid to the well-accepted jerk. So when Lisa Anne led everyone in a round of applause, I blanched, mumbled some excuse, and fled to the bathroom. Scott and I had scrupulously avoided each other ever since. On the rare occasion that the limited number of computers forced us to sit next to each other, we both pulled out our iPods.

It was actually kind of amazing that the two of us hadn't been forced together sooner.

I just wished my luck had lasted a little bit longer.

Rubbing my forehead tiredly, I told myself that armed with my plan I could handle Scott Fraser. It might even have been true if Mr. Elliot hadn't effectively derailed me fifteen minutes before.

"I'm sorry, can you repeat that?" I muttered when I finally noticed him looking at me expectantly.

That was one way to make it clear that I refused to be intimidated on this assignment.

Not.

"I said, what's your angle?" Scott sounded half bored, one quarter irritated, and one quarter smugly certain that I could never pull off a front-page story.

"I don't know yet," I admitted.

He crossed his arms, and I would have loved to say something—anything—to remove that stupid smirk from his face. Unfortunately, I had a feeling he was absolutely right: I wasn't ready for this.

"Do you have any ideas?"

"Erm . . . no?" I probably shouldn't have let my answer sound like a question.

"Well, that's helpful, Grammar Girl."

I glared at him. The only time our sportswriter, Brad, had

asked him to edit an article, Scott had waved dismissively in my general direction and said, "Grammar Girl can fix it." That stupid nickname had spread like wildfire and successfully removed the necessity for anyone on the newspaper to actually learn my name.

But I couldn't do anything juvenile for payback. I had to be the bigger person if I wanted to prove that I could do more than apply basic rules of punctuation. Then I'd be taken seriously when I suggested adding a fiction page to the paper.

I just had to nail this story first.

"Could we hold off on the animosity? I got this assignment all of *five minutes ago!* Just . . . give me a second!"

Scott's smirk never wavered. "Want me to come back sometime next week? Think you'll have processed it by then?"

I took a deep breath and pictured him as a toothy iguana that I could blow up with the help of a handy grenade. Much better.

"Regardless of what you think, Scott, I'm writing the front-page story. And since your reputation is on the line, you should want it to succeed every bit as much as I do."

I was bluffing, of course. Our stakes were nowhere near the same. If he took crappy photos it'd be disregarded as a fluke. If *I* bombed I'd be Grammar Girl for the rest of high school, or worse, I might be ignored completely.

But Scott didn't need to know that.

"You think you can mess up my place on the paper?" His grin widened as if the thought were too ridiculous for words. "Not in this lifetime, Grammar Girl."

Had it been anyone else I might have felt bad about lying right to their face to suit my own needs. But since it was Scott Fraser . . . not so much. I leaned forward and met his gaze evenly.

"We both know you're still considered the newbie. And a few decent photos for the paper—"

"*Decent!*" Scott interrupted.

"Yep. Average shots at best, really," I lied. "Definitely not enough to prove that you're consistent. So if *we* don't deliver a killer front-page spread, get ready to say hello to the bottom corner on page four."

Scott's smirk vanished.

Maybe I should reconsider joining the drama club. Sure, my sister starred in every theater production before she graduated, leaving a legacy I'll never be able to fill . . . but it might not be the worst extracurricular activity for me. If I could make Scott buy that line of total crap, then maybe I did show promise as an actress.

Or maybe I had a future as a psychologist, because I knew *exactly* how to maneuver Scott into helping me out. Time to pound on some of his new-kid fears and watch as his apprehension about the wildly unpredictable Mr. Elliot took hold.

At least, that's how it would have worked with *anyone* else.

He gave me a look of pure, smug confidence. "There won't be a problem with my photos. If you have a story, I'll have a shot. Come up with anything yet?"

I tried to recall Lisa Anne's instructions. She wanted something sexy for the front page. Something provocative. Something that positively reeked of scandal.

Yeah, I had nothing. But lying to Scott's face was becoming startlingly easy.

"Sure. I've got ideas."

He looked at me expectantly.

"I'll—uh, I'll just . . . go undercover."

He didn't even try to hide his derisive laughter. "Right. 'Jane Smith: Undercover Girl Reporter and the Case of the Missing Lunch Money.' "

He had a point. Going undercover sounded exciting in theory in a spy-next-door kind of way—but it's sort of pointless if you don't have an objective beyond writing . . . something.

There has to be a target before there can be an infiltration, which left me right back where I started: screwed.

"I can do this!" I insisted.

"Sure you can, Nancy Drew."

"Nancy Drew was a detective, not a reporter. Get your stories straight."

"*My* stories aren't the ones you should be worrying about, Grammar Girl. You're the one with a front page to fill. So either figure it out or scurry back to your editing cave. I don't care what you do as long as you don't waste my time."

I straightened my shoulders and mentally ground his precious camera into the gum-littered pavement sidewalks of Smith High School. "I'll have something for you by the end of the day. At the latest."

Hopefully.

He nodded. "Then I'll see you at lunch." And before I had the chance to veto *that* idea, he snagged his backpack and moved to an empty computer where he could tweak his photos in privacy.

Nothing like digging up a front-page story under the sharp photographic lens of an archnemesis while having lunch with my newly famous friends.

Oh yeah. Nothing could possibly go wrong there.

Chapter 4

"Uh . . . Jane? Don't freak out, but I think Scott Fraser is stalking you."

Isobel's eyes widened in surprise when I merely tried to brush off her words with a shrug. But she couldn't just leave it alone. Instead, her voice lowered to a whisper. "Wait, did you actually talk to Mr. Elliot today? Is that why Scott Fraser is—" Isobel cut herself off and planted her hands on her hips. "I'm missing something, right?"

I peered over Isobel's shoulder and saw Scott standing patiently in line for a sandwich, his trusty camera slung around his neck. I scanned the cafeteria slowly so he wouldn't think I was paying any extra attention to him. No need to inflate his already overblown ego. Although it was hard to be inconspicuous with Isobel pushing up her glasses so that she could get an even better look. None too discreetly, I might add.

"It's complicated. I'm sort of an undercover reporter on probation right now. Scott's hanging around to supply the photos."

Isobel's whole face lit up. "Jane, that's fantastic! Congratulations!"

I was too nervous about my ability to avoid Lisa Anne's wrath to feel like celebrating my promotion. Not yet. Not until I had dotted my i's, crossed my t's, and handed my grammatically perfect article to Mr. Elliot himself.

"Thanks, Isobel. Now I just need a story. Something controversial."

Isobel looked dubious. "Uh, Jane? You don't *do* controversial."

All of this "Jane, *you* can't do *that*" crap was starting to seriously piss me off. Sure, I expected it from Lisa Anne and Scott, but I had hoped that Isobel would have showed a little faith in me. Especially considering that I *had* spoken up in class.

And, okay, I hadn't mentioned my idea to add a fiction page to the paper. But I would . . . eventually.

"*I* don't have to be controversial," I pointed out, perhaps a bit too defensively. "I just have to find the story. Two completely different things."

"And Scott's going to be tailing you for the photos?"

"Yep."

Isobel nodded thoughtfully. "Well, frankly I don't know how you're going to get anything done with him watching your every move."

"You mean because he's such a jerk?" I shrugged. "I'll deal with it."

"Actually, because he's so cute. It's distracting."

I stared at her in disbelief. Isobel has always been the rational member of our group, who observes everything objectively.

"Nothing about Scott is cute. Trust me, beneath that thin veneer of polish lies a raging egomaniac."

She studied him carefully, almost clinically. "You're right: He's not cute."

"See!" I reached for the ketchup to add some to my french fries. Our high school cafeteria leaves much to be desired in the way of nutrition.

"His features are too classically shaped to be 'cute.' He has a strong nose, but it doesn't appear disproportionate. The disheveled, short, dark brown hair, green eyes combination usually falls under the 'hot' category—and either he has an incredible metabolism or he gets some kind of physical exercise on a regular basis. The guy is in excellent shape."

Isobel wasn't wrong, and I had definitely noticed. Which didn't mean anything. Stuff like that is bound to happen when your hormones don't get the message that the insanely hot guy adjusting his camera is slime.

Backstabbing slime, to be specific.

"Yeah, well, I tend to choose substance over surface. I'm picky that way."

Isobel shrugged. "So have you told Mackenzie or Logan th—"

"Move your ass, fatty!"

No, I didn't say that to Isobel. That honor would have to go to Alex Thompson—football player, Notable, and the all-time-reigning king of the jerks at Smith High School. His mile-long rap sheet makes my grievances with Scott look petty in comparison. Although even if Alex Thompson's only crime had been outing my best friend Corey in our freshman year of high school—I would still have hated his guts.

The memory of that afternoon still haunts me sometimes.

I had been standing right next to Corey when Alex Thompson yelled, "Here comes the homo!" in the cafeteria.

Corey blanched, his skin taking on a deathly waxen sheen as the *entire* school tittered uncomfortably. At him. Nobody stood up and yelled at *Alex* for being a jerk. They just stared expectantly at Corey—probably hoping that he would burst into tears, since that would make the story even more intense.

And I knew that within hours the whole school would be abuzz with speculation on Corey's sexual identity. That changing for P.E. in the boys' locker room tomorrow might no longer be a safe option for him. Not with all the rumors that he was secretly trying to sneak a peek at everyone around him.

"Are you going to *cry*, fairy?" Alex continued mockingly. "Pathetic."

I was gripping my stupid plastic cafeteria tray so tightly my knuckles turned white, caught in the crosshairs between the bully and my best friend, and yet . . .

I did absolutely nothing.

Alex Thompson had a nasty smirk plastered across his face—daring us to try to take him down. And I just stood there, utterly powerless, staring at this broad-shouldered football player who was capable of such senseless cruelty.

If Corey hadn't dragged me away, I probably would have stayed glued to that spot, gaping at Alex in horror. I wasn't even able to find my voice outside the cafeteria. I had just nodded numbly when Corey swore me to secrecy. I didn't even try to talk him out of hiding it from Mackenzie.

I merely nodded and pulled him into a hug. And when Alex Thompson bodychecked Kenzie in the cafeteria line— two *years* after his altercation with Corey—I proved that I was still too much of a nonconfrontational wimp to speak up.

Instead, I did my brilliant imitation of a statue.

So I shouldn't have been surprised that Alex Thompson would insult Isobel in the cafeteria—especially since it was one of his favorite locations for dweeb hazing. Still, I had hoped that Alex would back off now that Logan—aka the captain of the hockey team and Kenzie's boyfriend—had ordered him to quit messing with us. Which was still something of a sore subject with Kenzie, since she doesn't like other people fighting her battles.

Normally, I would agree with her, but when it comes to bullies like Alex Thompson, I care a lot more about ending the geek hazing than about the kind of relationship precedent it sets.

But either Logan's message didn't stick or Alex didn't think Logan's shield of protection extended to Isobel. After all, she was a *freshman* and hardly connected to either Logan or Mackenzie.

Easy pickings.

And maybe if I hadn't spent the last few days mentally psyching myself up for a confrontation with Mr. Elliot, he would have been right.

"Excuse me?" I squeaked, before fighting to keep my voice level. "What was that?" I gave him my strongest, most withering glare (which I had aimed at Scott without any positive results only a few hours earlier) and hoped with every fiber of my being that he would mutter: *I didn't say anything,* so that we could let the matter drop.

"I said: *Move your ass, fatty!*"

Except this time he didn't just say it. He practically yelled it for the whole cafeteria to hear. Isobel was seconds away from tears as she pushed her glasses up higher on her nose with shaking fingers. Worst of all was the dull, resigned expression in her eyes—as if she had known all along that her day had been too good to last.

That's when I snapped.

I dropped my tray on the counter, pulled back my fist, and slugged Alex Thompson right in the face.

Hard.

The bright shock of pain that radiated from my hand took me by surprise. All I could think was: *Holy shit, that hurts!* The whole thing felt like a surreal out-of-body trip, like something out of a cheesy body-swap movie. If it hadn't been for the pain and the murderous look on Alex Thompson's hard-as-granite face, I might have even been able to convince myself that I had made the whole thing up.

Except then his fist came hurtling in my direction. I threw my hands up, but was unable to block the punch, the force of which sent me sprawling backward. My mind was numb, but my body sure felt it when I connected solidly with the cement of the cafeteria floor. Searing pain had me gasping for breath as I hauled myself off the ground. Everyone around us started chanting, "Fight! Fight! Fight!"

Well, everyone except Isobel. I think she was too shocked to speak.

Alex moved in for another attack, making my (rather limited) Women's Self-Defense training kick in and my brain switch off. I punched, pinched, clawed, grabbed, and kicked as much of him as I could reach. I only dimly felt the arms separating us as I struggled to get in one last good swipe, but the Autoshop teacher had an iron grasp and forcibly dragged me away. I heard Kenzie and Logan shout my name, but I didn't actually see them since Scott switched to flash, temporarily blinding me. I had heard the incessant *click, click, click* of his camera during the fight, but I hadn't paid much attention to it. Actually, I hadn't given it a second thought. When a football player built like a tanker has a fist plummeting toward your eye, the smaller details in life tend to fall by the wayside.

The last thing I saw inside the cafeteria before I was hauled out, caveman-style, were my three best friends (and Logan) trying to run to my aid. Well, that and Scott snapping more photos of my dramatic exit.

And Isobel wondered why I didn't like the guy.

Chapter 5

"So, Jennifer, do you want to explain to me what happened in the cafeteria?"

I looked at the guidance counselor, Mr. Shelder, in disbelief. What did he expect me to say: *Sorry, I figured it'd be a good idea to attack the biggest guy on the football team for no reason. My bad.* But being nice little Jane Smith, I couldn't let the sarcasm out. So I did what I do best: I kept my feelings tightly locked away inside.

"Um, I'm Jane. Not Jennifer. And Alex Thompson insulted my friend, so I punched him in the face."

"I see." Mr. Shelder jotted down a note and looked at me with his best *concerned counselor* look firmly in place. "Are you often this protective of your friends?"

"No. Usually, I'm spineless."

"I'm sure that's not true," he said soothingly. "There's no shame in avoiding conflict. Especially when an altercation could potentially become physical."

"Yeah, it's real noble of me to let jerks treat my friends like garbage."

The bitter words tumbled out of my mouth before I could stop them, and I stared at the dingy tile floor in discomfort. I couldn't bring myself to look directly at Mr. Shelder, because

I knew exactly what I would see if I met his gaze: poorly masked condescension. I could hear it in his voice already. He would probably return home, shaking his head, and muttering something stupid like, *"Teenagers. Why must they make everything so dramatic all the time?"*

"Violence is never the solution, Jenny."

That was easy for him to say. He wasn't the one who pretended not to notice when our lunch spot was referred to as the table for "gays and strays." As far as I was concerned, this was one bout of violence that should have happened years ago. I was a little surprised it hadn't. I tentatively skimmed my index finger around the edges of my bruised eye as it throbbed mercilessly.

"Right," I agreed, without even bothering to correct him on my name. Again. I couldn't drum up the energy to care. Not when the pounding of my eye could keep pace with Ready-Set's fastest rock song. I tried to figure out which one of their hits best matched the beat while I tuned out Mr. Shelder.

"Good. I'm glad you're ready to apologize. It's really the mature way of handling situations like this."

That pulled me out of my pain-filled preoccupation.

"Wait, *what?* No way am I apologizing to that—" Mr. Shelder gave me his best look of disciplinary disapproval, the one that was supposed to evoke guilt in good girls like me. But I guess I'm not such a good girl anymore since I wasn't even fazed. No way in hell was Alex Thompson going to get an apology from me.

Not after all the crap he had said about my friends.

"Janice, be reasonable now. You know I can't just let this go. You attacked a football player a week before the big game. Ordinarily I would have already notified the parents."

Of course, my offense wasn't that I'd hit someone—it was that I had hit a *football player* before some stupid school-rivalry game. If Mr. Shelder were to call *my* parents, he would have to discuss it with the quarterback's family as well. Something I suspected he would want to delay until *after* the game. After all, he didn't want to be forced into sidelining our star player over a simple misunderstanding in the cafeteria. High school really sucks.

"But because this is a first-time behavior from you, I hope detention will be a sufficient deterrent if you are ever tempted toward violence again."

I slung my backpack over my shoulder. "I'll be sure to check myself before I wreck myself next time. Better yet, I'll reprimand him using my indoor voice."

The silence that filled the room triggered my guilt reflex. It wasn't really Mr. Shelder's fault that I was in this mess. If he went out on a limb for me and actually tried to change the dynamic at Smith High School, it might put his job in jeopardy.

"Sorry," I mumbled. "No more fighting. Behave myself. Write a nonviolent story for the school newspaper. Got it."

"Good. Wait, what was that about the school paper?"

"Nothing. Just ignore me." I winced as my own words sank in. "Shouldn't be hard for you to do."

And with that I walked out of his office—only to be confronted by my friends.

"Jane, you're officially my hero! That was phenomenal! The way you sucker punched him in the face..." Corey whistled appreciatively. "Most beautiful thing I've ever seen."

Isobel still didn't appear to have found her voice. She just stood there in the hallway gaping at me. Unfortunately, Kenzie has never had a problem speaking her mind when it comes to me.

"Are you deranged? What were you thinking? Oh, I forgot. *You weren't thinking!* Seriously, Jane, what part of *enormous football player* did you *not* understand?"

Logan put a comforting hand on her shoulder. Even after a

month of watching Kenzie's eyes turn dreamy whenever Logan was around, it still struck me as strange to see them actually doing couple-y things. My best friend dating a Notable who treated me like a geeky kid sister . . . yeah, that was one change that definitely required some adjustment time. "Mack, breathe. Jane, how are you feeling? Besides your eye, what hurts?"

The searing pain I felt in the cafeteria hadn't lessened, and I struggled not to resent that my so-called friends were yapping at me when they could be doing something *helpful*. Like shooting me with a tranquilizer gun so that I could be unconscious for the worst of the ache.

Or handing me some Tylenol for my headache.

Either was preferable to being on the receiving end of Kenzie's lectures.

"How . . ." I cleared my throat and tried again. "How bad does it look?"

"Badass!" Corey proclaimed. "Just like the way you took on Alex Thompson! You attacked him like a territorial she wolf on the Discovery Channel or something."

I heard a snort and had to swivel my head so that my good eye could locate the source.

Scott. *Of course.*

"You've got a problem, man?" Logan demanded, his eyes a cold, hard gray I never wanted to have directed at me.

Sometimes it's nice being friends with a high school hockey captain. Especially when a major pain-induced headache makes rational thought unbearable.

Scott just ignored Logan and spoke to me instead.

"Interesting way to get a story, Grammar Girl. Nice plan. Nothing impresses teachers quite like getting your ass kicked by a football player. Foolproof."

"You were trying to get a story? Why?" Corey asked as he draped a protective arm around my shoulder. I winced as he pressed down exactly where Alex had landed a wayward punch.

Every single inch of me hurt.

"Jane's working on a piece for the school paper," Isobel informed him, picking one hell of a time to speak up. "See, she's planning on starting—"

"Isobel," I interrupted warningly. I didn't want Scott to know about my ideas for the paper—definitely not before I had a chance to run them by Mr. Elliot. Creating a fiction page was a long shot, but it wasn't *impossible*. At least, it wasn't if Scott didn't have any opportunity to prejudice Lisa Anne or Mr. Elliot against it. "Not right now, okay?"

Everyone noticed my not-so-subtle head nod in Scott's direction.

Scott didn't appear even remotely fazed by all the sudden attention. He grinned. "Don't stop on my account. You were saying?"

"Um . . . that violence is never the answer. Jane, you shouldn't have hit Alex." Isobel didn't speak with her normal level of conviction, and I knew she was still shaken up by what had happened.

But I had absolutely no idea what I could say to make it better.

"Look, I've already heard the 'turn the other cheek' speech," I told her tiredly. "I get it. Really."

"I don't think turning the other cheek was necessary." Scott examined me narrowly before he snapped another photo. "Both sides of your face look equally bruised to me."

Logan couldn't hold himself back any longer. "What the hell is *wrong* with you?" he demanded. "Get that damn thing out of her face!"

"Logan." Kenzie put a firm hand on his shoulder to make sure he didn't try to land a punch of his own. "Take your own advice and calm down."

He turned on her hotly. "Alex was punching Jane, *our Jane*, and that jackass just stood there taking pictures!"

I didn't really know what to make of the whole "our Jane" thing, but the rest of it was accurate. Except . . . Scott was doing exactly what Mr. Elliot and Lisa Anne wanted. What he probably thought I wanted too.

He was doing his job.

Not that I was going to defend him.

"I *knew* I forgot to bring something to school with me today—my noble steed. Good thing you were able to come riding to the rescue, Logan. She'd be lost without you."

It's never a good idea to piss off a high school athlete, even one as laid-back as Logan Beckett. They tend to punch really freaking hard, a lesson I had just learned the hard way from Alex. Although Scott looked like he might be able to hold his own if it came to blows. Not that his muscles bulged in a protein shake/pumping weights kind of way. They were just very nicely shaped.

Like the rest of him.

I really must have smacked my head hard when Alex knocked me down in the cafeteria. That was the only logical explanation for why I was standing there daydreaming about Scott's arms while Logan was poised to kick some butt.

"Logan," Kenzie repeated, a definite warning underlying her tone. The situation was quickly getting out of control, so I forced myself to face down Scott before anyone could do something stupid.

"A white knight is still better than an ass," I blurted out. "So . . . lay off."

Scott's lips twitched into something that resembled an amused grin, and I knew I had just blown any chance I may have had for him to see me as a force to be reckoned with. Still, my comeback seemed to go a long way toward mollifying Logan. His shoulders finally relaxed as he returned his attention to me.

"Do you think you have a concussion, Jane? Say the word and we'll blow off school and go to my house."

Scott raised an eyebrow. "Are you a nurse now too?"

"Both of my parents are doctors." Logan's clipped tone made it clear that he was trying to keep himself in check. "My mom is sleeping off a night shift, but I'm sure she can take a look."

"I'm fine, Logan. Really. No doctors needed."

"And you can't just 'blow off' school!" Kenzie said indignantly. "Your tutor is *not* okay with you randomly skipping class!"

Of course, since *Kenzie* is both Logan's girlfriend and his tutor, she'd know her own official position.

"This would fall under extenuating circumstances." Logan grinned for the first time since he'd seen me get pummeled. "Look at her."

"Hmm . . . good point."

"Hey!" I said. "I'm right here!"

"She does look pretty bad," Corey agreed as another wave of headache-related pain rushed through my system.

"Still right here, guys!"

Isobel shifted uncomfortably, her eyes locked on the dent in the locker right behind me. "You didn't have to do that for me, Jane. Really. It was no big deal."

And that's when I realized my black eye would probably fade a lot sooner than the blow to Isobel's self-esteem. It wasn't fair. Alex had no right to pick on a nervous freshman girl whose biggest ambition for high school was probably fading into obscurity with her fellow geeks.

But that's high school.

"I did it for me." I suspected she could tell I was lying. I *had* done it for her. But that still didn't make it the wrong thing to do. "The guy's a jerk."

Isobel pushed her glasses higher up on her nose, and I knew she was every bit as uncomfortable discussing what had just happened as me. "You didn't need to punch him."

I shrugged. "Nothing else came to mind."

"Just . . . don't do it for me again, okay?" I winced as another wave of pain rolled through me. My thrashed limbs sure wished I had been more like Gandhi and less like Mohammed Ali. I forced a grin anyway.

"I'll take that under consideration."

The five-minute warning bell sounded, and my friends melted into the surging crowd of students hurrying for class, although not before Logan sent Scott a glare that said: *You hurt her, I kick your ass.*

And I'll enjoy doing it.

"So we're done then?" Scott asked casually. He tapped his camera when I stared at him blankly. "You've got your story, I've got my photos. Your master plan is complete."

"That was *not* my master plan," I insisted, even though I doubted he would believe me. "I didn't show up to lunch thinking, *Hmm, I think I'll get into a fight with a football player today!*"

"But you don't regret it. Even if you could go back and change how things went down, you wouldn't." He made it a statement, not a question.

"Sure I would." I gestured to the eye that was definitely going to have one hell of a shiner. "I would've ducked, for starters."

A quick grin flashed across Scott's face, before it disappeared just as abruptly as it had arrived.

"You never answered my question."

"Which one? You asked a few." I rubbed my forehead and fervently hoped that I didn't have a concussion. I already had way too much homework to slog through without that slowing me down.

"Are we done with the story?"

"I think I've got more than enough material about bullying." I shouldered my backpack. "And now I have to get to class, or risk double detention."

Scott nodded, but prevented my hasty departure by reaching into his own backpack and handing me a can of Pepsi.

I stared in confusion at what looked like a peace offering. "Um . . . thanks? Not really my drink of choice but . . . uh, thanks."

Not the most gracious of thank-you speeches, but I half expected him to shake the can, pop it open, and spray it right in my face.

Instead, he took a firm grip on my hand and directed it upward until the beverage pressed against my swollen eye. I hissed momentarily from the bite of pain, until the chill of the can numbed away the worst of it.

Or maybe that was just wishful thinking on my part.

"Wait, why are you being nice now?" I demanded before I could lose my nerve.

He grinned. "That's for the kick-ass photo shoot. You make a pretty good model, Grammar Girl."

I would've glared at him for the Grammar Girl part, but my eye didn't permit it.

"And you're back to being yourself. See you later, Scott."

He tossed me one last amused look before strolling into the nearest classroom. Alone at last, I hobbled to my next-period class thinking about Scott's last comment. Me? A model? I was the least model-like person at Smith High School. Models get noticed wherever they go—like the queen of the Notable crowd, Chelsea Halloway. Now *she* could have made the scene in the cafeteria look like an upscale photo shoot. Even under our school's crappy fluorescent lighting her long blond hair looks like something out of a freaking shampoo commercial.

But maybe I wasn't quite as boring in front of a camera as I'd originally thought.

That was kind of cool.

Chapter 6

Detention is nothing like *The Breakfast Club.*
I sat down in my hard plastic chair hoping there would be some group bonding, maybe a little dancing, a few heart-to-heart moments set to eighties music. John Hughes shouldn't have given me such high expectations. I stared at the graffiti carved into my desk, isolated in a room full of slackers, while a bored-looking Spanish teacher focused more on paper grading than on inmate guarding. Most of the kids were either listening to music or texting their friends, probably about the overwhelming lameness that was detention at Smith High School. With nothing better to do with my time, I flicked my iPod onto shuffle and started working on the newspaper story.

There was quite a ruckus in the cafeteria this week.

Ruckus? That was my big opening line?

I slashed it out and tried again.

The Truth Behind the Padding: What You Didn't Know About the Smith High School Football Team.

That sounded like they were slipping socks into their jockstraps.

Cafeteria Menace Strikes Again!

Lame.

My head started spinning, so I sipped my soda and hoped

that the sugar infusion would help me organize my thoughts. I knew the worst was over. Considering everything that had happened, I definitely had a story. I just had to find it. My shoulder ached and the right words refused to come. Not for anything that Lisa Anne or Mr. Elliot might want to read, anyway. If they'd allow me to hand in fiction . . . well, that would be a different story. I can happily scribble away for hours if I'm not expected to produce something *serious*, like an essay comparing famous books written by dead white guys to other famous books written by, oh that's right, more dead white guys.

I tapped my pencil against my desk and told myself to snap out of it. The only way I would ever get anyone to support my idea was if I built up my credibility as a staff writer.

Tuesday afternoon and the cafeteria line was long.

That had to be the worst opening line yet.

Ignoring my notebook, I rested my battered face on the cool surface of my desk and waited for my incarceration to end.

"Hey!" The tip of one bright red Converse sneaker nudged me. "Are you the girl who punched Alex Thompson?"

My head jerked up, brushing my notebook with enough force that it landed with a loud thump under the very shoe that had disturbed me.

I slid my gaze up to see my fellow detentioner. Detentionee? I wasn't clear on the correct title. Slouched in the chair next to me, wearing loose jeans, chipped black nail polish, and layers of silver necklaces, was one seriously intense girl. She didn't look goth, precisely, but she hadn't exactly restrained herself when applying her eyeliner. Girls that hardcore generally ignore me.

Then again, everyone generally ignores me.

"Um, yeah." I nodded, then had to shove my bangs out of my face. "That's me."

She leaned forward, her voice lowering. "How'd it feel?"

"Actually, it felt pretty good." I pointed at my increasingly colorful eye. "Well, this part not so much. I'm Jane."

Maybe *The Breakfast Club* wasn't quite as off base as I thought.

"Sam," she replied. Then her chocolate-brown eyes narrowed into an intense *don't mess with me* look. "Never Samantha."

"So what did you do to land in detention?"

"Me?" She might have thought her wide, toothy smile looked innocent, but it was pretty obvious to me that it contained nothing but mischief. I couldn't help grinning back. "I was busted sneaking into the boys' bathroom."

"Oh."

I had no idea what I was supposed to say to *that*.

"By Mr. Taylor." She rolled her eyes, as if landing on the wrong side of our superconservative principal was no big deal.

"I don't mean to pry but . . . what were you doing in there?"

Sam shrugged. "Pry away. It's not exactly a secret that I've been taping condoms to the bathroom stalls for months. This time he got lucky and caught me red-handed."

I laughed. "I'm sure Mr. Taylor loved that." It was no secret that our principal tried to squash student activities that ran contrary to his own views.

"Detention is a small price to pay for my convictions. Plus, this will make a great college essay. Fighting the system and all that." Sam pulled out a condom from her backpack. "Need one?"

"Um . . . I don't think so." I nervously eyed the little packet. If Kenzie was sitting in detention with us, she would have found it absolutely hilarious that Jane Smith, romance novel connoisseur, couldn't so much as look at a condom without blushing a brick red.

Or maybe she would be too distracted pocketing one for herself to even notice.

I instantly tried to erase that thought.

Just . . . no.

Unfortunately, Sam didn't appear to pick up on my discomfort as she tossed the condom Frisbee style onto my desk. "Why's that?"

"The closest thing I have to a boyfriend is a friend who happens to be a boy. And since he's in a serious relationship with a really great guy . . . your, uh, well . . . it would be wasted on me."

Sam laughed. "You still might want to keep it, just in case."

I stared at her in disbelief. "In case he stops being gay?"

A loud snort escaped her. "In case you decide to have consenting penetrative heterosexual sex. Or you can use it for dental da—"

"Got it!" I hurriedly cut her off, my cheeks turning three shades darker. It seemed unfair that she could say stuff like "consenting penetrative heterosexual sex" without sounding even the tiniest bit insecure, and yet I couldn't handle another second of our conversation. I knocked the packet off the desk and into my open backpack in one fluid movement—not because I wanted it, but because I didn't want anyone to see it sitting there.

"Never hurts to be prepared, I guess."

Sam nodded and then gave me a once-over. Boring jeans. Plain shirt. Ordinary silver studs in my ears.

"No offense, but if it weren't for your bruise, you would look way too straight-edge."

This time it was my turn to shrug. It wasn't like Sam was telling me anything I hadn't heard a thousand times before—and the words stung far worse when they came from my Notable older sister.

"None taken."

But when Sam picked up my notebook, I couldn't hide the way my whole body tensed.

"What's this?" Sam raised an eyebrow and flipped it open to the story I had scribbled when I was supposed to be paying attention in my AP Calculus class.

"It's nothing. Really. Can I have it back?"

But Sam began to read aloud.

"*Jane Smith lived a boring life. . . .*" I winced, but Sam either didn't notice my discomfort or chose not to care. "*. . . until the day she felt compelled to defend a friend with her fists.*"

"You can stop anytime now."

"Don't interrupt. This is getting good."

Jane fell in love with fighting. She began to crave the kick of power behind each punch. She lost herself in the thrill of battle, the rush of adrenaline, the beauty buried beneath the crunch of bones. It didn't come without a cost: realignment surgeries, suspensions, extensive parental lectures. Her frequent hospital stays made it impossible for her to graduate from high school on schedule, and she was forced to watch the ceremony from the bleachers.

Alone.

Jane Smith never attended college. The only job she ever managed to hold down was at a sleazy bar where her fists were her first and last line of defense. Her nights were spent pouring drinks, slapping away randy hands, and breaking up drunken tussles while tone-deaf girls in skin-tight skirts abused Shania Twain's biggest hits on the karaoke machine. Jane's days were spent in a dingy apartment with a revolving door of men who all had one thing in common—none of them stuck around.

Jane Smith died trying to separate two belligerent patrons at the bar. More specifically, she died when a knife accidentally collided with her eye. As the world dissolved into a pool of red, Jane prayed that she would never again have to hear "I feel like a woman!" *howled into a microphone. Never have to hustle drunks out after last call. Never have to return to her barren apartment and her sleazy one-night stands. And for the first time in her life . . . Jane Smith got her wish.*

"Did you write this?" Sam asked curiously. "It seems way too twisted for you."

"Yeah. I wrote it today because . . . well, it's just something that I do, imagining ways to die."

Something I also preferred not to share with anyone.

She raised one inky eyebrow. "The Shania Twain karaoke was a nice detail. I liked it."

Those few brusque words were quite possibly the nicest compliment I had ever received. Writing fictional deaths was one of the few things that made me feel like I had control over my destiny, especially when my sister was around. It was the one place where I could create a future for myself that didn't include comparisons to Elle.

But while I loved doing it . . . I never knew if any of it was *good*.

My work wasn't exactly something I could pass around for a writing critique, unless I *wanted* to spend a lot more time in the guidance counselor's office.

Which I really, *really* didn't.

"Thanks. It's what I do when I get bored in class."

"Wicked," she muttered, her eyes locked on mine. "How do you usually die?"

"Um . . . it varies. Nothing I *actually* expect to happen. Death by boredom, death by pencil sharpener, that kind of thing. I don't have a death wish or anything."

"Then why did you get so freaked out when I started to read it?"

I hesitated. "It's just . . . I know it might be stupid, but my writing is important to me. That's why I'm trying to get our school newspaper to have a fiction page."

Sam's raccoon eyes widened. "You write with all those pretentious journalism kids?"

The sad truth was that I couldn't even say in all honesty that I wrote with them.

"I'm the go-to grammar girl," I admitted sheepishly. "But not all of them are pretentious."

"If you say so."

I mulled it over. "They're just a little intense. They'll warm up . . . eventually."

"Well, good luck. I don't envy you. I wouldn't want to work with that Lisa Anne Mont-something girl. She freaks me out. No one should have that many extracurricular activities."

"Ah, but she's applying to *Harvard*," I said, as if that explained everything, which it kind of did. "I'll be fine."

She slumped back in her seat and shrugged. "Maybe. I tend to be a bit on the pessimistic side. After all, things can always get worse."

I grinned and pointed to my black eye. "Really? Because I'm pretty sure that getting my butt kicked in the cafeteria counts as an all-time low. Actually, I take it back. This detention is me hitting rock bottom."

I really believed that too.

Until I found out firsthand that actually hitting rock bottom hurts way more than a punch to the face. Even if it never leaves a bruise.

Chapter 7

My mom wasn't exactly thrilled to pick me up from school.

Luckily, she was too preoccupied with my face, specifically the dark blue bruise forming over one eyelid, to harp about the inconvenience of shuttling me home every time I miss the bus.

Or maybe not so luckily, considering the way her jaw dropped open when she caught her first good look at me.

"What happened, Jane? You look like you've been mugged!"

Sadly, that wasn't an inaccurate description.

I did my best to shrug the whole thing off. "Nothing, Mom. I had a small accident in the cafeteria. I tripped."

Into the fist of a two-hundred-pound football player.

I just kept that last part to myself.

"It looks worse than it is, I promise."

My mom examined my face while we idled at an intersection, and I found myself mentally trying to will the traffic light to switch to green so that she would have to pay attention to the road.

No such luck.

"You fell?" she repeated in disbelief.

"Mm—hmm." I kept my voice noncommittal. I didn't want her to guess the truth, but I also didn't want to lie. Still, when she asks, "How was your day, honey?" she doesn't want *"Gee, well, today I got into a fistfight"* to be the answer.

It *can't* be the answer.

So even though that was exactly what happened, I carefully skirted the truth.

"You know me, total klutz. I'm just surprised it didn't happen sooner."

That was all it took to get my mom assuring me that, *No, I wasn't a klutz. It was all her fault for letting me drop out of ballet lessons when I was seven, and that if only I had continued I would be every bit as graceful as Elle.*

A lecture that I had grown so accustomed to hearing that I could tune it out effortlessly.

Our car rolled past the neatly lettered SMITH mailbox and the white picket fence before pulling into the garage.

"Why don't you go use the makeup I got you for your birthday? I'll call you when it's time for dinner. How does that sound?"

Like something only an alternate-reality version of myself might be interested in doing.

I bit the inside of my cheek to keep myself in check. "Uh . . . sure. That sounds great, Mom."

Shoving open the car door, I tried to make a hasty getaway to my bedroom. The last thing I wanted was to be stuck deflecting more questions or nodding along to more lectures.

I didn't make it past the kitchen.

"God, what happened to your *face?* It looks like roadkill. More so than usual, even."

Oh, the joys of having an older sister. Scratch that. Oh, the annoyances of an older, more popular sister taking time away from college (and her precious sorority sisters at the Theta Beta Omega house) while she waits for her internship helping the homeless to begin. That's right: *helping the homeless.* She can't even be straight-up vapid and shallow the way sorority girls are in the movies. Instead, she lounges on the sofa in the living room simultaneously filling out grant proposals and watching crap television. And mocking me whenever possible.

Not like any of that is a challenge for her.

"Thanks, *Lane*." I put a heavy emphasis on her full name just to annoy her. Lane and Jane Smith. I seriously don't know what our parents were thinking when they picked out our names. Of course, my sister had found a way to make it work for her. She started signing everything "L" back in middle school. That was it, just one initial. L. Smith. But the abridgment stuck to the point that even my parents found it a more natural fit than her given name.

Now it feels weird to even think of calling her anything else.

Unfortunately, my name isn't quite as flexible when it comes to nicknames. I mean, theoretically I could have started signing things J. Smith. But since my associations with the name "Jay" are restricted to birds or middle-aged men with receding hairlines . . . I wasn't exactly tempted to make it permanent. Or even temporary.

My sister has always been the lucky one.

Elle crossed her arms and smirked. "I'm just telling you the truth. It's not *my* fault you look like crap."

Definitely time to escape to the privacy of my bedroom.

"I'm so glad you're home, *Lane*," I called back over my shoulder as I climbed the stairs to my room. "And only two weeks and two days before you leave. Not that I'm counting or anything."

And then I slammed my door shut so I wouldn't have to hear her reply.

It was only when the lock clicked into place that I was able to release the breath I had been holding and my tension began to ebb.

I love my room.

Back when I was six I convinced my parents to let me have

my grandma's bed after she passed away. I risked what the other elementary school kids, including Kenzie, termed "death cooties" because it was the most luxurious thing I had ever seen. The large wooden frame included four spindly posts that spiraled upward before disappearing into a canopy of rich golden-yellow fabric that draped and billowed above me.

And it was all mine.

Mainly because by the time Elle realized that "death cooties" weren't a big deal, my dad had sworn that he was never moving that *blasted bed* so much as an inch ever again. That was the only time I could think of when my sister had been jealous of *me*.

I flopped down on the bed and stared at the fabric pattern I've admired every morning for the past eleven years. It was comforting knowing that the exact same view would greet me the next morning. Especially because it felt like nothing else in my life was stable anymore. Not when my friends were on a first-name basis with rock stars, and football players were probably planning on stuffing me into trash cans.

Which was why I wanted to enjoy the familiar view in peace while I could still see out of one unbruised eye.

My cell phone started ringing.

So much for that plan.

"Isobel told me everything," Corey announced, instead of saying hello like a normal person.

"About landing the front page of the school paper?"

"Yeah. Someone's been a busy girl. Apparently, you're working on an article right now. Funny how you never mentioned it."

"Oh."

"Yeah, 'oh' is right! I thought we agreed that when it comes to big news, I'm *always* your first phone call. What happened to that, *friend?* Suddenly, I'm not good enough for you?"

I grinned. No one does fake indignation quite like Corey. "Nope. You're not important to me at all."

"That's what I thought." I could hear the smile in his voice.

"It's not like I've told you all my secrets and embarrassing moments or anything. Oh wait . . . yes, I have."

"Well," he said melodramatically, "I don't recall my phone ringing *this* time."

I rolled my eyes and instantly regretted it when a jolt of pain shot through me. "Consider me properly chastised."

Although I couldn't help wondering when exactly I had been expected to fill him in on *my* life. It's rather hard to connect with somebody who spends the majority of his time waiting for someone else on Skype. Even when he's away from his computer, he's always checking his phone to make sure that he didn't somehow miss a call from his superbusy rock-star boyfriend. Lately, talking to Corey felt like trying to get a six-year-old with attention deficit disorder to put away his crayons.

But I couldn't say any of that without offending him.

And upsetting my best guy friend was the very last thing I wanted to do.

"Okay, now that we've straightened that out, I'm so excited for you! Jane Smith using her skills for the good of all geek-kind. I love it. So, what breaking news are you going to report?"

"Wow, slow down. I'm not exactly interviewing dictators and presidents here, which is definitely for the best. I would probably choke and somehow wind up serving a twenty-year prison sentence."

"Nah . . . forty to life at least. For treason."

My fingers itched for a pen so that I could scribble down another fake death. It was almost ridiculously easy picturing myself in a bright orange jumpsuit, insisting that it was all one big misunderstanding as Lisa Anne instructed a guard to return me to my cell. But this time, I did my best to shake off the image.

"Care to describe those skills you mentioned? My ego could use a boost."

"Oh, you know," Corey said airily, even though obviously I didn't. "You always know when it's 'my friends and I' or 'my friends and me.' "

His words brought a sharp, acidic taste to my mouth, but I tried to play it off.

"Armed with talent like that, I must be one step away from a Pulitzer."

Corey laughed and the tension in my shoulders eased slightly. "You know what I mean, Jane. You pay attention to the details and crap."

That was one way to put it, but Corey wasn't finished. "Plus, you're really good at listening to others."

Yeah, well, when your best friends are too wrapped up with their boyfriends to ask about your *day, you tend to get a lot of practice listening.*

But I couldn't say that either.

"Is that a nice way of saying I eavesdrop?" I joked instead.

"Yes."

"I can live with that."

"Look, Jane, you'll rock the assignment. I'm betting the thing is half written already."

I thought back to my failed attempts during detention. "Not so much. The story is proving to be . . . resistant. Maybe I should ditch it entirely and write about your whirl-wind celebrity romance instead." I deepened my voice in a halfway decent imitation of a brusque reporter. "Tell me: What's it like to date America's hottest young rock star, Tim-othy Goff?"

Corey snorted. "It's not exactly a 'whirlwind' romance when you see him more often on television than on Skype."

I could practically feel the exasperation rolling off him. "The long-distance thing not working out so well?"

"It's just . . . we've spent a total of nine days together, five of which were with Mackenzie and the rest of his band. I mean, he came up to see me over New Year's, which was . . . *amazing*. But he's back in LA working on a sound-track project that's meant for a slightly younger demographic than their other stuff. I guess there's a lot of pressure for them to come across as *family friendly*."

"I take it that having the lead singer come out as gay isn't part of that image?" It wasn't exactly a difficult conclusion to reach. The frustration in Corey's voice was a pretty big giveaway that everything here was *not* okay.

"Exactly. Tim keeps telling me that the sneaking-around part is temporary and that he wants to take us public. And I believe him. I really do, *but* . . . I think his definition of temporary is different from mine."

"Months?" I asked sympathetically.

"Try *years*. And I know it's stupid, but I want our Facebook profiles to make it clear that we are together. Taken. Committed. Instead, he couldn't even kiss me to ring in the new year in case someone snapped a picture." Corey took a deep breath. "Let's face it: He could date any guy he wants, which *eventually* he will figure out. And when that happens, well, I'll probably find out via the front page of *People* magazine."

"You don't actually believe he'd do that," I insisted.

"You're right." Corey sighed. "Tim's too nice to blindside me that way. He'd dump me via Skype instead."

"You're being ridiculous."

"I'm not so sure, Jane. If you were a celebrity, would *you* want to date someone in high school?"

I couldn't contain my snort of disbelief. "First of all, me, a celebrity? Never going to happen. I'll leave that to Kenzie. Secondly, if I were to meet an attractive boy who was smart, funny, and kind, who liked me back, then yeah, I'd want to date him. Gee, I wonder who fits *that* description!"

"It's not that simple."

"Sure it is!" I argued, pacing around my room. "You're just being stupid and insecure. That's my job, remember?"

Corey laughed. "Stupid. Yeah, that's exactly how Mr. Taylor will describe you at our graduation ceremony. Right before you give your valedictorian speech."

"I'm not the valedictorian yet," I countered. "And you know that doesn't mean anything. It's not exactly hard to get A's here. I *never* speak up in class, and so far that hasn't made a difference. The only reason you don't have a 4.0 is because you keep blowing off assignments to go into Portland."

"True. Speaking of blowing off assignments . . . got any plans for tonight?"

"Just homework and nothing that can't be postponed. Why?"

"Okay, then hear me out."

There was such a long pause that I checked to make sure we hadn't been disconnected. "Corey?"

"Look, you're being such a badass now. I just thought you might want to consider changing up your look. Baggy sweatshirts and ill-fitting jeans aren't exactly trendy."

"Uh . . ."

"If you want people to take you seriously, you can't look like your closet has been on lockdown since middle school. Trust me, if you walk into school tomorrow looking like a million dollars, you could easily become Smith High School's next big thing."

His words made my blood run cold. "But—but I don't *want* to be . . ."

Corey just ignored me. "Listen, Jane. You're going to be the center of attention tomorrow. That's just what happens when the school good girl sucker punches the bully. The real question is whether you're ready to make the situation work in your favor."

I sucked in a huge breath, while I did my best not to completely freak out. This was what I wanted, wasn't it? A little more attention from my peers. Some respect.

That concept had been significantly less terrifying when it was theoretical.

"Well, I guess if you put it that way . . . I'm not so sure."

Corey laughed. "That's why you've got me. Just sit tight, Jane. We'll be over there soon."

I stared at the phone. "Um, are you using the royal 'we,' or are other people actually coming over to my house with you?"

"I'm bringing everyone," he replied vaguely. "Don't get all melodramatic about it."

Right. Because *I* was the one blowing the situation out of proportion.

But Corey wasn't quite finished. "Stay put, Jane. We'll fix everything. You'll see."

"Corey, wait, what are you—"

But he'd already hung up on me. Note to self: Never let the most impulsive person you know shake up your life.

Even if that person happens to be your best friend.

Chapter 8

I'd underestimated Corey.

That's what I discovered when he barged into my house while I was loading up the dishwasher after dinner, with Kenzie, Isobel, and their mutual friend Melanie sheepishly trailing behind him.

Melanie looked particularly uncomfortable entering my bedroom, probably because she was hyperaware of the fact that the two of us weren't exactly friends—just two girls who happened to know a lot of the same people. And while I knew Kenzie and Corey never would have befriended her if she wasn't sweet and nice and all that good stuff . . . I couldn't help feeling a tiny twinge of resentment that she was one of the many reasons *my* best friends no longer had as much time for me.

But I couldn't start obsessing over it since all four of my visitors began dumping bags full of clothing onto my bed. My AP Calculus textbook slid to the floor with a muffled thump while I stared at the growing mountain in disbelief.

"Um, so what's going on here, guys?" I asked apprehensively.

Corey beamed. "We're here to bust your rut."

"A rut? I don't think I'm in a rut. Well, maybe a small one—actually, now that I think about it, my rut is barely a dip. Not even worth noticing."

I slowly panned their faces to see if any of them were buying it.

Apparently not.

I fought down a sudden rush of claustrophobia and focused on Isobel, who was shifting her weight uncomfortably.

"You're in on this too?" I found that hard to believe. Isobel is even less fashionable than me. Of course, she also doesn't have a Notable older sister who critiques all her outfits on a scale between hideous and dumpster dive.

Elle's words may sting, but she has prevented me from wearing a few things I would have regretted.

Argyle tights with denim shorts. Not a good look.

"I'm just here for moral support," Isobel said, eyeing the pile of clothing warily.

"Um . . . thanks. But I really don't think this is necessary."

"Are you kidding me?" Corey exclaimed. "Do you have any idea how long I've wanted to do this? Don't answer that. Now sit, and I'll take care of everything."

"But . . . where did all of this come from?"

"I was famous for two weeks, remember?" Kenzie replied as she tossed a pair of jeans to me. "These are the designer clothes that were too small on me. And since you cowered when Corey gave me *my* makeover, I'm thinking of this as karmic retribution."

I couldn't help grinning. Kenzie's the only person who could say, *Yeah, I'm throwing you to the wolves* and make me laugh while getting ripped to shreds. Okay, gross mental image. But when you've been best friends since elementary school, you can't get mad over one makeover. Especially since she was right: I had chickened out when she was the focus of Corey's attention. Of course, that was only because I didn't want Corey focusing on me next.

Karmic retribution sucked.

"Now, are you going to put those on or do I have to force you?" Corey demanded.

"Like you could."

He had a few inches on me, but my mom's idea of good, clean, family fun is to discuss caloric intake while hiking. On the plus side: I know all about weight loss.

Then again, who really wants to know that much about broccoli?

He sighed. "Just get in the pants."

I waited for him to turn around first, not because I cared if he watched me change since (1) he's just a friend, (2) he's in a relationship, and (3) he's gay. However, my mom is prone to entering without knocking, and I prefer to avoid awkwardness like that whenever possible.

"So, uh . . . how was detention?" Melanie asked tentatively as she sat down in the chair by my desk.

Even when she was nervous it came across as sweet instead of geeky.

"Not bad." I toed off my sneakers and started unbuttoning my jeans. "Do any of you know Sam?"

"You'll have to be more specific." Corey scrolled through the music on my iPod, which meant any second Lady Gaga would start pumping out of my speakers. I kept her on a playlist just for him.

"She's got short black hair, lots of jewelry, compact frame, intense but in a good way. Oh, she also tapes up condoms in the bathrooms."

"Oh, her! She's in my AP U.S. History class." Kenzie looked thoughtful. "She seems cool but rather . . . extreme."

"Yeah, well, she saved me from boredom." I zipped up the new jeans. "Okay, so what's the consensus?"

Corey pursed his lips. "Well, *obviously* the shirt has to go. Here, try this one on." He tossed me something silky and blue.

"You sure about this?"

He glowered at me. "Yes! Now, could you please stop asking that and just *do what I tell you?*"

"Okay." Definitely not the time to ask if he thought the shirt showed off more cleavage than our school dress code (strictly speaking) allowed. I just kept my mouth shut as I wrangled it into fitting correctly even as the butterflies in my stomach viciously beat their wings against me instead of fluttering.

"And . . . how do I look now?"

Foolish. Gawky. Like I'm trying too hard.

Kenzie grinned. "You look amazing and nothing like yourself."

Corey pushed me across my room toward my mirror. "Meet Jane Smith 2.0."

"Great. I've always wanted an upgrade," I said sarcastically before I took a deep breath and faced my reflection.

The whole look was subtly glamorous.

The dark gray jeans fit like a glove, and the shirt gleamed a watery periwinkle. The texture of the pebbled silk had me fighting the urge to stroke the material forever. It also showed far more cleavage than . . . oh, anything I'd ever worn before.

I tugged at the hem. "You guys don't think I look, erm . . . slutty?"

"Are you kidding me?" Corey exclaimed. "You look phenomenal. Now try this on." He thrust a deep purple dress at me. "We have a lot of work to do."

"We do?" I traded my outfit for the one in his arms.

"Shoes, hair, makeup, accessories—the works. What'd you expect?"

Isobel, Melanie, and I all exchanged nervous looks, although I don't know why Melanie was concerned. If Scott had spotted Melanie, he definitely would be asking her to model for him. He would probably be tripping all over himself to talk her into it. The only explanation for why that hadn't happened that I could come up with was that as a transfer student in his junior year, he might not be paying much attention to underclassmen.

I had a feeling that two minutes with Melanie would have him reconsidering that policy.

"Sorry to bail so early, but I've got to head home." Melanie waited for Corey's back to be turned before she mouthed, "Good luck!"

Then, with a quick little wave, she skirted the pile of clothes that had now taken up residence in front of the door and vanished.

She was too nice for me to even resent her properly.

So instead I focused on obeying all of Corey's commands, with the end result that I eventually collapsed on my bed, the slightly freaked-out owner of an entirely new wardrobe from Kenzie's designer castoffs. Kenzie kept insisting that she *wanted* to get rid of the stuff, but I couldn't help imagining the price tag attached to each Valentino dress and BCBG blouse.

It was only when Isobel found a pair of funky gladiator sandals for herself that I started to get into the whole makeover thing. I didn't even try to roll my eyes when Corey insisted we cover up all evidence of my fight with pounds of makeup. Not even when he pulled out the stuff my mom had purchased as my birthday present in the hope that I would become more feminine like Elle. The old photos of my mom rocking a cheerleader uniform paint a very clear picture: Like mother, like . . . one of her daughters.

Corey finished applying my eye shadow before he handed over the tube of sealed mascara.

"I'm amazed you've never touched this stuff. Your mom has a real eye for makeup."

Nodding seemed dangerous, given how easy it was for me to jab myself in the eye with the wand. "Um . . . reality check? It's not like we go clubbing on the weekends."

Isobel waggled her toes in her new shoes. "Just because you don't go to clubs doesn't mean you can't wear makeup."

"Well, yeah," I agreed. "I guess. It just doesn't seem like *me*."

Corey rolled his eyes. "That's because you give a whole new meaning to the term 'wallflower.' "

Okay, that sort of stung.

"She punched Alex Thompson today," Isobel pointed out. "Not that I'm thrilled about what happened, but . . ."

"She held her own," Kenzie finished when Isobel trailed off. "Logan said he was impressed by some of your punches. I warned him that you've also got a mean right hook."

I grinned and decided not to comment on her abrupt change of attitude from this afternoon. Maybe she had just needed a few hours to cool down.

"And if you show up tomorrow in one of these outfits, your social standing is going to skyrocket," Corey enthused. "Just don't forget about us when you're hobnobbing with the Notables."

I snorted. "*Hobnobbing?* Yeah, right. Chelsea Halloway and I are going to become lunch buddies. Get real."

"Well, my work here is done." He flapped a hand in the direction of the mirror. "Go admire yourself some more."

It was strange feeling like I was at the part in a movie when the camera zooms in to capture the expression that says it all: a mixture of doe-eyed innocence, confusion, amazement, and nerves on the plucky heroine's face. That's kind of how I looked—a little panicky, but pretty nonetheless. And "pretty" is not a word that ever gets applied to me. Unless I put a lot of work into it and hit "cute," I usually land squarely in the "all right" category.

But the girl staring back at me in the mirror looked more like the leading lady instead of the trusty sidekick.

One thing was obvious: I wasn't going to be Invisible anymore.

Chapter 9

I was careful to follow Corey's instructions the next morning.

Well, most of them.

I put on the dark gray jeans with the pebbled silk blouse, then added a chunky necklace because despite what Corey thought I wanted to display a little less cleavage. I applied makeup until my bruise was barely visible. My goal was to become virtually unrecognizable. I wanted to fool myself into feeling like a top-secret spy poised to break into an underground vault, crack a high-level security system, and gain access to nuclear launch codes.

All of which sounded less stressful than walking through the doors of my high school.

"Jane?" My mom stared at me when I entered the kitchen like I'd been replaced by a Jane Smith from a parallel universe.

"Yeah?"

My outfit clearly had her flustered. "I, well. You look . . . oh, sweetie. You look nice." Then her eyes started watering. "*Very* nice."

Oh no.

"My little girl is all grown up," she snuffled. "Do you have your camera, Janie? We should take pictures."

"No, it's, uh . . . not charged, Mom," I lied without guilt. She was acting like it was my first day of high school all over again. If I'd known that she would make such a big deal out of it I would've done my primping at school.

"Morning, ladies." Then my dad saw me and pulled up short. "You're not going to school like that, are you?" he demanded, jerking his gaze from me to my mom, then back to me again. "She's not going to school like that, right?"

I grabbed my frozen waffles from the toaster and decided to leave before my mom started sobbing, my dad ordered me to change, or Elle commented on my new look.

"Here—" He pulled off his sweatshirt and handed it to me. "All yours. Keep it. Wear it. Enjoy."

"I've got to go. I'll see you later, Dad."

On impulse I pulled him into a hug. I don't know which one of us it was supposed to reassure, but I left him blinking in confusion while my mom continued to sniffle. All I wanted was to sprint back upstairs, tug on my discarded pajamas, and sink beneath my covers. I couldn't let go of my dad's sweatshirt. It was like being handed a stuffed animal before going to sleepover camp for the first time. I knew it was weak, but I just couldn't resist taking it with me. On impulse, I zipped up the sweatshirt so that it entirely concealed my upper body. Cleavage issue resolved. I felt guilty for chickening out—but not guilty enough to unzip.

Especially when I climbed onto the bus only to be met with open-mouthed staring. The news of my fight with Alex Thompson must have spread like wildfire. Either that, or everyone around me had witnessed the whole thing firsthand in the cafeteria. I wondered how the story was being relayed. I definitely preferred to be known as the *totally awesome girl who punched the jerk from the football team* versus *the freaky girl who randomly went berserk in front of everyone.*

All the attention made me appreciate Corey's meddling the night before—I couldn't have hidden my bruises otherwise. The rest of his style upgrade . . . well, I'd just keep that under wraps until I felt a little more confident.

In the meantime, I tried to distract myself with another fictional death, since Isobel was nowhere to be seen.

Jane Smith lived a very boring life . . . until she accidentally incited a fight. That's when people began to take notice. Only instead of swaggering the hallways, Jane skulked in the shadows and sprinted behind corners. Yet hundreds of pairs of prying eyes followed her everywhere. Fully freaked out, Jane misguidedly sought a hiding place by crawling into an air duct.

She died from starvation when she was unable to squirm out.

Hmm . . . death by air duct lacked a certain *je ne sais quoi*. Maybe—

"Smith!" Mr. Elliot roared, interrupting all thoughts of fictional deaths the second I walked into class. As he stormed toward me, everyone nearby shrank away. *"What the hell were you thinking?"*

I knew Mr. Elliot wasn't going to lower his voice. He didn't care if the entire school heard him blast me. I just hoped he would segue into one of his motivational *you need to show more leadership* rants instead of anything more personal.

No such luck.

"Fighting with a football player! You better have a damn good explanation. And don't you *dare* say this has anything to do with your story! *The Smithsonian* does *not* condone this kind of behavior!"

My mouth gaped open. I knew word must have spread among the students, but I kind of expected the faculty members to be too insulated due to their budget-cut drama to pay any attention to it.

"How did you hear about that?"

He looked at me with disgust. "Word travels when you *attack* someone, Smith."

"I didn't just spontaneously attack him!" I protested.

"You mean you planned it?"

"Of course not!"

Mr. Elliot's scowl never lessened. "Did he punch you first?"

"Well . . . no. I was, uh, taking initiative?"

I trailed off as Mr. Elliot began a deep-breathing exercise that sounded rather like the snorting of an outraged bull.

"Why did it happen, Smith?"

I weighed my words carefully. "Irreconcilable differences? It was . . . personal. Although I could type some—"

He slammed his hand down on a nearby table. "You are *not* writing about that for my newspaper!"

"Are you sure? Because I thought maybe if I—"

"Fraser!" he bellowed, cutting me off. "Get over here!"

I closed my eyes briefly. *This isn't happening,* I told myself. *This. Can't. Be. Happening.*

Scott glanced up, then walked over without looking even slightly cowed. It was like he hadn't noticed Mr. Elliot was practically foaming at the mouth.

"Congratulations, Fraser. Due to Smith's utter *stupidity,* you now get to consult on her piece."

"*What?*" I gasped. "Mr. Elliot, I can handle this!"

But he just ignored me and continued speaking to Scott.

"You want to show me what you can do, Fraser? Go for it. From here on out, I give you complete authority to shape this story."

"But this is *my story!*" I protested weakly. It was my chance to prove that I could be more than Grammar Girl or Mackenzie Wellesley's little friend.

Mr. Elliot turned to me. "You should've thought about that earlier! Just be grateful I'm not making you cover the football team for the sports section, Smith."

I hate the whole *girls don't like sports* stereotype. Plenty of girls are die-hard sports fanatics who would absolutely love to get that assignment. Then again, plenty of girls also hadn't been on the receiving end of a football player's fist.

"I'm fine with sports," I blurted out. "I'm happy to interview Logan Beckett about the hockey team. It'll be a hard-hitting piece. Just . . . please don't put Scott in charge."

Scott leaned back against a desk, as if he were perfectly content to just enjoy the show. Even though he had to realize that it would force us to work together even more closely.

"Not going to happen, Smith," Mr. Elliot told me coolly. "Consider this your punishment for making the school principal ask if I was *encouraging my students' violent behavior!*"

Okay, I could see why he'd be mad . . . not that he ever needed an excuse to yell.

"Look, I'm really sorry about that, Mr. Elliot. But please, you can't—"

The flash of a camera momentarily rendered me speechless. I blinked a few times to clear the blotches of color from my vision while Scott proceeded to snap another shot.

"Say cheese."

"Mr. Elliot, please don't do this to—"

He didn't even give me a chance to beg. "The two of you better make an excellent team."

Then he marched off to lecture someone else, leaving me alone in my own personal worst nightmare. Scott lowered his camera, revealing a Grinch-like smirk.

"Well, this is an interesting development, *partner.*"

Chapter 10

"We are *not* partners."

"You're right," Scott said, shocking me with his sudden acquiescence. "As the consultant, I'm really more of a boss than a partner."

Oh no.

"You are not my boss!"

"Sure I am. Although I'd be happy to call Mr. Elliot over if he wasn't specific enough for you."

The thought of Mr. Elliot yelling at me in front of everyone *again* had my stomach flipping in tight little somersaults. "That's okay."

His grin widened, and I knew right then that Scott Fraser had to be the devil. He must have had one hell of a time hiding the triple sixes on his forehead.

"Excellent. So let's talk story concepts then."

"Why are you doing this?" I demanded. "You had no interest in my story yesterday. One fight and suddenly you're a team player. What's that about?"

He straightened. "I'm here for the photographs. End of story. Which is why, whether you like it or not, I'm taking charge."

"Oh yeah?" I challenged. "You and what army?"

A pretty lame retort, but it's not easy whipping out snappy

comebacks when an athletic-looking, overcontrolling jerk *informs* you that he's in charge. I struggled against the urge to smack that smug look right off Scott's face. Not that I would. Cafeteria incident aside, I've never hit anyone in my life.

Well, unless you count wrestling with Elle for the TV remote.

"Somehow I doubt I'll need my friends in the SEAL teams to get your cooperation."

He didn't look like he was kidding, but that didn't mean I was about to back down.

"Look, Scott, I have way too much at stake here to blindly follow orders."

He ignored me. "The paper comes out on Tuesday, so your article needs to be ready by Monday at the absolute latest. That's a tight deadline to meet even for people who know what they're doing. And my photos will make your story look like amateur hour if you don't follow my lead."

My back stiffened at "amateur hour." Okay, so I didn't crank out front-page articles like Lisa Anne. . . . That didn't mean my work sucked. In fact, the only reason *The Smithsonian* wasn't riddled with errors was because the articles crossed my desk for proofing first.

But my name wasn't on the byline, so nobody cared.

"Listen, Your Royal Snobbiness, *my* article will be just fine!" I snapped.

Scott smiled, but there was nothing comforting about the expression. He looked like a sleek black panther who knew he was stalking an injured sloth.

"I'm going to make sure of it."

I rolled my eyes. "Look, I've got it under control. I can't write about the fight, so I'll . . ."—I scanned the classroom for flyers—"go to the drama club meeting at lunch."

Scott didn't appear impressed with that bit of quick thinking. "That'll make a thrilling story. I can see my cover shot now. 'Grammar Girl: A Portrait of Mundanity.' "

"I am not mundane!"

"You're so dedicated to your stupid routines that you've practically got a schedule stapled to your forehead," he scoffed.

"Fine, what do *you* recommend? Let's hear those oh-so-brilliant ideas of yours."

"Try something new." He leaned closer and the dark intensity in his eyes was kind of . . . attractive.

What was *wrong* with me?

"Try something your friends haven't already pre-screened and selected for you."

I took a step back, hoping that some distance from him might help clear my head. "So what you're saying is that instead of listening to my friends, who have yet to steer me wrong, I should trust *you*? Gee, why didn't I think of doing that sooner?"

He shot me a pointed look. "You won't get a good story if your friends are always coddling you."

"Excuse me, if they're always *what*?"

"Oh come on, even you must have noticed it. '*Oh no, our dear little Jane is in trouble! We must save her!*'" Scott clasped his hands together while his mouth curled in disgust.

"They aren't like that!"

"Sure they are."

I wanted to tell him exactly where he could shove this evaluation of my life—but I held myself in check. It didn't matter what he thought of me. All I had to do was write one freaking story . . . and hope that was enough to redeem me from the journalism doghouse.

"Since you're my consultant, I will consider all of your specific recommendations," I said loftily. "But kindly keep your opinion of my personal life to yourself."

Scott grinned. "I don't think I will. You forget: I call the shots now. If you've got a problem with that, take it up with Mr. Elliot."

"That's coercion!"

His smile only deepened. "That's journalism."

"I will hold you in contempt for this."

Scott's beat-up leather jacket barely moved as he shrugged. "I'll live. So drama club at lunch and then what I want after school."

"I can't do that," I told him, relieved that I didn't even have to make up a lie to avoid him. "I work after school on Wednesdays, Fridays, and Sundays. That's non-negotiable."

He nodded. "Okay. Where do you work?"

I looked at him suspiciously. "Why?"

"Just making conversation."

"Fiction Addiction Used Bookstore."

"Do you like it?"

"Yeah, I do, actually." Just thinking about the store got me smiling. "I still can't believe I got the job."

I braced myself for him to say something snarky like, *Yeah, I have no idea why anyone would want to hire you!*

But he didn't.

Instead, he smiled back and it struck me that for the first time since I'd overheard him talking about me with Lisa Anne, we were actually having something that resembled a nice conversation.

"Were there a lot of applicants or something?"

"Not to my knowledge. But my boss is very . . . *particular* about how her store is run. She won't accept any books with boring covers. She says that it's her store, and she can judge them however she wants."

"Sounds like an unusual woman."

I laughed. "Oh, she's that for sure."

"Good. If I'm forced to go somewhere I always prefer there to be interesting people around."

I stared at him in outrage. "You're kidding me. You started that conversation so you could stalk me at work? Was that supposed to be some kind of *charm offensive* or something?"

"That depends on whether you found me charming."

"Not so much."

"Then clearly it wasn't."

I wanted to blame my lack of a comeback on my slowly building headache, sore body, and emotional whiplash. Already I'd had to deal with a sentimental mom, an uncomfortable dad, an irate teacher, and now a jerk turned dictator—I didn't want any of the above to follow me to work.

"You're not going to the bookstore with me."

"Sure I am." Scott's cocky grin was out in full force. "To the store *and* to the drama lunch. I'm going to make damn sure that we get a story worthy of the front page. See you later, Grammar Girl."

I could hardly wait.

Chapter 11

I shouldn't have done it.

I knew better than to open my writing notebook during my English class. But I *really* didn't want Scott Fraser tailing me all the way to work, and I thought if I had the bare bones for a drama club story written, then I might be able to dodge that bullet. And, okay, I didn't exactly have a *story* yet . . . but that didn't mean I couldn't prepare some snappy headlines.

Drama Club: Where Not Everything Is Staged.

Lame.

I tapped my pen restlessly while Ms. Helsenberg lectured on about *Doctor Faustus*. Okay, so maybe Scott had a point about the drama club lacking real potential. Lisa Anne had made it clear that she wanted something sensational. Something shocking.

I could only think of one story with that kind of potential:

Rock Star's New Relationship on the Rocks?

Timothy Goff, the front man of America's hottest indie band, ReadySet, is known for holding back information when it comes to his private life. Rumors have connected him to many of Hollywood's young starlets, including singer Tay-

lor Swift (a rumor that was neither confirmed nor denied by their publicists), but now the truth is finally out! Goff has been quietly dating eighteen-year-old Smith High School student Corey O'Neal, whom he first met backstage at a concert. The two were introduced by YouTube sensation Mackenzie Wellesley, and the couple remains close by regularly texting, calling, and Skyping each other. Still, the distance has definitely become a barrier.

"It's not exactly a 'whirlwind' romance when you see him more often on television than on Skype," O'Neal complains. "I want our Facebook profiles to make it clear that we are together. Taken. Committed."

Let's hope these two lovebirds make it work.

I'm not sure why I even bothered writing the story.

It's not like I could ever turn it in. If Corey wanted to keep his relationship with Tim a secret, my lips (or in this case, my pen) would never spill it. His relationship, his decision—nobody else's. The last thing I wanted was for some magazine editor to spin it into something salacious and then plaster *that* all over the newsstands.

I would just have to come up with something else.

Still, I paused to consider my writing. Stylistically, it was almost as strong as the story where I was . . .

"Stabbed in the eye in a bar fight."

I jerked up in my seat. "What?"

And that's why I shouldn't drift off during class.

"Christopher Marlowe," Ms. Helsenberg said slowly, as if that were perfectly obvious—which it would have been if I had been paying even the slightest bit of attention. "He was stabbed in a bar fight under suspicious circumstances. It's possible he was a spy."

"A spy," I repeated foolishly. "That's interesting."

"I think so," Ms. Helsenberg agreed. "If you're really interested, find me after class, Jane. Now, where was I? Right, Marlowe . . ."

I was so busted.

There was no way I could tell Ms. Helsenberg the truth: *Sorry, not really interested. I read ahead of the syllabus, and Marlowe's death worked its way into my writing. Surprised me for a second there. All better now. Guess I'd better go.*

Yeah, I didn't think that would go over too well. Especially since I knew Ms. Helsenberg would try to capitalize on even the smallest display of student interest . . . and I didn't want to disappoint her.

"So, Jane, let's talk," Ms. Helsenberg said cheerily as she planted herself directly between me and the door.

"Um, I'd love to, but I should really get going. There's only a fifteen-minute break between classes and—"

"I'm sure you'll be fine. You can always run if necessary."

"Sure, but—"

"I'm curious as to why today's class was the most I've heard from you all year."

"Um, I guess I find death interesting," I admitted sheepishly. Then I remembered that when speaking to an authority figure it's generally best not to imply an unhealthy interest in anything even remotely creepy. "Strictly in the hypothetical, of course."

"I see. So you're doing all right?" It sounded like real concern.

"I'm fine." The words were automatic.

"Are you sure? I heard about—"

"My little fight yesterday," I finished for her. "That's already blown over. No big deal."

And if you believe that . . . *then my dog totally ate my homework.*

"It sounds to me like you might need a creative outlet, Jane. Have you ever considered acting?"

"Acting," I repeated. "Me?"

"Sure, you can try on a new persona without making anything permanent."

"Uh, that sounds . . ."

Awful. Terrible. Like a disaster waiting to happen.

"Interesting. I planned on going to the drama club meeting today, but it wasn't—"

Ms. Helsenberg waved dismissively. "Oh, just come to the auditions for *Romeo and Juliet* tomorrow. I'm providing my Shakespearean expertise, so I'll see you there at three o'clock."

"Wait, what?!"

"You better start running now."

I stared at her in confusion. "Running? You think I should join the track team too?"

Ms. Helsenberg smiled. "I think you should get to your next class, Jane. You don't want to be late."

"Right. Class."

She gently propelled me out of the door as students filtered in for her Shakespearean Lit class. "See you Thursday."

I wanted to say something like, *Yeah . . . about that. Not going to happen. But thanks for trying!*

But too many students were eyeing me with blatant curiosity for me to get the words past my throat. So I just nodded and scurried away like she had recommended.

Then I spent almost the entirety of my next class trying to figure out what to do for lunch.

The high school play audition sounded a lot more promising than a drama club meeting, so my original plan was out. Which left me debating the merits of giving Scott a heads-up or letting him find out the hard way when I didn't show.

I would have been seriously tempted to stand him up if I hadn't known that he would find some diabolical way to pay me back in full.

So I texted him.

His response was succinct: **Fine.**

I pocketed my phone, feeling ridiculous for expecting more. The last thing I wanted was to spend any more time than absolutely necessary with the guy. So for me to be disappointed that he hadn't bothered trying to guess my new lunch plans was patently absurd. Ditto for hoping he might express some concern over my return to the scene of the fight.

Then again, I was anxious enough about walking into the cafeteria for both of us.

I couldn't do it.

Corey's makeover had barely gotten me through my bus ride.... The last thing I wanted was to be the center of the entire school's attention. The very thought of standing in line near Alex Thompson or any of his football team buddies was enough to make me queasy. And knowing that Corey would insist I take off my dad's sweatshirt didn't help matters.

I hid out in the library.

Then I went through the rest of my school day on autopilot. I didn't have to think about my routine because it was just that . . . routine. As much as I hated to admit it, Scott had a point when he called me predictable. I wanted him to be wrong about everything: his stupid photography, his assumptions on my personality—all of it.

But none of that changed the fact that this time he had pegged me.

Not something I particularly wanted to linger on as I shoved two of my notebooks into my locker before I headed downtown—without waiting for a certain photographer. If he was that serious about shadowing me at work, then he knew where to find me. And if I wasted time waiting for him, I might be late. My mom had been unhappy enough about picking me up from school the day before; no way would she be willing to shuttle me to Fiction Addiction for at least a month. I could probably call her en route, begging for a lift, and she would suggest that I run faster. Having a physical trainer for a mother definitely has its share of disadvantages.

Then again, as long as I leave immediately after school, I usually enjoy the walk to work. I can crank up my music without Elle yelling at me to "Turn off that emo crap!" And back when Kenzie and Corey had been primarily ignored by the Notables at our school, I could call one of them up and talk all the way to the store.

I missed those days.

Especially since the walk today wasn't soothing my nerves in the slightest. If anything, I was only growing more anxious about my stupid newspaper story with every step. Which meant it was time to call Corey for advice. I knew the story I had written during class was unprintable, but it was possible he knew something that could be leaked. He had mentioned something a few weeks ago about ReadySet eyeing a potential sound-track job. . . . That might satisfy Lisa Anne. I tried to convince myself that it didn't count as cheating to use my friend's celebrity contacts to impress Mr. Elliot. It wasn't like I had befriended Kenzie in elementary school because I predicted that someday she'd be an overnight YouTube sensation.

So maybe it was okay if new clothing wasn't the only perk of our friendship.

The possibility pulled me up short, and I tugged off my backpack so I could begin fumbling inside it for my cell phone. Corey would have no trouble coming up with a brilliant idea that would stun even Lisa Anne Montgomery. I was sure of it.

That's when a firm, masculine hand gripped my shoulder.

I froze in absolute terror.

Alex Thompson. It was either him or one of his football buddies. And judging by the strength of his hold, whoever it was wouldn't be satisfied with a little catch-and-release action. More like *catch and shove the geek girl around* action ... if I was lucky. My gut twisted as I mentally berated myself for ever being stupid enough to think that the fistfight had ended in the cafeteria. Alex would never accept being publicly sucker punched by a girl without getting revenge.

Just like I would never accept a thrashing without a fight.

Releasing a piercing battle cry, I swiveled into his grasp and jackknifed my knee into one well-toned stomach. I felt a quick rush of satisfaction at the solid contact and the surprised grunt of pain from my attacker. The grip on my shoulder weakened as he doubled over.

"That's right, scumbag!" Adrenaline pounded through my system like I had just chugged three energy drinks.

"Not so brave without your posse of friends, are you!" I taunted as I stomped down hard on a Converse-clad foot. Maybe it wasn't the best idea to insult an aggressive jerk, but I was beyond caring. "Take that!"

But this time the elbow that was supposed to sideswipe his face was caught in his hand. In a deft move my self-defense classes hadn't covered, he pivoted and drew my arm up behind my back.

"Damn, Jane!" said an all-too-familiar voice. "What the hell is wrong with you?"

My whole body went slack. "Scott?"

"Yeah. Were you expecting someone else?"

"No," I said quickly. "Let me go."

There was a long, considering pause. "I don't think so. You might try to throw another punch."

I tried to yank my arm out of his grasp and succeeded only

in wrenching it. Two fights in two days. That had to be a new record for Smith High School. Although we were a few blocks away, so maybe it didn't technically count as fighting on school grounds.

Not that it made me feel any better about the situation.

"Scott, I'm sore, I've got a blinding headache, and I think I can now add 'paranoid' to my list of winning personality traits. Please release my arm so I'm not late for work too."

My cool, rational tone appeared to do the trick as he lowered my arm before he unclasped me entirely. I spun around to face him.

"Thanks," I said with forced politeness. "I'm sorry I hit you. It was an accident."

"Some accident. That's one hell of a knee you've got there, Grammar Girl."

I couldn't help smiling at the obvious irritation in his voice. "That's what you get for sneaking up on people."

He stared at me in disbelief, his green eyes flashing with indignation. "I called out your name *three times,* which you would've noticed if your music hadn't been loud enough to drown out a twenty-one-gun salute."

"Oh." I glanced down at the sidewalk where my iPod lay sprawled out like the victim of a sudden hit-and-run. Selecting a playlist for my walk to work was so ingrained I didn't even notice it anymore. Or much of anything else, apparently. "Sorry. My bad."

"Damn right! What the hell had you wound up that tight anyway?"

"Nothing."

He shoved his rumpled dark brown bangs out of his eyes and took a good, long look at me. I tried to lock my knees so he wouldn't notice the sudden shaking. I wanted to blame it all on the adrenaline rush from a heated, albeit short-lived, tussle, but a lot of it was from fear. I hadn't been attacked, but that didn't mean a large group of irate football players weren't still out there gunning for me. Maybe Alex Thompson was just biding his time until he was good and ready. Not so reassuring.

"Are you okay?" This time when he asked, his voice was gentler than I'd ever heard it before—which meant he must have noticed the trembling.

"I'm fine."

What else could I say? *The way my luck has been going, I'm probably going to be beaten up tomorrow. Thanks for asking, Scott. And how have you been lately?*

I thought not.

He nodded. "Look, I'm only going to say this once. If you're in serious trouble, then you should tell your guard dogs about it."

I tried to imagine how my friends would react if they knew my level of Alex Thompson–related fear: Kenzie would panic, Corey would look concerned, Isobel would feel guilty, and Logan would arrange for a hockey player to escort me down the halls between classes. Good intentions, but they would smother me. I'd never noticed it before, but my friends can be a bit overwhelming . . . when they aren't so busy planning romantic dates for two that they ignore me completely.

"I'm fine," I repeated. "Just a touch jumpy. I'm going to buy some mace. Maybe a stun gun. That should do the trick."

"That's all we need: you armed and dangerous. You'd probably zap some little old lady asking for directions."

I laughed, but it still sounded shaky even to my ears. "Don't worry, Scott. I'll make sure it's you before I zap."

"I bet." He stooped to pick up my iPod before he slung my backpack over his shoulder. "How far away is this bookstore?"

"Only another ten minutes. I can carry that," I said, gesturing to my bag.

"Let's just walk it off, Grammar Girl."

And since our fight really had brought all my aches and pains from yesterday right back to the surface, I decided to let him haul my textbooks without protest.

Hey, he volunteered.

Chapter 12

I considered the bookstore my second home . . . only quirkier.

Every wall was painted a different color, nothing in the place matched, and the twisting maze of bookshelves should have struck me as bizarre. Instead, I'd always found it comforting. Probably because as a kid my choice was either to hang out there or join my sister for ballet classes. Elle then threatened to throw a royal tantrum if I didn't pick Fiction Addiction. She needn't have worried. Even at that age I saw Mrs. P's School of Ballet for exactly what it was: a secret program designed to mold Notable girls. From there it's just one short step to world domination, or at least total control of Smith High School's social scene. Case in point: Chelsea Halloway.

And my older sister.

So I wasn't exactly thrilled with the idea of sharing my safe zone with Scott Fraser. In fact, the nearer we came, the more determined I was to defend the store.

If he makes one wisecrack about the décor, I'll punch him, I decided impulsively. *One snarky comment about getting the owner checked for color blindness and his shiny camera will be ground into the sidewalk.*

I couldn't even convince myself that I meant it.

Which left me with no other option than to grab onto his leather jacket and wait for his full attention before I attempted to communicate the gravity of the situation.

"Mrs. Blake is working with me today. If you so much as look funny at her, I'll, uh . . . I'll make sure that you don't get any good photos."

Scott looked thoroughly unimpressed with my threat. "Relax, Grammar Girl. I won't make you look bad in front of your boss."

I gave him a long, hard look to make sure he wasn't just trying to placate me. "Good, because if you—"

"Hello-o, Janie," Mrs. Blake called out, waving at us through the store window and effectively cutting me off. "Why are you bickering with that young gentleman out there?"

"Not. One. Word," I ground out to Scott.

"Sure, *Janie*."

That wasn't any better than being called "Grammar Girl."

Still clutching his jacket, I propelled him into the store in front of me. "We aren't bickering, Mrs. Blake. This is Scott. He's a . . . friend who works on the school newspaper with me."

I did my best not to choke on the word "friend." Unfortunately, Mrs. Blake took my hesitation to mean something else entirely.

"Oh, will you look at that!" she cried out, clasping her hands together so that all of her rings clinked musically. "My little Janie has a beau! And such a handsome one too! I can see why you've been so picky now, Janie dear. I bet you had your sights set on this one."

"Uh, no, Mrs. Blake. No sights whatsoever."

"Oh, I see. Well, I suppose it is more romantic that he picked you out from the crowd, but I don't see anything wrong with making the first move. Although to be fair, when Frank and I got started, I let him think he was steering the dates." She winked. "But we went to *my* favorite restaurants."

"Uh, that's nice."

I probably should have come up with something better to say, but I've never known how to handle Mrs. Blake when she gets going on a subject that interests her. The worst was back in middle school when she regularly asked if my "monthly visitor" had paid me a visit yet. I couldn't say, *None of your business* because that'd be like yelling at Julie Andrews. Or being mean to Betty White.

"Frank is your husband?" Scott asked.

"Oh no. I had three of those before we got together." She winked again, but this time it was directed at Scott. "Frank was my partner."

Scott turned his grin on her—the one that had propelled him onto *The Smithsonian*'s elite staff team in a week while I went virtually ignored for three years. "He must have been a very lucky man."

"Aren't you the charmer!" Mrs. Blake declared. She might be eccentric, but she's always been astute when it comes to people, which was why I had expected her to give Scott a much cooler reception. I hoped it was because she wanted to like whomever she thought I was dating.

Not that we were dating. Obviously.

"The two of you make the sweetest couple. Why, it's just like my psychic told me! I asked her about you the other day, Janie. She said you were in store for a fabulous romance. About time, if you ask me." She beamed while I forced myself not to wince.

"I guess Annette has, uh, finally gotten something right," I lied. I couldn't believe I was saying it, especially to Mrs. Blake. But if I didn't produce a boyfriend soon she was going to start creating online dating profiles for me. The woman gives a whole new meaning to the word "persistent." So I ignored the startled look Scott shot me as I slid my arm around his back. He tensed momentarily and then relaxed into the halfway hug as if he had expected it all along. As if he had always known it was only a matter of time before I'd be unable to resist his appeal.

Yeah, right.

Although it did feel really nice to have his body pressed against my side. I decided not to focus on that part.

"Yep, Scott's my boyfriend." I tried not to choke.

"And Janie's my little ray of sunshine."

I wanted to step hard on his foot again. It may have been my lie, but that didn't mean I wanted him to be having fun at my expense.

"I'm so happy, I'm at a loss for words," I said, mentally adding, *except for words like "discomfort" and "irritation."* "So . . . did Annette mention anything new about lucky number four?"

"Number four?"

Mrs. Blake smiled at Scott and went into an explanation I'd heard a hundred times.

"I met my first husband in college back when we were both impetuous and full of *joie de vivre*. Then he took a corporate job that started sucking all the *joie* out of my *vivre*. The divorce was perfectly civil, and I met my second husband in a library. We were both reaching for a copy of *Pride and Prejudice*." She sighed gustily. "My favorite. The two of us were together for fifteen years."

"What happened to him?" Scott looked so interested in her story, I couldn't tell whether he was putting on a good show for an old lady or whether he found her as enjoyable as I did.

"Oh, we divorced too." She shrugged and waved her hand dismissively. "It was wonderful while it lasted, and we've stayed very close friends. He actually introduced me to Frank years later. But that was after William."

"William?"

"Now *he* was a mistake, but a wonderful learning experience nonetheless." She lowered her voice to a whisper. "Never marry someone based solely on the sex."

"I'll keep that in mind," Scott said, clearly struggling to keep a straight face.

I wanted to drop my arm the instant she mentioned sex, but Scott just squeezed my shoulder and pulled me closer. "Especially with this one. She's a tiger."

Okay, that was taking it too far.

Mrs. Blake looked at us speculatively. "The two of you are just darling. Working together on the school newspaper . . . and is that a camera you've got there, Scott?"

"Yes, ma'am."

Ma'am. The guy was definitely pulling out all the stops to charm her. Which technically he didn't have to do since it's not like the two of us were actually dating. He could just wander the shelves and send her a vaguely friendly nod. After all, he was really only there to discuss the next move for our story.

"How wonderful! You should take some photos of me! Now wouldn't that be a hoot and a half. Just give me a moment to get gussied up and I'll be ready to go."

Mrs. Blake is something of a diva.

"That's really not necessary," I protested.

"A lady should always freshen up her lipstick for the press."

"Sure. Fine. But we're not taking photos for the press. I'm straightening the shelves today." I gestured around the store. "I'll just see if anyone needs help first."

Mrs. Blake beamed at me. "Such a hard worker, our little Janie. I don't know what I'd do without her." She patted her golden-blond hair, which retained its shape due to her liberal use of hair spray. "Now why don't you show your new beau the memoir section?"

The memoirs reside in a hidden little alcove at the very center of the maze of bookshelves, so it's usually deserted—unless people use it for a semiprivate romantic interlude. Mrs. Blake and I had taken to calling it the make-out memoir section, or M.O.M.S. for short. It seemed appropriate, given that most of the women we caught mid-lip-lock were members of the PTA.

I did my best to pretend that my boss hadn't suggested I go make out with my fake boyfriend.

"No, that's okay. Not for us, thanks. Uh, time for me to work. We'll be in the kids' section."

I yanked Scott away from her before she could be any more explicit with her suggestions.

It was only when we safely reached the kids' section that I could slump against a wall and close my eyes. "Just . . . Don't. Say. Anything."

"I don't see why you're so concerned. She doesn't exactly strike me as frail."

"I never said she was."

"Then why were you so nervous? Afraid she wouldn't approve of me as your new *beau?*"

I shook my head slowly. "Okay, first of all, never say 'beau' again. Secondly, that whole pretend-dating thing never happened. Erase it from your memory. Now."

"I don't know, I might be your cosmic destiny." Scott smirked as he leaned toward me.

"Forget the psychic stuff too. The closest that Annette Lovegood has ever come to predicting the future is guessing which one of her cats is meowing for kibble. Mrs. Blake mainly goes there to be supportive."

"So why does she ask about your love life?" His grin widened. "Does Janie have trouble finding a date?"

"Don't call me Janie. Can't we just pretend the last few minutes didn't happen? I only lied to stop Mrs. Blake from trying to fix me up with her best friend's grandson," I admitted. "Not because I think there is anything wrong with my preference to remain single."

Well, I guess *preference* isn't quite accurate. Did I want a boyfriend? Sure. But it's not like you can pull up to a drive-through and say, *Hi, I'd like to order one boyfriend. Smart, sweet, and funny with a lot of physical attraction. Yes, fidelity is important to me. And I'd like friendship on the side. Two bucks? Perfect. I'll just pull up to the window.*

Not so much.

Although it's entirely possible that the primary culprit behind my permanent single status was my inability to tell when guys were flirting. Kenzie and I even turned it into something of a game. I'd walk her through an incident to check if there were any "flirty vibes" I missed. And then she usually rolled her eyes and said, *No,* the maintenance guy was *not* flirting with me when he was changing a lightbulb in the library.

My mistake.

"Sounds like good little Jane Smith isn't getting many suitors."

I crossed my arms defensively. "What, are we in the eighteen hundreds or something?"

"No gentleman callers for you." His green eyes shone with a mocking glee.

I gritted my teeth. This was ridiculous. I didn't have to justify myself. I didn't have to stoop to his level and continue the conversation.

"Maybe I'm not interested in gentleman callers."

Where had that come from?

He straightened and raised an eyebrow. "So, female callers, then?"

I considered how to react for the briefest of moments before I stepped forward and bit my lip provocatively the way my sister did back when she was dating her Notable boyfriend Jeff.

"If I kissed a girl . . ." I let my voice trickle down to a whisper and moved even closer. "I wouldn't mention it as a cheap ploy to turn you on."

"Uh. Okay."

It appeared I had been able to temporarily short out some of his brain cells.

Score one for me.

"I've got work to do." I picked up the books that were lying on a kiddie table and let my body brush lightly against his. Okay, so I was power tripping. But it's not like I get to rub shoulders with really hot guys every day. And maybe I was feeling a bit defensive over my lack of a love life. Telling myself that my worth wasn't determined by male interest was easy—believing it was harder. Especially now that Kenzie and Corey had entered serious relationships while I sat at home every night.

My friends had fallen in love, and I hadn't even experienced good old-fashioned lust yet. Well, maybe a few mild cases, but nothing major.

And it was definitely in my best interest to use all the leverage I could get with Scott.

Only this time, I guess I oversold my hand. Scott swiveled so that the parts of me that were barely brushing him before were definitely touching now. I felt a spike in my heart rate, and this time it had nothing to do with a football player hunting me down for vengeance.

"Why, Grammar Girl, are you trying to seduce me?"

I instantly pulled back, but I still couldn't resist grinning. "Who, me?"

He only narrowed his green eyes as if I were a puzzle where none of the pieces fit together properly. That beat being dismissed as predictable by a long shot.

"Now what would good little Jane Smith know about something like that?" I asked, throwing his own words back at him and widening my own blue eyes to look as innocent as possible. I picked up another book and playfully whacked him with it. "I need to work. Don't you have an ego to polish somewhere?"

He pulled out his camera and snapped a photo of me before I could object. Then he looked down at the screen. "Hideous. Really terrible. You look like—"

I laughed and waved the book menacingly. "Watch it."

"No, I think we've got a real winner for page one right here."

In that moment I really wanted to pretend that I'd never overheard his conversation with Lisa Anne.

But I couldn't.

Scott Fraser had already stabbed me in the back once before—I wasn't going to let him do it again.

Chapter 13

Work was fine.

I cleaned up the kids' section, made a beverage run to Starbucks, and assisted customers until the store closed—all of which I accomplished with a certain photographer snapping photos behind me. Scott was good about backing off when customers needed help. He even distracted a little boy with a LEGO spaceship while I gave his older sister some book recommendations.

But it wasn't like we shared our life stories while shelving. For someone who willingly agreed to shadow me for hours, Scott wasn't exactly a fountain of information about himself. Maybe because he was so focused on his photography. He kept making adjustments to get the perfect shot, but by the time the click came I was a knot of tension. All the scrutiny made me self-conscious. So I flinched and winced and repeatedly pointed out that working at a bookstore wasn't exactly front-page material.

But every time I asked why he had decided to come in the first place, he shrugged and gave me more directions. Turn left. Look right. Gaze a little higher up. Higher. Got it.

He fired out the orders while I did my best not to cower behind a book.

Still, it was only when Mrs. Blake insisted he take photos

of us together that I grew seriously apprehensive. Mrs. Blake would never pose and let the matter drop. She'd demand copies and then tack them up in the tiny room that served as the employee lounge. And no matter how badly the pictures turned out, they would go right next to the one of Mrs. Blake hugging her granddaughter, Joy, who had recently gone goth and now refused to smile. The sight of Joy's sullen face staring back at me from the fridge always creeps me out.

Nevertheless, I was stuck waiting for Mrs. Blake to refresh her lipstick while Scott debated the merits of various locations within the bookstore.

"Stand over there," he directed me as he stared through the lens of his camera. "Actually, move more to the right. Closer to the historical fiction. No, wait, never mind."

"Okay, stop. Put down the camera," I ordered. "Mrs. Blake is going to make us shoot it in the memoir section. Might as well spare yourself the trouble and just wait."

He lowered the camera. "What's so special about the memoir section?"

"Look, it's just a thing. Mrs. Blake is going to demand we take the stupid photos in the M.O.M.S. She thinks it has romantic powers."

"Because she finds moms romantic?"

I couldn't help grinning at his obvious confusion. "No, that's our private acronym for the memoir alcove."

"Okay. So what does it stand for?"

No way was Scott going to drop it now. And if I didn't supply him with the answer, he'd ask Mrs. Blake. And *she* would have no trouble giving him all the details. That would be far more awkward in the long run.

"Make-out memoir section," I mumbled.

"Sorry, I didn't catch that."

"Make-out memoir section!"

He smirked. "Mrs. Blake wants you to kiss me."

"No," I corrected. "Mrs. Blake wants my boyfriend to kiss

me. And since I don't *actually* have one of those, she'll just have to live with the disappointment."

"Sounds like you'll be the one disappointed."

Somehow I didn't think my fledgling flirting skills were ready to handle that comment. So I chose to ignore it.

"Look, we'll go to the memoir section—"

"Make-out memoir section," Scott interjected. "It's usually best to refer to a place by its full name."

"We'll go there, take the stupid photos, and be done with it. And these shots have to be good because the fridge is scary enough already. Joy's picture makes her look possessed . . . although that may have been beyond the photographer's control."

"Did you just say something mean? I thought comments like that were prohibited for good little Jane Smith. Big step for you, Grammar Girl."

"Shut up, Scott." I paused dramatically. "Clearly, I must no longer have a problem being mean. And I've got two fistfights to prove it."

He shook his head, and I knew he wasn't buying it. "One of those fights was with me, Grammar Girl. Doesn't count."

"Sure it does! I kicked your ass."

Maybe that wasn't the smartest thing to say. Scott instantly straightened.

"I had your arm behind your back! If that's your idea of kicking someone's ass, then you seriously need some professional help."

"I could've gotten out of it," I lied. "No problem."

"Oh, really?" Scott set down his camera. "Want a rematch?"

"No, I'm good." I backpedaled.

He stepped closer. "I'm fine with picking it up where we left off. I believe it was your right arm I had immobilized."

"All right, Mr. DeMille, I'm ready for my close-up!"

Never before had I been so grateful to see Mrs. Blake. She

wrapped one ring-laden hand around Scott's arm and tugged him through the maze of the store. Right to the make-out memoir section. As if the proximity to all those true love stories would compel Scott to grab me and commit some massive display of PDA.

So not going to happen.

Still, I wondered what Kenzie would say if I mentioned the flirty vibes Scott had been sending earlier. She'd probably burst out laughing and tell me to get my imagination under control. Too bad Mrs. Blake hadn't responded that way.

"I'm just so excited," she declared, before puckering her lips into a pout for the camera. "Annette Lovegood always says that the sensitivity of the universe sometimes jumbles her predictions. But she also said that I would have a passionate intrigue after a loved one formed a stable, meaningful relationship." She did a quarter turn and put a hand jauntily on her hip. "Maybe now my next good one will show up."

"And this would be number five?" Scott asked as he adjusted his lens.

"Lucky number four. It's all about having the right order of husbands. See, I had a mean one, then a nice one, then a mean one. . . . Time for another nice one!"

I'd already heard this before, so I wisely kept my mouth shut.

"What about Frank?"

Mrs. Blake repositioned me into a better pose before answering. "Oh, Frank doesn't count. Mean one, nice one, only counts if you *marry* them. It's a technicality, sure, but I like it. Now with Janie here—"

"So, uh, did Annette comment on anyone else's love life?" I interrupted, wanting to keep the conversation as far away from me as possible.

"Sure! Why, just last week she foretold Joy giving me the sweetest little great-grandchildren."

"J-Joy?" I sputtered. "She's what? Fifteen?"

"Fifteen and a half coming up next week."

Scott and I just stared at her.

"Well, I don't expect it to happen right this second. It must be one of those out-of-sequence events. Annette told me very clearly that the spirits get confused sometimes. Something about different types of psychic energies . . . Oh, I can never keep it straight."

"Interesting. Do you see a lot of your granddaughter? Jane, tilt your head to the side a little more. Great."

I obeyed the command before I remembered my plan not to be such a pushover. If I kept allowing myself to be easily maneuvered, I wouldn't be taken seriously on the school paper. Then again, following instructions was practically a hard-wired response for me. Stopping cold turkey sounded next to impossible. I couldn't recall the last time I had purposefully ignored an order—or if I ever had.

"Joy comes into the store every Saturday afternoon and helps me sort books. Then we get frozen yogurt together." The very mention of her granddaughter put an extra layer of sweetness into Mrs. Blake's smile. "We're working on a novel together." Her eyes darted from Scott to me so quickly, I wondered if I had imagined a furtive expression flickering across her face. "It's still in the planning stages."

"Okay." Scott didn't appear to be listening any longer. "Now, Jane. I want you to put your arm around Mrs. Blake's waist. Try not to stand so rigidly. Just like that, perfect. Don't move."

"What's your story about?" It was easier to relax into the position when I ignored the way my pretend-boyfriend's disheveled brown hair and camera obscured his face and focused instead on the perky grandmother next to me.

"Oh, it's about a teenage girl," she said airily. "Scott, can you believe our Janie hasn't told me anything about you? Why, I was sure she would call me the second she started dating. I can see that we have a lot of catching up to do. Tell me how you met."

"Hmm," he mumbled distractedly as he tried to capture the perfect shot.

"Um, we met in journalism class." I wanted to keep the story as close to the truth as possible. "I was editing. Scott was standing around while everyone else worked."

That caught his attention.

"It was my first day," Scott said defensively, "and out of nowhere, Jane told me to sit down before I got into trouble."

"And you didn't take my advice."

"I didn't think you were serious."

I tried to remember what exactly Mr. Elliot had hollered at Scott that day. Something about stepping up his game . . . and making himself useful for the first time in his pathetic life.

Of course, Mr. Elliot hadn't realized at the time that Scott was new.

I shook my head slowly. "I don't joke around when it comes to Mr. Elliot."

"Well, I know that *now*. You weren't much help at the time."

My arms crossed automatically as I glared at him. "What? That wasn't *my* fault!"

Who, me? Defensive? Never.

"Oh, this is so romantic." Mrs. Blake clasped her hands together.

I didn't see anything romantic about being blamed for something that wasn't even remotely my fault. Okay, maybe I should have tried harder to save him from Mr. Elliot since he was the new kid . . . but he wasn't exactly a defenseless toddler. Scott had handled it just fine without me.

He sighed, obviously playing it up for Mrs. Blake. "Mr. Elliot *reamed* me while *Janie* stared silently at her computer screen."

"As if I could have said anything to make it better!"

"But once the crisis was over," Scott continued as if I hadn't spoken, "Jane turned to me, introduced herself, and cordially welcomed me to hell. That's when I knew she was special."

Actually, that was sort of sweet. Especially since I knew that he was trying to tell Mrs. Blake as much of the truth as possible. Okay, so the part about finding me special was a lie. If he had been really honest he'd have said: *That's when I knew she was a neurotic nutcase.*

But it was a nice alteration.

"Right. That's how we met," I blurted out. "I think we're done here. And will you look at the time? My mom will be here to pick me up any minute. So—"

"But how did you ask her out?" Mrs. Blake demanded. "I want the full story for Joy so that we can . . . well, you know what gossips we are sometimes."

Yeah, I did know. I had intentionally switched to working Sundays in order to avoid the two of them together for that very reason. Well, *that* and because the way Joy stares at me kind of freaks me out.

"Uh, well . . ."

"It's a great story, but we'll have to save it for another time." Scott continued snapping photos. "Ditch the sweatshirt, Grammar Girl."

I instinctively unzipped it before I remembered what I was wearing underneath.

"Well, isn't this pretty!" Mrs. Blake cooed as she rested her hand on the pebbled silk of my sleeve. "It feels so nice. Why, Janie, where did you get it?"

I did my best to ignore the way Scott soaked in this alteration before he started snapping in a flurry of activity. I didn't blame him. I bet my blue shirt photographed much better than a beat-up sweatshirt. It just made me feel more exposed. No wonder my dad had freaked out on me earlier.

"Kenzie gave it to me."

"Oh. And is she still dating that lovely boy I met a few weeks ago?"

"Logan. Yeah, they're still together."

Scott smirked. "I can't picture Hockey Boy in here. Not unless he was tricked into thinking he'd get to meet Wayne Gretzky."

There was nothing even remotely flirtatious about the death glare I shot him. "For your information, they were looking at books on U.S. history."

"Oh, so Hockey Boy's girlfriend was the one interested in the books." Scott nodded as if that explained everything. "She can do a lot better."

"Her name is Mackenzie Wellesley, not 'Hockey Boy's girlfriend.' And *Logan* had a great time checking out our books on painting. He's actually a very talented artist."

I don't know why I felt the need to defend Logan. It's not like he cared in the slightest what Scott Fraser thought of him. But their interaction made absolutely no sense to me. Scott hadn't been at Smith High School long, barely over a month, and yet in that time he had somehow managed to alienate the nicest guy at school.

"Sure, beneath those hockey pads beats the soul of a tortured artist," he scoffed.

"What is *wrong* with you?"

"Erm, why don't I take a photo of the two of you?" Mrs. Blake probably thought she was interrupting one of our lovers' quarrels.

Yeah, right.

But the reminder that we still had an audience effectively silenced us both. I couldn't believe that I had even temporarily forgotten she was there. Mrs. Blake isn't exactly the type to blend into the background.

Scott sheepishly handed her his camera. "Sorry about that, ma'am. Difference of opinion."

And just like that, he was completely redeemed in her eyes.

"Oh, I understand. William had this friend, *Jennifer*." She pursed her lips in distaste. "I never did like that woman. She wore the most atrocious perfume, really cloying stuff. Eau de desperation, I used to say to William. Then I came home one day and the pillows reeked of it." She shrugged. "Ah, well. It was for the best in the end."

I turned to Scott, but he didn't look like he knew how to respond to that either.

"Uh, let's take that picture," I covered gamely, even though the last thing I wanted was to stand anywhere near Scott. I did it for Mrs. Blake. I followed her every instruction and let Scott drape his arm around my waist. I even smiled nicely for the camera.

My brittle grin was still frozen in place when my mom entered the memoir section . . . and caught sight of her little girl entangled in the arms of an unknown boy.

If this was karmic retribution for one small fib, I'd never lie to a sweet old lady ever again.

Chapter 14

"Uh, hey, Mom."

I couldn't come up with anything else to say. Although, there aren't all that many options when your mom stumbles upon you hugging a green-eyed hottie in a bookstore while your boss is instructing you to "snuggle closer." Maybe something along the lines of, *This really isn't what it looks like* would have been better. But then I'd have to explain what exactly I meant by *that*, and Mrs. Blake's feelings would be hurt. I racked my brain for a way to gracefully extract myself from the situation.

"Oh, Susan, how wonderful to see you! I take it you've already met Janie's boyfriend."

Oh, hell.

"I can't say I have," my mom replied, glancing pointedly at the arm Scott still had wrapped around my waist.

I found myself too stunned to move. Unfortunately, Scott was not similarly affected.

"Scott Fraser. It's nice to meet you, Mrs. Smith."

My mom shook his extended hand and then looked at me as if she expected me to yell, *Psych!* Even my mother acted like it was impossible for me to have a boyfriend. She clearly found it inconceivable that any guy could be interested in this one of her daughters *that* way.

Which was doing wonders for my self-esteem. Oh, wait. Not so much.

"Hi, Scott. It's nice to finally put a face to the name. I've heard so much about you."

I inwardly winced at my mom's words. Scott and I both knew that if I had said anything about him at home . . . it wasn't complimentary. Well, at least I wasn't the only liar in my family. "You'll have to come over for dinner sometime."

"Mom, that's un—"

"—believably generous of you," Scott cut me off. "I'd love to get to know Jane's whole family. Hear all the embarrassing stories."

That last part was said with a grin that looked awfully self-satisfied to me.

"Well, this week is crazy, but . . . how about on Monday? Are you free then, Scott?"

Sorry, I can't make it. I have plans. Big test coming up. I'll have to take a rain check.

Any of those excuses would have worked.

"That sounds wonderful. I'll be looking forward to it."

"Wonderful! Then it's settled."

Apparently, I didn't get a say in whether or not *my* fake boyfriend was invited to dinner. Then again, that was probably because only Scott and I knew the whole thing was a sham.

But just because he wanted to tinker with my life didn't mean I had to play along.

"You know, Scott might not have time for dinner at our house. He has a pretty hectic weekend scheduled."

My mom gave me a long, hard look. "Is there anything more important than family time?"

It wasn't actually a question.

"Of course not, it's just . . ."

"Jane is worried that I won't have enough time to work on the school paper." Scott effortlessly pulled me into the crook of his arm, which felt oddly comforting given that *he* was the one responsible for this latest set of complications. "It'll be fine, sweetie."

Sweetie? This was definitely hell.

"Oh, I'm sure *you* will be fine," I gritted out. "I just think that we need to discuss boundaries for *the article*. Make sure it doesn't make anyone uncomfortable."

He grinned. "Interesting, whereas I think more digging is in order to get the full scoop."

The subtext of all of this went completely unnoticed by my mom and Mrs. Blake.

"Jane, we need to get going. I have to pick up some things from the grocery store for dinner. Scott, it was nice to meet you, and we'll see you Monday night."

"Absolutely. I'll see you later, Jane."

The jerk had the nerve to wink at me. I had to bite my tongue to keep from growling back.

"Sure thing, Scott."

Then I was propelled out of the bookstore and into the supermarket, where my mom simultaneously purchased veggies for our stir-fry and interrogated me about Scott. It wasn't easy fielding her questions since I didn't have the answers to most of them. I didn't even know the most basic information about him. Stuff like what his parents did professionally and whether or not he had siblings.

It didn't get any less stressful when she moved to the more personal questions either—like how long I had been hiding this secret relationship from everyone.

Talk about a minefield.

I think I covered pretty well. I said that we had started a *thing* together a few days ago, and I wanted to keep it low-key until we knew each other better. I said that I didn't want her to get all excited over nothing if it didn't pan out.

But maybe I should have stuck with *no comment*. Maybe that way she wouldn't have gotten all teary-eyed in the

frozen food section over how quickly her little girl was growing up and putting on makeup to impress her new boyfriend.

Of course I couldn't say, *Oh no, Mom, that's just to hide
the black eye I got from a psychopathic football player.*

So I loaded up the grocery cart while she wiped at her watery eyes and welcomed me into "womanhood." I hated lying
to her, but I didn't know how to take it back. Not without
mortifying one or both of us.

I just hoped she wouldn't make too big a deal out of it,
which was why I begged her to keep it to herself.

She barely managed to pass Elle the stir-fry before she
dropped the bomb.

"Jane's got a boyfriend!"

Yeah, that went over about as well as a case of head lice at
an elementary school.

"You've got a *what?*" Elle demanded, nearly spewing
apple juice in her surprise. "Yeah, right!"

"I do!" I insisted, even though . . . I didn't. But I hated the
way they assumed I was pranking them about this when I've
never lied to them before. I mean, *come on!* It isn't like I was
born with an extreme social disorder or a case of leprosy. It
was ridiculous the way my family acted like I had just announced, *Well, tomorrow is the coming of the Messiah.*

My dad looked pained. "So . . . does this mean we need to
have the talk?"

I knew exactly what talk he was referring to, and I definitely didn't want to have it. Not over dinner, not with him,
not ever.

"Nope. I'm fine, Dad. Really, they cover all of that in
school these days."

Elle snorted before she heaved a long-suffering sigh.
"Don't worry, Dad. I'll make sure she knows all about STDs
and contraception."

What I *actually* needed someone to explain was how my

sister could imagine that I would appreciate her discussing that stuff with me, because *that* was beyond me.

I focused on spearing a piece of red pepper with my fork. "No explanations necessary."

My mom and dad traded looks. "You haven't already . . ."

"NO!" I could feel my cheeks heating up in embarrassment. "Can we please drop this?"

"See, Mom! If she's not mature enough to have this conversation, then she definitely isn't ready for sex."

I glared at Elle. "Not wanting to discuss my sex life *over dinner* doesn't mean I'm not mature enough to . . . do it."

"Aw, she said, 'do it.' Isn't that precious?"

"Shut up, *Lane*."

Her jaw stiffened. "It's not my fault you're not ready to be in a *meaningful, lasting relationship.*"

Translation: You'll never be ready to have what Jeff and I had together.

That had me so annoyed I barely noticed when my fork slid from my fingers to my plate with a clatter. "Okay, enough. Scott and I have just started spending time together. We're not exactly searching for the cheapest hotel room we can rent by the hour. And I promise that if we do have sex, I'll be as safe as possible. Not that it's any of your business, but I'm carrying a condom around with me as we speak."

Technically, that wasn't a lie, since the condom Sam gave me was still in my backpack upstairs. I just didn't plan on using it with Scott—or anyone else, for that matter. My dad shot my mom one wild-eyed look, but he didn't comment, probably because he didn't want to say anything that would send me looking for one of those cheap hotel rooms.

I'm not sure what shocked the family more: the announcement that I had a boyfriend or a condom.

"Can I be excused? I've lost my appetite."

My parents nodded their permission, probably because as soon as I left the room they could begin discussing these latest developments. Not that I had any interest in eavesdropping. If I heard my mom sniffle over her little girl reaching womanhood one more time, I was going to lose it.

So I bolted for my room, cranked up my music, and flipped open the ancient family laptop to see who was online. I was hoping to find Kenzie on Skype, but she must have been focused on her homework or out on a date with Logan—either way, she wasn't online. A week ago, I probably would have started in on my homework like a good girl. Then again, a week ago I also wasn't getting lectured about safe sex over the dinner table.

I decided to waste some time on Facebook. There was nobody I particularly wanted to message, but I thought it might be a good way to unwind from the awkwardness of my family dinner. Or at least I *did* until I began wading through a slew of pointless status updates, most of which were painfully long quotes from random people and pictures of food.

Still, it wasn't like I had anything better to do.

I was still clicking through photographs of Kenzie and Logan together, when Scott logged on. I would never have voluntarily friended him if Mr. Elliot hadn't required everyone in the journalism class to add each other. He claimed it would foster a sense of solidarity. All it had actually accomplished was a shared sense of outrage at the total breach of privacy. Not that anyone was about to confront Mr. Elliot on it.

After spending the past two days with Scott and his stupid camera tailing me, he should have been the last person I wanted to contact. Except he was also the one who had let this whole fake-boyfriend thing get so out of hand.

Which is why I skipped all preliminaries and got right to the point.

Jane: **What were you thinking?**

Scott: **Care to specify?**

Jane: **Dinner! Really. You thought that was a GOOD idea?**

I have a much easier time expressing my frustration with people when I can type it—partly because it's less likely I'll get punched in the face.

Scott: **You're a relatively good model when you follow directions. So I'm using you for my portfolio.**

Jane: **Portfolio? What are you talking about? What does that have to do with dinner?**

Scott: **I'm looking forward to a family shoot.**

Of course, if Scott Fraser agreed to something, there was always something in it for him. In this case, that something was the elusive holy grail of photography: a perfect shot.

Jane: **You do realize there is more to life than photography, right?**

Scott: **Do you have a point, or are you just wasting more of my time?**

I glared at his words for a moment before I responded with a little more force on the keyboard than was necessary, strictly speaking.

Jane: **Yes, I have a point! You need to come down with an illness.**

Scott: **Do I now?**

I could practically sense his smirk spreading.

Jane: **Yes, something nasty but not fatal.**

Scott: **So you don't actually want me dead. Good to know.**

Jane: **No, just disfigured and pox-ridden, please.**

Scott: **When exactly did you want this unfortunate illness to strike?**

That was an easy question to answer.

Jane: **BEFORE THE DINNER!**

I took a deep breath and then continued typing.

Jane: **You don't understand: They're already grilling me about you. Where you are from. What your parents do. If you have ever held down a job. It's insane. Run while you still can!**

Scott: **I'm from LA via a bunch of other places. Dad is a**

journalist. Mom is in social work. Mainly I've worked waiter/dishwasher/barista-type jobs. A few gigs as a wedding photographer. You want to know more, you have to ask me yourself.

Wow, that was a lot more information than I had ever expected to get out of him.

Jane: **You really don't want to do this.**

Scott: **Consider it done.**

Jane: **Fine. But you'll regret it.**

Talk about the understatement of the century. Five minutes with my sister making passive-aggressive comments, my dad obsessing over my condom, and my mom choking up over my life changes, and Scott would never come within twenty-five feet of me again.

Scott: **You're boring me. What's the plan for tomorrow?**

I didn't know whether to laugh or glare at the words on the screen. The guy was so blunt and rude and . . . interesting. Even though I hated half of what came out of his mouth, I never knew what he was going to say. At least he wasn't predictable.

Jane: **I'm having lunch with my friends. I plan on checking out the auditions for the play after school, though. Hopefully, I'll find a story there.**

Scott: **See you then.**

Jane: **At the auditions?**

Scott: **All of it.**

Oh, hell no.

Jane: **You're not after more photos of Kenzie, right? You seriously need to stop bugging her.**

Scott: **I'm taking photos of you, not Mackenzie. Or did you somehow forget that** *we are stuck working on a journalism assignment together?*

So maybe I was being a bit overly protective of my friends . . . or maybe he was getting prepared to stab me in the back again. It wouldn't be the first time he tried to use me for access to Kenzie.

Jane: **You seem to be making a habit of inviting yourself along to my meals.**

Scott: **Afraid I can't manage a civil meal with your goons? I mean . . . friends.**

Jane: **Where are you getting this goon stuff? They're really not.**

Scott: **Right. Some *other* hockey players warned me to keep my distance.**

I stared at the words in disbelief.

Jane: **WHAT?**

Scott: **I thought you called out the hit squad.**

Jane: **NO!**

Although I had mentioned his whole "she doesn't have what it takes to be a reporter" thing. I remembered it vividly because it was the first time in a long while that Kenzie had asked about my day, and I had seized the opportunity to vent. But I never expected any of it to go beyond our lunch table.

Apparently, part of it had.

Scott: **Easy on the capitalization, Grammar Girl. Caps lock is not the solution.**

Jane: **WHAT HAPPENED?**

Scott: **Nothing.**

Oh, sure. A conversation between Scott and hockey players where *I* was the topic of conversation: no big deal. Except that it was also the most exciting thing ever to include me—pre-lunchroom fight with Alex Thompson—and I hadn't heard anything about it until now.

Jane: **What did Logan say to you, Scott? If you even think about holding out, I will use the sappiest pet names I can come up with over dinner on Monday. Consider that, honey-dumpling sugar-pie!**

Scott: **Never call me that again.**

Jane: **WHAT HAPPENED?**

Scott: **Your white knight and his friend mentioned that people who upset you don't tend to have the most agreeable
high school experiences. They left it at that.**

Jane: **I'm going to kill him.**

All I had to do was tell Kenzie and then Logan would be a
dead man. Primarily for not including us in his decision to
warn off Scott before he had leaped to my defense. Not that I
had any intention of mentioning it to either of them until I
had sorted out my emotions. Was I irked at Logan for his in-
volvement? Pleased that he obviously cared enough about me
to confront Scott? Annoyed that he thought me incapable of
standing up for myself?

I didn't know.

I couldn't brush off the fact that Logan must have assumed
I was incapable of standing up for myself. Or maybe it was
the fear that he was *right* that bothered me. Sure, I had punched
Alex Thompson in the face, but I hadn't even done that for
myself. Not really.

I did it for Isobel.

Scott: **Can I watch the fight?**

Jane: **No. So does this explain your coldness toward me, or
are you naturally like that?**

I probably could have phrased it better, but at that point I
wasn't thinking too clearly.

Scott: **It comes naturally.**

Jane: **Great.**

Scott: **See you at lunch then.**

Jane: **Right. Wait, what?**

But he'd already logged off.

Chapter 15

I was very careful with my school prep the next morning. And not in my usual way, by double-checking that all my textbooks and assignments were perfectly ordered in my backpack. Instead, I took one step closer to becoming a *Seventeen Magazine*–reading, makeup-wearing, certified girlie girl, by assembling my own outfit. My sister would be so proud if she ever managed to watch me succeed at anything without wincing.

This time I had a better idea of the look I wanted to achieve—something significantly tamer than what I had worn beneath my dad's sweatshirt the day before. Something I could wear in public without inwardly wanting to cringe. Especially since I planned on attending the auditions for the school play. I needed a look that said, *Oh, I could totally handle being up on stage. I just* choose *not to perform.*

Despite the fact that I'd rather be deployed with Scott's SEAL friends than speak in front of an audience.

Hopefully, nobody would think of me as a wimp for declining Ms. Helsenberg's invitation to try out if I wore Kenzie's very stylish boots. I toughened up the look by pairing her dark-rinse skinny jeans and BCBG military-style jacket with my Beatles *Rubber Soul* shirt. That, plus my stupid *hide the black eye* makeup routine, and I was good to go. I glanced over at the clock in disgust.

It had taken me well over an hour to prepare for school.

The whole process made me nostalgic for the days when I would stumble out of bed, throw on whatever was cleanest, and be out the door in fifteen minutes. It was weird realizing that those days I missed, yeah, they had ended roughly two days ago.

At least I still had Isobel. She greeted me with a confused smile as I boarded the bus.

"Did I miss something? The last time I saw you, Corey was trying to go for a more, erm, feminine style. Now you look like an assassin."

I tried to play it cool. "I thought the clothes went with my black eye."

"So you're telling me that this look is meant to hide the fact that a football player punched you in the face this week?"

I lightly touched my face and felt the now-familiar dull throb of pain. Still, it could've been a hell of a lot worse.

"What, this ol' thing? Why would I want to hide it? It's no big deal—my badge of honor." I used up all my reserve of false bravado. "The clothes make it look more normal, right?"

"R-ight."

I slouched against my seat. "How bad is it?"

Isobel smiled sympathetically. "You're not fooling me with the clothing and the makeup, but that's probably because you don't have a convincing attitude. And I couldn't help but notice that you bailed on lunch yesterday."

I knew exactly where this was going.

"You can't avoid the cafeteria, Jane. Trust me: If that were a viable option I would have done it already."

She had a point: Hiding in the library the day before had been a moment of weakness. Even if I had only done it to avoid making myself an easy target. The only way I was going to convince anyone that I could stand up for myself was if I stopped cowering.

"You're right, Isobel. No more hiding. It won't be so bad. Compared to finding a newsworthy story and breaking up with Scott . . . it's a minor-league concern."

"You have to *what?*"

It felt like my brain was spinning. "I'm going to call Corey for advice. Lisa Anne wants something sexy and controversial, and if there is one member of our group with access to something like that, it's him. It's not wrong of me to depend on him, right? That's just utilizing a source."

"You're dating *Scott?*"

"No!" I stared at her in disbelief. "Where did you get that idea?"

"You just said that you have to *break up with him!*"

"I did?" I was having a hard time keeping track of my own words. "It's nothing. I pretended that we were dating to get Mrs. Blake off my back. Then my mom showed up. So now I have to fake break up with him, but I can't let it look staged because if Elle ever finds out she will never let me live it down."

"Wow, breathe, girl."

I sucked in some air. "But none of that matters. I'm going to focus on this article, and that will make everything better."

She shoved her glasses higher up on the bridge of her nose. "You just told me that you're in a fake relationship with one of the hottest boys at school. You're right: totally doesn't matter."

I laughed. "No, it doesn't, because it doesn't *mean* anything."

Isobel hesitated. "Not that I want to add any more complications to your life right now, but . . . I'm not convinced. I don't think you would even *pretend* to be in a relationship with someone if there wasn't an underlying current of interest."

"Yeah, there was definitely a current of interest . . . in getting Mrs. Blake off my back!" I scoffed. "There's nothing going on between me and Scott Fraser."

Okay, except maybe for some flirting in the bookstore. But that seemed more like a reflex for him than an actual display of interest.

Isobel bit her lip thoughtfully. "I don't know. That's still quite a stretch. I just think—"

Whatever she was about to say was lost in the shuffle of students as we disembarked from the bus.

"Jane!"

My head snapped up as I searched for whomever had called out my name. A small part of me hoped it was Kenzie. That she had been waiting by the bus ramp for a chance to walk me into school.

Then my eyes connected with Sam from detention.

"Uh, hey, Sam," I replied, hoping that she wouldn't notice the sudden flush of embarrassment on my face.

I couldn't stop thinking about the condom she had given me . . . and the way I had announced it to my family.

"Have you, uh, met my friend Isobel?" I had trouble visualizing the two mixing in the same social circle. Especially since Isobel is a khaki-shorts-and-oxford-shirts kind of girl, while Sam clearly favored her knee-high leather combat boots.

"No, I haven't." Her eyeliner-rimmed gaze assessed Isobel slowly. "I'm Sam."

"Right." Isobel pushed up her glasses again. "I figured that part out."

I knew that she didn't intend to be sarcastic because that might provoke someone like Sam . . . and alienating *anyone* was the absolute last thing Isobel wanted.

The words just seemed to tumble out against her will.

Sam grinned. "You're the girl Jane got into a fight over."

"Uh—" Isobel turned red. "Yeah, well, I was the catalyst.

Actually, I'm not so sure about that anymore. My theory is that Jane wanted to do something dangerous and that she used Alex Thompson's behavior as a convenient excuse."

"What?" I protested. "That's not what happened!"

She shrugged. "It makes sense to me. Although it's really more of a working hypothesis than a theory right now. But I still appreciate that you feel strongly enough about me to jump to the rescue, Jane. It was stupid, but nice."

"Your hypothesis needs a lot of work," I grumbled.

"I will take that under consideration."

Sam laughed. "The two of you are freakishly similar."

I wasn't sure how to respond to that particular statement. I mean, sure, Isobel and I were both complete geeks in the same social circle, but beyond that . . .

"Nope," Isobel disagreed, before I had so much as opened my mouth. "We're actually very different. For example: Jane is torn between remaining in the background and joining her friends in the spotlight. I'm not."

This was getting to be *way* too much psychoanalysis first thing in the morning, and I half expected Sam to laugh it off and change the subject.

Instead she looked intrigued. "So you have no interest in getting attention?"

"Oh no, I get plenty of attention." Isobel shrugged. "It's just limited to stuff like my AP scores."

"Aren't you a freshman?"

"Yes."

"Then how could you have any AP scores?"

Isobel suddenly appeared very interested in examining her shoelaces. "I took two courses last year in middle school."

"Why would you do something like that?" Sam demanded.

She shrugged. "I had nothing better to do."

It was pretty obvious from the way Sam's mouth hung open that she hadn't anticipated that answer, but it made sense to me. In fact, that was exactly how I felt about homework most of the time. I didn't study hard before my tests because I wanted to impress colleges with my valedictorian status. That's the kind of reasoning that Lisa Anne probably used. Studying was just the only thing for me to do . . . and at this point everyone expected it of me.

Sam whistled. "We really need to get you a social life."

"Uh, sure. I mean . . . what does that entail for you, Sam?" Isobel sagged a little in relief when she finally formed a question.

"Usually that entails socializing, but I got an extra week of detention for passing out condoms yesterday. Then again, you never know the friendships you'll form in detention." Sam grinned at me. "Every now and then I meet someone cool. I'm also a founding member of the baking club. Any interest in joining? We've got a meeting at lunch today."

I shook my head apologetically. "I have to eat in the cafeteria today. Time to return to the scene of the crime."

"What about you, Isobel? Interested?"

Isobel looked stunned. Probably because she doesn't often get invited to things—even low-key events like baking club meetings. Meanwhile, I was still trying to process the mental image of Sam in a floppy baker's hat. I guess there were way more layers to my new raccoon-eyed friend than I'd initially thought.

The bell rang, and I had to scurry off to journalism before I heard Isobel's response. I found myself hoping she declined. I knew it was selfish, but I didn't want her to go without me. It was just that . . . my oldest friends didn't have much time for me anymore. I didn't want that to happen with my newest ones too.

But I had way more pressing issues to focus on when I entered the classroom and Lisa Anne pulled me into a secluded corner. The whole thing felt very mafia-esque, especially when she cracked her knuckles impatiently.

"How's the article going?"

So much for easing into the conversation with small talk. I guess, *Hello, Jane. How are you today?* was too much to hope for coming from Lisa Anne.

"Erm, great!" I lied. "It's really starting to take shape."

In my nightmares.

She shot me a look that made it clear she wasn't buying it.

"What's it on?"

"The high school play?" I couldn't keep my voice from wobbling.

"Oh, how sweet," Lisa Anne said mockingly. "Except we're not in elementary school anymore. I want something hard-hitting, Grammar Girl. Or do I have to remind you again what's at stake?"

"No. I've got it."

"You get me that story by Monday, or I will personally—"

"—destroy my writing career," I finished for her. "I've got it."

She looked momentarily rattled by my interruption, but she recovered quickly. "Good, because I'm not covering for you."

As if I ever thought she would.

I restrained the urge to roll my eyes. "Understood."

"So how are you working with Scott?"

Now where had that come from?

"Fine," I hedged. "Why?"

"As our best staff photographer, it's imperative that his talents are being utilized to their fullest potential."

"Uh . . . okay."

"Your article has to showcase his work."

I was starting to think her list of demands would never end. It had to be fresh and fun, modern and mature, smart and sexy, and now it also had to be a showcase for Scott's photography. It sounded like she expected me to be a freaking magician so I could also whip a rabbit out of my hat.

But if I commented on it, I could kiss my fiction page good-bye.

"No problem."

"Good. Oh, and Jane? Scott can take pictures of anything he wants. Is that clear?"

"Uh, no." I shook my head. "I'm sorry, what are you talking about?"

Lisa Anne couldn't even be bothered to meet my eyes. Instead, she concentrated on straightening the collar of her shirt so it was perfectly aligned with her form-fitting sweater. "He's creating a portfolio based on his photos of you." She rolled her eyes in a way that implied, *There's no accounting for taste.* "And even though I personally think he has chosen the wrong model, *The Smithsonian* is giving him its full support. As am I."

I wondered if that was her way of attempting to capture his attention. As a flirting technique I thought it had potential, since the only thing Scott appeared to care about was his stupid camera. Something I should have kept in mind when he'd mentioned a portfolio on Facebook, but instead I had dismissed it as his warped idea of a joke. Surely he valued his photography too much to waste time documenting someone he actively disliked. So I assumed he was making up a portfolio to mess with my head. Apparently, none of it had been a joke.

And I definitely wasn't laughing.

Lisa Anne held up a hand to silence any potential protest. "A good newspaper requires teamwork. I expect your full cooperation on this."

The *or else* hung heavy in the air. It wasn't hard to fill in the blank. *Or else you'll be sent right back to copyediting. Or else you will be ignored for the rest of high school.* And

Lisa Anne would ensure that every one of those threats became a reality if I didn't agree to go along with Scott's every whim.

Of that I had no doubt.

I surveyed the journalism classroom until I located Scott. I couldn't believe he had the nerve to meet my gaze without flinching after orchestrating his photographic *coup d'état*. I gritted my teeth.

Game on.

Lisa Anne continued lecturing me about teamwork and professionalism until she spotted one of the smokers trying to sneak out of the classroom. Instead of watching her verbally roast the guy, I seized the opportunity to march over to Scott. In one smooth move, I yanked out a chair and sat down gunslinger style: eyes forward, back straight, jaw set in contempt.

"You went running to Lisa Anne!" I snapped. "Seriously, Scott? *Seriously.* That was your brilliant plan to convince me to be your model? Not smart."

Scott's green eyes were partly hidden by his dark brown bangs, but they didn't look guilty to me.

Nope, his expression was just as arrogant as ever.

"We should probably talk about this when you're not so upset."

I rolled my eyes. "What is there to discuss, Scott? You got what you wanted because you forced me into it. Don't pretend to care about the blackmailing technique you used now."

He leaned back in his chair. "Okay, calm down, Grammar Girl. You're blowing this whole thing out of proportion."

"Right. My mistake. I should be *thrilled* to have absolutely no say in any of this!" My voice cracked, but my anger had me beyond caring.

"You're acting like you were sold into bondage."

"I know this isn't slavery, Scott. But it *is* indentured servitude. And from where I'm sitting that still completely *sucks!*"

"You're making way too big a deal out of this."

I folded my arms. "No way would you be saying that if the positions were reversed."

When Scott finally spoke, his voice held none of the humor I had heard yesterday in the bookstore. "If it were me, I'd concentrate on getting the job done. But if you want to whine about it, by all means continue."

"I'm not going to model for you."

He didn't appear any more rattled by that statement than by anything else I had said.

"Look, I didn't plan on using you for my portfolio. I thought you'd have failed this project already and my talents would be redirected elsewhere. But apparently 'transition' is a popular theme for art schools, and since I've got such great shots from the fight"—he shrugged—"I'm going to continue following you everywhere—whether you like it or not."

Then he turned his back on me, logged into one of the computers, and began toying with his photos from the cafeteria. I couldn't help glancing past his shoulders at the screen and was rewarded by a glimpse of an action shot featuring a virtually unrecognizable version of myself with a raised fist and eyes shooting bloody murder. It was disconcerting, not just because I looked so different, but because I looked *strong*. My expression belonged on someone fearless about to charge into battle in defense of her homeland. And even though I didn't particularly want *that* look captured on film, I couldn't deny that it showcased his photography skills nicely. I just couldn't tell *him* that I wanted a copy without the acknowledgment going to his head. And no way did I want to encourage his insufferable ego to even greater heights—especially not after Lisa Anne's decision to give Scott approval power.

Not when he took so much enjoyment out of messing with every aspect of my life.

I might not have wanted to write the front-page story, but

I sure didn't appreciate having Scott in charge of what I could say. As far as I was concerned, Scott and Lisa Anne already were a match made in hell. I had no trouble picturing some future argyle-wearing devil-spawn daughter of theirs snapping photos of her classmates leaving restrooms with toilet paper stuck to the bottom of their shoes and then cackling evilly at the prospect of placing it on the front page. I shook my head to clear away the image.

The only way to make them back off was to write the story of the century.

Way easier said than done.

Chapter 16

I must have looked miserable when I plunked down my cafeteria tray because Kenzie unwrapped her arm from Logan's shoulder and really focused on me for the first time in weeks.

"What's wrong, Jane?"

Just as if things between us had never changed.

Except she didn't have the faintest idea what was going on in my life. She didn't know about Scott posing as my fake boyfriend. She didn't know how badly I wanted to have an important role on the paper. She didn't know how much I missed her.

"I've been ordered to model for Scott," I said bluntly. "It's nothing. I'm fine."

Logan sat up straighter and stopped nudging Kenzie's knee under the table. The two of them tried not to be nauseating with their public displays of affection . . . but they didn't always succeed.

"What happened?" Logan demanded in his concerned-big-brother kind of way.

"He's working on his portfolio and . . . you know what? We can get back to that later. Right now, I'd much rather have you tell me what *exactly* you said to Scott a few weeks ago."

I couldn't believe that I was interrogating Logan about it over lunch. But since the words had already slipped out, I had no intention of trying to take them back. The concern on his handsome face was wiped away in an instant, leaving only a carefully shuttered expression in its place.

"Logan?"

He couldn't stand disappointing Kenzie, and I knew that it was only a matter of time before he cracked under our interrogation.

"It was nothing," he said staunchly.

"I thought we agreed you weren't going to say anything to Scott," Kenzie reminded him. "Just like you aren't going to confront Alex about his fight with Jane."

"It wasn't planned."

I gave him the firmest look I could muster, which in his case wasn't very tough. It helped that Logan was dating my best friend, but the guy was still a *Notable*.

And everyone at Smith High School was well aware that glaring at a Notable could be hazardous to your health.

I'm just surprised the Surgeon General hasn't issued any official warnings about it.

"If it wasn't planned, then what was it?" I asked him.

Logan sighed and crossed his arms. "You sounded really upset about his journalism crack, okay? So when Spencer and I happened to see him in the parking lot . . . we may have mentioned that we don't think kindly of those who mess with our friends."

Kenzie jabbed him with her elbow. "That's getting involved!"

"It was no big deal."

"Yes, it was!" I protested. "It was a very big deal. He's on the school paper with me! Now thanks to you, that has become about a million times more awkward! God, what else did you do? Let me guess, it was *your* genius idea for him to start calling me 'Grammar Girl' too!"

That last part was pure sarcasm, but instead of rolling his eyes, Logan looked guiltily at the french fries on his plate.

"Spencer and I may have mentioned something along those lines."

"*What?*"

The guy really needed to learn when he was only digging himself deeper. "We may have said something about . . . not going near you or, um"—he faltered as he took in our horrified expressions—"not getting to know each other on a first-name basis."

"You have *got* to be *kidding me!*" I put my head down on the table and seriously considered whacking it against the hard surface a few times.

Kenzie grabbed Logan's shoulders. "*What were you thinking?*"

"It was no big deal, Mack," Logan repeated.

For the first time I wasn't jealous of Kenzie's relationship—I wouldn't have relished trying to explain why it is generally considered a bad idea to warn off other guys behind your girlfriend's best friend's back.

"I bet that's when he began referring to me as Grammar Girl." I felt numb. "For future reference, when I say, *I'm just venting, don't get involved,* that is not code for *Please intimidate the guy I have to see every single day in class!*"

Logan didn't appear to have anything to say to that, probably because he had never imagined good little Jane Smith yelling at him.

Kenzie cleared her throat. "Jane? Are you sure you're okay?"

"I'm *fine!*"

Logan and Kenzie traded skeptical looks as I focused on stabbing the pasta on my plate.

"Hey, guys." Corey slid into the seat next to mine. "How are you, Jane?"

"She's fine," Kenzie answered quickly, probably because I

looked like I was reconsidering my decision not to beat my head against the table.

"Oh good. So you're not worried about that story anymore then?"

Logan raised an eyebrow. "What story?"

"Jane's struggling a bit in journalism," Kenzie explained as she reached over to steal a french fry from Logan's plate. I felt a small kick of jealousy. I wanted to be in the kind of relationship where I could elbow my boyfriend for being a blockhead, sneak a fry, and then continue playing footsie under the table.

"It's not worth freaking out over, Jane. It's just the school paper. It doesn't mean anything."

It doesn't mean anything.

I couldn't believe she was being so blasé about it. When her botched attempt at CPR got four million hits on YouTube, did I tell *her* not to worry about it?

It's just the Internet, Kenzie. It doesn't mean anything.

No, I did not.

My problems with *The Smithsonian* were nothing compared to being the punch line for every late-night comedian, but that didn't make them any less real to me. I still needed my best friend's support, even though I was already too pigeonholed into the role of sidekick to get it.

I didn't trust myself not to say something I would regret, so I kept my mouth shut and scanned the cafeteria. Logan's best friend, Spencer, and all his hockey teammates sat at the Notable table presided over by Chelsea Halloway. At least half of the guys looked like they would willingly quit the team just for a date with her. Saturday night . . . Sunday afternoon . . . I bet most of them would willingly sell a kidney for a private Wednesday lunch.

Chelsea knew it too.

Her two lackeys, Fake and Bake, tittered away nearby as

she gracefully tossed her hair over her shoulder and accepted a diet soda from one of her many admirers.

Her every move looked like a choreographed dance.

I couldn't help wondering how she made being popular look so effortless. Chelsea Halloway might not excel under academic pressure, but I had yet to catch her ever appearing anything less than perfect. It was like she was genetically predetermined to get everything she wanted—or almost everything. Although she hadn't managed to get back together with Logan.

And, according to Kenzie, that hadn't been for lack of trying.

Not that she appeared to be suffering. In fact, Chelsea looked perfectly content to flirt with every cute guy in her vicinity. On the rare occasion that she glanced over at our table, she merely sent Logan a vaguely pitying smile.

You picked the wrong girl, and we both know it.

At least that was how I always interpreted the look.

"Earth to Jane!" Corey elbowed me right in the stomach.

"Sorry. I was sucked into the Notable vortex. What did I miss?"

"You didn't answer my question."

I sighed. "You're going to have to repeat it if you expect an answer."

"Are you still freaking out over your journalism story or what?" Corey demanded impatiently.

"Oh, that." My stomach muscles coiled into even tighter knots. "Yeah, it's not going so well."

Corey patted my knee and made some sympathetic noises before launching into a recitation of his own drama. Not that he had anything *new* to report.

Oh, I'm having trouble getting in touch with my ridiculously hot rock-star boyfriend. Poor me!

I wasn't even sure that should count as a problem.

Long-distance relationships can't be easy, but . . . Corey's whining was getting old fast. Especially since, contrary to what he thought, not *all* of his friends were deliriously happy in committed relationships.

Some of us were lying to little old ladies to avoid being fixed up with grandsons.

Or maybe that was just me.

Still, I was just starting to feel guilty for not taking Corey's relationship issues seriously enough when his face spread into a broad grin.

"On the plus side . . . Tim is flying up to Portland tonight!"

Corey couldn't have just started the conversation that way. Oh no, he had to build the tension first.

"No way!"

"That's great, man."

I nodded along with Kenzie and Logan. "I'm really happy for you, Corey."

The guy was positively beaming. "His manager, Mitch Monroe, has been talking about doing a collaborative track on their upcoming album with Wilco. So when he heard that Wilco was looking for someone to step in as a replacement for an opening act, the guys jumped on it."

Meaning that Corey's separation from his boyfriend was about to be temporarily relieved.

"When is the concert?" Kenzie stole another one of Logan's fries as he playfully batted her hand away.

"Friday. As in, *this* Friday."

"And you didn't mention it to us earlier!"

Corey's grin only widened. "I just found out myself. And did I mention that the manager wants to meet you?"

Kenzie looked momentarily surprised, then shook her head. "I'm done with the spotlight, Corey. I mean it."

"Yes, but that's not something we're mentioning to Mr. Monroe—at least not until he hands you the backstage passes. We all scored tickets!" He pulled out two tickets from his backpack and handed them to Kenzie and Logan. "The guys want to see you again. And they want to meet Logan since they've heard *so much about him*." Corey rolled his eyes to indicate that Kenzie hadn't been able to shut up about him during their bus trip from Portland to LA.

I hadn't been invited to join them then.

They had never asked me. In fact, they never even *considered* it. Instead, they had assumed that my parents wouldn't give me their permission and that even if they *did* . . . I would probably want to stay at home with my Calculus homework.

Not so much, actually.

But I couldn't accept an invitation that was never extended to me in the first place. Just like I couldn't invite myself along to this new ReadySet concert, even though it was exactly the kind of thing I should be scoping out for my article. Something I expected Corey to have considered.

I stared at the tickets clutched in Kenzie's hand as I tried to process what had just happened. I should be happy for Corey that Tim was coming to Portland. I should be happy for Kenzie that she was going backstage with her boyfriend. And, most importantly, I should *not* be upset that my best friends hadn't thought to include me. I opened my mouth to say something supportive like, *Wow! That sounds amazing. You guys are going to have so much fun!* when a tray laden with food thumped down right next to me. I looked up to see . . . Scott.

Uh oh.

Chapter 17

"Sorry I'm late."

I had entirely forgotten about Scott's plan to accompany me to lunch. Probably because accusations that include *indentured servitude* aren't usually followed up with a friendly meal. He also had no business sitting in on *my* time with *my* friends—regardless of Lisa Anne's opinions, I was still entitled to a private life. Although I found it doubtful that his presence at our table had anything to do with me. He was probably just trying to piss off Logan by joining us.

I suspected that angering Logan was all the motivation Scott needed.

"Uh, hey. I didn't expect you to show."

Scott merely nodded and took a massive bite out of his slice of pizza. That's when he noticed the tickets in Kenzie's hands.

"Are we going to a concert, Grammar Girl?"

"I—uh, wasn't really invited."

It hurt to admit. I probably would have sounded less pathetic if I had made something up. *I can't make it. Too much homework. I have my great-aunt Millicent's memorial service to attend—I would skip it, but the two of us were really close.*

Why yes, I will be adopting three of Millie's fifteen cats. How did you guess?

Any of that would have been less humiliating than answering his inevitable question.

He studied me too intently for my great-aunt Millicent story to work. "Why weren't you invited?"

"I, uh—because I, well," I stuttered.

Because my friends didn't consider that I might want to go.

I couldn't say that. Even if it was the truth.

"I didn't think you'd want to go, Jane." Corey's brow was furrowed in concern. "You always do your homework once you get off work on Fridays."

I doubted it was possible to make me sound any more painfully predictable.

"Oh, sure. I mean, you're right. That's what I do. It's fine."

I couldn't seem to escape that word. I half expected someone to create a video montage of me just saying it over and over again.

Fine, fine, fine. Me? Oh, I'm just *fine.*

But I didn't want Corey to feel bad about the situation. After all, he hadn't been *intentionally* rude . . . he just didn't see the point in inviting me to something that I wouldn't want to attend.

Although it did make me wonder what other opportunities I had missed.

"Good thing we're free this weekend, isn't it?" Scott took another bite of pizza as the table descended into awkwardness.

"I can call Tim and look into getting another backstage pass. No promises, but I can try."

Scott grinned. "Why don't you make it two passes? I'll be attending as Jane's plus one."

"No, you won't," Logan growled, unable to hold himself back any longer. "You aren't going anywhere with her."

"Really? Why don't we ask Jane? I have a feeling she's going to side with me this time."

I didn't know what I was supposed to say. Corey probably wanted me to back out of the concert, Logan wanted me to blow off Scott, Scott wanted to use it for his photography—or to further annoy Logan—and Kenzie...I hadn't the slightest clue what my best friend thought of the whole situation. This time, I definitely couldn't please everyone.

"Er...I—" My friends looked at me expectantly, and I felt my resolve begin to crumble.

It's fine. Really. Enjoy the show!

I probably would have said it if Lisa Anne's threats hadn't still been ringing in my head. Scott didn't have to say a word—I knew this was my best shot to deliver the kind of story she wanted...and that meant Scott had to tag along. "Two tickets would be great."

"Okay, I'll get on that." Corey pulled out his cell phone and started texting Tim. "I know the guys have been working on their Wii skills in the hopes of having another face-off with you, Jane."

The only time I had met the rock stars of ReadySet, I had crushed them with my superior gaming skills. The guys weren't exactly known for being gracious losers, which might explain why the two straight members of the band displayed no interest in dating me afterward.

I grinned. "Yeah...they still don't stand a chance."

"Are you that good?"

Coming from anyone else, I would have dismissed it as a normal follow-up question without an ulterior motive. But Scott was always working an angle...unless I'd been wrong about him from the very beginning.

Because *that* was likely.

Still, I didn't see the harm in answering. "I'm great when it comes to anything with a controller."

His grin was full of challenge. "I bet I could beat you."

A lot of guys think that their childhoods spent playing Super Mario Bros. can compete with my gaming abilities. They also tend to pout when I prove them wrong.

Kenzie smiled at Scott indulgently. "Jane annihilates everybody when it comes to Wii Tennis. Don't take it personally."

"I take it the two of you have frequent battles."

That particular statement sure seemed laden with subtext to me, but Kenzie didn't appear to notice anything suspicious about it.

"Hell no. I can't compete there. Jane's better off just playing against herself."

Scott nodded, his attention fully focused on Kenzie. "So do you play any sports?"

"Not unless you count Rollerblading."

"Interesting."

I didn't know what to make of their exchange, but at least Logan had restrained himself from shooting Scott more death-ray glares. Not that he was suddenly all smiles and double rainbows . . . but he did appear to be silently reevaluating Scott. I wondered what he thought of him now. Then again, Logan didn't exactly have a good track record when it came to assessing the character of others.

I mean, the guy had dated *Chelsea Halloway* for a year. . . . *That* had to count as a mistake.

He had also initially dismissed Kenzie as little more than a socially inept history geek.

Okay, so maybe he hadn't been *entirely* off the mark that time.

Still, it was weird sitting there while Scott and Kenzie chatted away like old friends. I had expected Kenzie to show a little more solidarity with me after the whole "she doesn't have what it takes to be a reporter" thing. Then again, Kenzie probably thought she was being helpful, given the whole Logan/Scott parking lot debacle.

Mackenzie Wellesley, my very own ambassador of good-will.

Although I soon discovered that I preferred her verbal conversation with Scott to the nonverbal one she launched the moment the guys were suitably distracted comparing college sports teams.

She jerked her head slightly in Scott's direction, then raised an eyebrow.

I've been asking her opinion about the accuracy of my guydar for *years* while she rolls her eyes. Now she suspected there was something lurking under the surface with *Scott?*

Any suspicions I might have had on that front had ended when he'd approached Lisa Anne behind my back—again.

Yeah, nothing romantic was ever going to happen between the two of us.

I told her as much with a subtle shake of my head. At this point, Scott could even say, *Jane, darling! I'm so deeply sorry I said you couldn't hack it as a reporter. At the time, I was overwhelmed with the strength of my ardor for you . . .* and I would politely inform him where he could shove his stinking apology.

Okay, I might not have the guts to say it to his face, but I would still think it really loudly.

The whole thing was a non-issue since Scott would never apologize, even if I confronted him about what I had overheard. The guy would probably just dismiss me with a shrug before snagging *my* free backstage concert ticket.

Then again, once I nailed my concert story, none of that would matter.

Grammar Girl would cease to exist.

Just as long as I survived observing the play audition. Not something I relished even before my journalism incentive had been removed. For a happily-ever-after addict like me, *Romeo and Juliet* sort of . . . sucks. I mean, it's about a thirteen-year-old girl who freaks out and kills herself when she thinks her boyfriend is dead. Not exactly my idea of a good time. And I tend to call that behavior *creepy,* not romantic.

So watching a group of competitive, high-strung theater kids auditioning for a play I genuinely hate sounded about as appealing as attending a country club luncheon with Lisa Anne.

Not that I had a choice.

That's what I kept reminding myself when I hesitantly slipped into the theater after school . . . only to find it full of devoted performers doing tongue-twister warm-ups with the kind of fanatic fervor usually reserved for religious zealots. Ms. Helsenberg appeared entirely focused on handing out audition pieces, and I nearly seized the opportunity to bail. Unfortunately, my attempt to avoid a stampede of eager audition-ers had only propelled me deeper into the madness, leaving little room for a stealthy retreat.

My exit strategies were rapidly shrinking to include only spraining an ankle, faking a terminal illness, or hollering "Macbeth!" until the superstitious among the drama department demanded my removal from the building.

"Mac—" The intense beady-eyed stare from the girl next to me had me quickly rethinking my plan. "—kenzie is one of my best friends. You haven't seen her around by any chance, have you?"

She barely spared me a head shake before hurrying over to the stage.

Compared to drama club, my time in detention had been downright social.

A flash caught my attention, and I turned to find Scott chatting up two girls who were happily mugging for his camera. The guy could probably declare himself the foremost expert on Dungeons & Dragons and still have girls flocking to him . . . but the camera didn't hurt. It probably allowed him to use tons of lame compliments without sounding like a total creeper.

Do you mind if I take your photo? You're so photogenic. Have you ever considered modeling?

Gag.

Then again, I knew firsthand how effective that stupid modeling line was at making a girl feel special. Or maybe it was the delivery. I had almost believed that Scott meant it when he handed me the makeshift ice pack.

Apparently, the drama girls were every bit as susceptible to his flattery, since they continued posing for him and the camera—it was impossible to tell which one intrigued them more. It was only when one of the girls shifted so that her boobs were even more prominently displayed against the tightness of her shirt that recognition kicked in.

Fake.

Chelsea Halloway's regular wingwoman.

I tried my best not to panic when I spotted Chelsea casually flirting with the hottest of the theater boys. The Notable queen probably didn't even know my name. And as long as I sat in the darkest part of the auditorium, I might be able to keep it that way.

She might not identify me as Kenzie's geeky best friend.

That was the only way I would be leaving the theater unscathed. Otherwise, I had no doubt she would happily use her Notable powers to destroy my social life. Not that it would take that much effort.

"Jane!" Ms. Helsenberg placed a welcoming hand on my shoulder. "I'm so glad you made it. I was worried you wouldn't show."

"Uh, wouldn't miss it," I lied. "So where do you want me to sit?"

"Don't be silly. Now I just need you to fill out these forms before you run through a scene. A little singing and you'll be done. Simple."

"Sing?" My heart started pounding even harder. "I can't sing. Really. Even my parents don't think I could hit a note—*any* note—even if my life depended on it. And . . . wait, is this a *musical* production of *Romeo and Juliet*?"

"There are a few musical numbers, but nothing too elaborate," Ms. Helsenberg said calmly. "You can sing anything. A few bars of 'Happy Birthday' and it's over."

"I can't do it."

"That's simply the nerves talking." She cut off my protest by leaning in and whispering, "Some are born great, some achieve greatness, and some have greatness thrust upon them. Go be great, Jane!"

Then she waded into the crowd, convinced that her Shakespeare quote solved everything.

I glanced down at the forms she had handed me. Maybe Ms. Helsenberg would realize her mistake if I spelled it out for her. I inflated my work schedule and then scrawled *TONE-DEAF* in big block letters under the heading of *Music/Dance Experience*. Hopefully, that would be enough to make Ms. Helsenberg reconsider auditioning me.

And if that didn't work, maybe Scott could pretend we had urgent journalism business.

Ms. Helsenberg could hardly blame me for being called away by one of her colleagues. The tricky part would be convincing Scott to flee the theater with me, especially since Fake and her Not-able friend (the Smith High School equivalent of a B-lister) were still pouting prettily for his camera. He was looking rather pleased with himself, and that was before Chelsea sauntered toward them. Scott's grin widened farther when she murmured something in his ear.

I tried objectively to consider them as a couple.

Physically, they complemented each other well. His unruly dark brown hair contrasted nicely with her long, sleek waves of blond, and they both moved with natural self-assurance. Definitely a power couple. Scott's interest in photography also made their hookup inevitable. The guy was already snapping enough photos of Chelsea's perfect ballerina body to fill up an entire memory card exclusively with her.

Not that I cared. I didn't want Scott's attention, photographic or otherwise. As far as I was concerned, the guy alternated between annoying and insulting whether or not he had a camera glued to his face. If Chelsea Halloway wanted to play his manipulative little games, I wasn't going to stand in her way.

Good riddance.

Scott glanced over at me, smirked, and then said something to the girls that had peals of feminine laughter filling the theater. There was no doubt in my mind that I was the punch line when he raised an eyebrow in a silent challenge.

A challenge that wouldn't go unanswered.

Straightening my shoulders, I walked over to them without hesitation, although I berated myself for stupidity the entire way. Chelsea Halloway couldn't do any permanent damage to my social life as I had virtually nothing to lose. In fact, any calculated deviousness on her part might serve as the very catalyst that Kenzie and I needed to *talk*. Logan's perfect ex-girlfriend was one subject that Kenzie didn't feel comfortable chatting about with her boyfriend.

"Um, hi," I said brilliantly when I finally stood within the half circle of Scott's admirers. "Are all of you auditioning?"

Chelsea looked past me as if I had already bored her to the point of immediate departure. "Yes."

"Oh. That's great. Always good to audition."

Inwardly, I winced. Speaking like a stilted robot was *not* part of my plan to play it cool.

"Have a lot of experience auditioning, do you?" Chelsea asked snidely. "I never would have guessed."

Ouch.

She was right, though: I'd never been to a single audition. Mainly because Elle insisted that if I even *watched* her try out, I would somehow jinx her or do something superembarrassing in front of all her friends. Steering clear wasn't exactly a hardship. Not when the alternative was to receive nonstop death glares culminating in sororicide. Or even worse, being referred to exclusively as Elle's little sister. Theoretically, I could have auditioned after she graduated, but I knew there would be no escaping comparisons from her younger cast mates.

I might not be all that crazy about Scott's nickname for me, but I'd still pick Grammar Girl over Elle's little sister.

Yet strangely, my favorite part was always standing in the lobby after her performance, waiting for her to change out of her costume so I could give her the bouquet of flowers our parents had purchased. That's when she would give me a hug, and for a brief moment my older, more talented sister liked me.

That one moment meant more to me than any amount of time spent center stage.

But it also meant that I was now completely out of my comfort zone. I couldn't do tongue twisters or musical scales or high kicks . . . and Chelsea knew it just from looking at me. She's the queen for a reason. No one can crush the self-esteem of Invisibles with a single sentence quite like Chelsea Halloway.

Then again, after the debacle in the cafeteria, I wasn't exactly Invisible.

And I had the black-and-blue bruising to prove it.

So I put on my best poker face and reminded myself that Alex Thompson's fists might break my bones, but Chelsea's words could never hurt me . . . *too* much, before I said airily, "I've never auditioned personally. I let my sister take the limelight. Perhaps you know her? Elle Smith?"

Maybe Ms. Helsenberg was right about my acting potential, since this performance had captured the full attention of three popular girls, leaving Scott all but forgotten.

That tends to happen whenever a former reigning Notable comes up in conversation. A momentary hushed reverence fills the room before all the current Notables try to use the opportunity to cement their standing.

Oh, I remember her! I was her understudy for The Nutcracker *back when I was only in middle school.*

That kind of thing.

Although now the fifty million reasons why I kept that bit of familial trivia to myself came flooding back. It wasn't just because Elle had threatened to destroy my life if I spread it around—it was the *look*. The one that made it clear that Mackenzie Wellesley's boring best friend had no business being a *Legacy*. She should be disqualified—potentially disowned—on the grounds of extreme geekdom.

It hurt every bit as much as I suspected.

That was why, even though I knew my sister's reputation had the power to change mine . . . I hadn't ever intended to use it. Back when Kenzie and Corey were equally Invisible, I didn't see the point. Sure, if I didn't oversell my hand, my Notable connection could have been enough to position me within the inner sanctum, or at least within the Not-able crowd.

But then people would always be comparing me to Elle.

Not exactly the way I ever wanted to get people to notice me. Although now that Kenzie had accidentally out-Notabled the Notables, my position as a second-string teammate relegated to the sidelines felt inevitable. At least being dismissed by strangers couldn't possibly hurt worse than being ignored by my friends.

So I had nothing to lose.

"Elle is *your* sister?" There was no disguising Fake's surprise, which probably meant she wouldn't stay on top for long. A true Notable must remain elusive, which means they can't go around broadcasting their disbelief for everyone to see. I learned that one from observing Elle.

"Ever since I was born."

What did they expect me to say? *No, I just go around randomly making up siblings.*

I wondered if it was really so impossible for them to conceive of an Invisible sharing the same gene pool with a Notable that even our common last name didn't raise any red flags. I thought that should have been a pretty good-sized hint.

But if Chelsea was surprised, she didn't let it show. "How is Elle? I haven't seen her around in ages!"

The warmth in her voice left me confused, like Elle was a beloved babysitter or a mentor who had moved away. I couldn't tell if it was genuine or if it was just her way of maintaining her Notable credibility—not that Chelsea had any real competition for the title. Still, I've always seen my sister as a nightmare who critiques my clothes and criticizes my social skills. Not someone I would get misty-eyed over. Then again, Elle would never treat anyone besides me that way. Sister's privilege, according to her.

Bullshit, according to me.

"Uh, she's fine. She's doing great actually," I corrected myself. "She's leaving for an internship soon, but I'll be sure to have her call you."

Great. I'd been promoted from Invisible to the role of my sister's secretary.

"Thanks, I'd love to catch up with her." Chelsea's smile transformed her into someone who actually looked approachable. "Are you nervous about the audition?"

"Oh, you know. Just mildly petrified," I replied honestly, because Chelsea Halloway would easily be able to detect a lie.

Actually, anyone who glanced down at my white-knuckled grasp of the audition forms could see my nerves clearly enough. Chelsea's laugh lacked the mean-spirited edge I thought I caught in Fake's bizarre little titter. The Notable queen seemed honestly amused by my reply, as though she hadn't expected that I had it in me.

Kenzie had once confided in me that when she'd broached the subject of Chelsea with Logan, he had said there was a lot more to her than her looks.

Or something along those lines . . . Kenzie's memory of that night was rather hazy since that particular conversation took place after her first party. And her first time drinking.

According to Kenzie, it was also her *last* time drinking, because her bonding time with Logan's toilet remains her most vivid memory of the night.

I had laughed at the notion that there was more to Chelsea Halloway than her social position. I even pointed out to Kenzie that if Logan hadn't created an excuse for dating her—beyond her looks—he would have come across as completely shallow. As far as I was concerned, Logan Beckett wasn't a reliable witness when it came to this particular character testimony.

Now I wondered if maybe Logan had been right all along.

The flash from Scott's camera brought me back to my surroundings. He would probably want to call that particular photo "Beauty and the Geek." I tensed all over again.

"I'm nervous too."

Chelsea had to be lying. No way could she captain the dance team and star in every one of Mrs. P's dance recitals with my level of stage fright. But it was nice of her to say it. Especially since the only calculated objective I could see in it was to make *me* feel better.

The weirdest part was that it worked.

"Oh, me too," Fake chimed in quickly. "Butterflies every time."

Scott covered with a cough what sounded awfully like a snort of contempt, and I couldn't help grinning at him. I had a sneaking suspicion that we were in complete agreement when it came to Fake's acting skills . . . or lack thereof.

"I should probably get ready to perform," Fake's Not-able friend announced, but she didn't move to leave. She hovered, as if waiting for us to protest her departure, but I didn't have the faintest idea what to say.

Probably because none of it was aimed at me. The girl was clearly hoping for some Notable's acknowledgment of her existence, but she had already broken the cardinal Notable rule to never let anyone see how badly you want it. Although maybe the Notables would've overlooked that slip, if I hadn't walked over to them. Chelsea appeared marginally interested in me, and since Fake was obligated to find anything preapproved by her Notable leader *fascinating,* I had accidentally snagged the spotlight.

I doubted the Not-able would care that their popular-girl politics already had me reconsidering my position on sneaking out of the auditorium.

There had to be some way for me to make it out of this thing relatively unscathed.

At the very least, I wanted to avoid alienating anyone. I might not know the girl's name, but years spent living in Elle's shadow had drilled into me just how much it sucks to be overlooked by the popular kids.

"Um . . . break a leg." I tentatively smiled at her.

Her upper lip curled into a snarl. "Yeah, you too."

Only I don't think she was wishing me luck.

Chapter 18

Chelsea was the first to perform.

It made sense: She's the first at everything else at our school. And her performance only solidified her reputation for perfection, leaving little incentive for everyone else to audition. The best role even the most dedicated theater kids could hope for was probably Lady Capulet, since the drama teacher Mrs. Snider nearly declared Chelsea the new Juliet on the spot.

Something that didn't go over real well with a lot of the other girls.

Not that it should've come as a surprise. In fact, I thought it was obvious that Chelsea owned the role midway through her scene reading with Miles Kent. And anyone slow on the uptake should have figured it out when she busted out her rendition of "You Don't Own Me."

Complete with choreography.

Nobody in the auditorium could upstage her, although a number of girls certainly tried their best. One after another, they handed in the paperwork, ran through a scene, burst into song, and exited the stage shaking with adrenaline. I observed the entire process, cringing sympathetically every time a singer's voice wobbled. The number of people who had yet to audition shrank down to a very small pool of students—primarily freshman.

And then there was just me.

Only I had no intention of stepping forward. I was so much safer hiding next to Scott.

Mrs. Snider began to rise from her chair. "Thanks, everyone; we appreciate—"

"Wait, where's Jane Smith?" Ms. Helsenberg demanded. "Has anyone seen Jane Smith?"

"She's right here!"

I should have known better than to expect *Scott* to help me keep a low profile. I glared at him but was powerless to do anything more since all eyes were on me.

"Oh good! Jane hasn't left yet. Come on up here."

I couldn't disobey a direct order in front of everyone, so I stiffly forced myself to approach the stage. My mind jumped wildly to the time I suggested Kenzie find her inner vampire slayer before confronting the Notables. I thought if she had a less whiny Buffy-type persona shielding her that Chelsea Halloway wouldn't seem nearly as intimidating.

That plan wasn't the most effective.

In fact, it wasn't working at all.

When I finally stood onstage, my hands were shaking worse than the camera of a homemade biking video. Miles grabbed a copy of the script off the floor and began thumbing through the pages in search of our scene, while I tried to find my voice.

Surely there was *something* I could say that would get me off the hook.

Unfortunately, all the attention had me too scared to even think properly. I flinched when Scott snapped yet another picture from the audience before I focused exclusively on my scene partner. That actually kind of helped, since I knew Miles had the skill to make me look halfway decent. As one of the few legitimately talented guys auditioning, his job was fairly simple. He provided the potential Juliets with a real, live Romeo that they could essentially take for a test-drive.

Then Ms. Helsenberg and Mrs. Snider would know if the pair had any onstage chemistry.

Miles could probably convince an auditorium full of high school students that he was madly in love with a rock, if necessary. He was also *really* cute with a mop of curly blond hair that only emphasized his strong nose and chiseled jaw. I could easily picture his profile carved by a Renaissance sculptor. Trade in his jeans and striped polo shirt for period garb, and Miles would look like Shakespeare's ideal star-crossed lover.

Although the same could definitely not be said of me.

Miles blocked our faces from view with his script before he whispered, "Are you sure you're ready for this? I can help you get out of auditioning if you want."

I gulped and forced myself to meet his eyes, which were a dramatic mix of brown and gray. Honest concern radiated from him. Ordinarily, I would be too tongue-tied around a guy like Miles to reply, especially since I'd had a tiny crush on him ever since Kenzie, Corey, and I saw him in *A Midsummer Night's Dream,* but I had bigger issues now—like whether to accept his offer. I didn't doubt that Miles could find a way to get me out of this mess. He struck me as being cast in the same stand-up guy mold as Logan, which meant that his ethical code wouldn't allow him to stand idly by while a girl nearly hyperventilated. Although, unlike Logan, I wasn't picking up on anything particularly brotherly about his interest in helping me.

Especially when his gaze lingered on my new shirt. The hint of male appreciation I caught didn't exactly help with the whole shortage-of-breath situation.

But if I accepted his offer, I would be wimping out.

Not to mention, Scott would never let me live it down.

"I'm r-ready," I stuttered. "Thanks. I . . . nerves. Not really my scene." I flipped over the page of his upheld script. "No pun intended."

He laughed in honest amusement, and I found myself tentatively smiling in return.

"Whenever the two of you lovebirds are ready," Mrs. Snider called out. "Some of us have places to go and things to do."

"Right, sorry." I focused on finding the scene I'd chosen. "Uh, ready."

Drawing in a deep breath, I tried to imagine what it must be like for Juliet. Young, stupid, crushing on a guy she should want to avoid, and totally screwed over by fate. I could relate to more of that than I wanted to admit, even to myself.

"O Romeo, Romeo! wherefore art thou Romeo?"

My knees trembled as I read straight from the script. "Deny thy father and refuse thy name."

Translation: *Yeah, don't plan on inviting your family over for the holidays, lover boy. I don't have to meet them to know that they suck. All of them.*

"Or, if thou wilt not, be but sworn my love and I'll no longer be a Capulet."

Miles took a step closer to the stage, not even bothering to look at the script before he delivered his one line, "Shall I hear more, or shall I speak at this?"

I forged ahead, but the lines all felt flat in my mouth. It was obvious that I was simply going through the motions, repeating words that someone else had written. Even if the quavering in my voice could be overlooked, my performance was less than inspired.

I wasn't passionate enough and it showed. I could hear Mrs. Snider start tapping her pencil against the table in an unconscious gesture of impatience. Miles tried his best to salvage the scene by infusing his every line with enough passion for both of us.

Not even his expertise could disguise my complete lack of skill.

Although I did catch an unprofessional glint of laughter in his eyes when I fumbled over something about a maiden blush bepainting my cheek.

So maybe I wasn't the only one struggling to take Shakespeare seriously.

Time slowed to an excruciating crawl the whole time I stood onstage clutching my script in a death grip. The rational part of my brain knew that the entire audition lasted only a matter of minutes, but when we finished I could have sworn full hours had passed.

Days. Months. Seasons.

I just wanted to get out of there before I hit my midlife crisis.

"Okay, so . . . thanks!" I said to Ms. Helsenberg and Mrs. Snider, even though I didn't exactly appreciate being blackmailed into humiliating myself.

"Not so quickly, Jane. You haven't sung yet."

My stomach plummeted. "That's okay."

"Sing."

"I can't. So I'll just go sit down now . . ."

Mrs. Snider pinned me with a glare. "Everyone sings."

"But I *can't*. This isn't false modesty or anything. I'm physically incapable."

"Just a bit of 'Happy Birthday,' Jane," Ms. Helsenberg said encouragingly. "We're not asking for much."

"But I—"

"Just do it, already!" Mrs. Snider snarled.

I could hear the snickers already spreading among the other kids. They'd have a lot more to laugh about soon. My stomach twisted, and I thought I might hurl right there in front of everyone.

"Any song?"

"Just sing!"

"Okay." I took another deep breath.

This has to be rock bottom.

"Ain't no mountain high enough," I warbled weakly, forcing myself to continue with the rest of the lyrics.

The muffled sound of Miles's stifled laughter stung like hell. It also decided me. If I was going to be the object of ridicule, then I was determined to go out with a bang. Unfortunately, I blanked on all the other lyrics. I knew there was something about calling if you need me, but the details were all fuzzy. So I started from the top, this time using all the strength I could pull from my quivering diaphragm. The resulting racket had the girls in the front row fighting not to clap their hands over their ears. Kenzie likes to joke that my ability to consistently miss so many notes might prove to be a secret weapon. That if anyone ever tried to carjack me, I could belt out a few bars and let my Voice of Unearthly Discord take care of the rest.

She also maintains that I should reserve it for situations of extreme duress.

Everyone in the auditorium appeared to have reached a similar conclusion.

"Yes, thanks, Jane," Ms. Helsenberg said quickly when I completed my second pass, probably because she was terrified I might continue. "That was, erm, remarkable."

I had no trouble believing that my singing would generate plenty of remarks. None of them good.

My stomach roiling with humiliation, I bolted for the exit. I didn't even care if an auditorium full of people laughed at my hasty retreat. All that I cared about was getting as far away from this real-life nightmare as possible.

"Hey, Jane, hold up!'

Chelsea Halloway stood between me and freedom.

Deliberately sprinting away from her would completely screw up all the progress I had made earlier. Nobody intentionally ignores a Notable order unless they have some masochistic desire to be banished from . . . something. I wasn't on any of the invite lists, but that didn't make it any less of a bad idea. I pulled up short and turned around, bracing myself for an insult.

"That was brave."

"What?" I wasn't the only one surprised by Chelsea's compliment—Fake looked momentarily horrified before her expression twisted into a smirk.

Chelsea was being sarcastic.

Of course, that made way more sense. Except Chelsea looked sincere to me. I even thought I detected a spark of admiration in her eyes.

"I was a freaking *mess!*" I blurted out.

"Well . . . yeah. You weren't kidding about not being able to sing. Total train wreck."

Ouch.

"*But* it was brave of you to do it. Especially knowing how badly you were going to suck."

I winced, but couldn't stop myself from smiling back at her.

Chelsea Halloway thought *I* was brave.

"Well, you didn't suck. No surprise there." I expected her to toss her hair around and preen, but she didn't. Instead, she focused on me with an intensity that was unnerving. "I'm sure you'll get the lead."

"Thanks." Chelsea smiled, but it didn't reach her eyes until Scott came up behind me. Then she looked downright devilish. "We should hang out. I made some plans for tomorrow, but why don't the two of you join us for lunch on Monday?"

It sounded more like a royal decree than a question, but either way it wasn't something I could turn down. Strangely enough, I didn't even *want* to bail. Chelsea hadn't made any nasty comparisons between my disastrous audition and Elle's starring roles. No little jabs about being the failure in my family. Nothing.

If she honestly wanted to hang out, I wasn't going to turn her down. Especially since the sight of me at the Notable table with *Chelsea Halloway* would definitely make Kenzie jealous.

Maybe it would inspire her to actually call me, like she did pre-Logan.

"Absolutely. We're in."

Scott raised an eyebrow. "Apparently, I'll be joining you."

"I'll see you then." She turned and left the room in long, confident strides with Fake scurrying behind her.

"So did you get any good photos?"

I was too distracted by our brief encounter of the Notable-kind to realize that Miles Kent had joined our makeshift group until he spoke to Scott.

Then I became all too aware of his close proximity and struggled to act normal.

Scott tightened his hold on his camera. "Yeah, I did. A few of them look really promising."

"That's great, man." Miles shifted toward me so subtly I nearly didn't notice it. "Still think theater isn't your scene, Jane?"

I laughed. "After *that* performance, you shouldn't even have to ask."

"A little coaching and you might not be so bad."

I shot him a look of complete disbelief.

"Okay, a lot of coaching."

"It wouldn't make a difference, believe me. I'm a lost cause."

"Maybe you just need the right coach."

That's when it hit me that our whole back-and-forth sounded suspiciously like flirting. And I was holding my own. I hadn't stuttered or bolted or desperately introduced him to someone else in order to deflect his attention. His

easygoing nature put me completely at ease, and I found myself wondering what it would be like to date him. If I would
feel this self-confident all the time.

"Maybe I do."

My practice with Scott had totally paid off because for
once I said the right thing.

And it seems like it's working.

Miles leaned in closer. "I'm happy to provide my services.
How does after school tomorrow work for you?"

"Uh, sure." Nothing was going to prevent me from going
on a date. My very first date. Especially since it was *Miles
Kent* doing the asking. I almost expected to hear someone
yell, "And . . . scene. Nicely done, Miles!" because all of this
felt way too surreal to be happening. But if a genuinely nice,
superhot guy wanted to spend time with a total geek like me,
I wasn't going to complain. Instead, I struggled to play it
cool. "Tomorrow's fine."

Tomorrow will have to be fine.

"Then I'll pick you up in the parking lot."

"Uh, okay. Tomorrow. After school. Parking lot. Got it."

He grinned, and I felt my pulse rate speed up. "Great, it's a
date."

And then he strolled away looking all strong and confident
and totally swoon-worthy. All I could think was that after a
lifetime of watching romantic comedies, I had stumbled upon
the perfect leading man in real life.

And he had just asked me out.

"Jane!"

"Huh?" I hadn't even noticed Scott calling my name. My
powers of observation must have been temporarily obliter-
ated by my Miles-related adrenaline rush. Reality slowly
began to seep in. "Oh, my God. He just asked me out!"

Scott nodded. "I noticed that."

"I'm not ready for this! I have nothing to wear!" It
sounded painfully girlie, but it was the truth. I had stuff from

Kenzie, but nothing that said, *Wear me on your first date, please!*

"Go naked."

"Hah, you're hilarious, Scott. Oh wait, *no you're not.*"

"You'll figure out something."

"It's not just the clothes."

"What is it then?"

"Well—" Suddenly, everything came rushing out. "What if I have nothing to say? He's a really nice guy, but I have no dating experience, so what if he's wonderful and I choke and the whole date is just one long, endless pit of awkwardness that stretches before us and—"

"I'm sure you'll come up with something," Scott said, cutting me off. He looked bored by our topic of conversation and glanced toward the door, as if calculating how long he would have to spend with his neurotic excuse for a journalism partner before he could make his escape.

"I hope so. Tomorrow. Wow, okay. Why do I have the feeling there is something big I'm forgetting right now?"

He looked at me incredulously. "Because you also agreed to go to the concert. With me. And all of your friends."

"Right. *Right!* Okay, but this can work. I just have to fit in my date before the concert and after . . . work! *That* is what I forgot! I still haven't called Mrs. Blake." I grabbed his sleeve as another thought hit me. "I've never canceled on her before! What do I say? Should I lie? That's a bad idea, right? I mean, the last time I lied, I got stuck with you as my boyfriend."

Scott ignored my accidental jab. "Just tell her you have a date. She'll assume it's with me."

"Brilliant! Thanks. In case you didn't notice, I'm freaking out. It must be leftover nerves from my performance. I'm not usually this . . . jittery, or whatever."

"I noticed."

"Okay, well." I didn't know what else to say. "Thanks for

being so cool when Miles asked me out. And for not saying anything."

"Of course. So I'll see you tomorrow after school in the parking lot."

"Yeah, you'll—wait, *what!?*"

"Until your story is written and my portfolio is complete, where you go, I go."

"But this is *my date!*"

"I know. I can hardly wait."

And just like that, my brief spell of good fortune evaporated.

Chapter 19

I tried not to lie to Mrs. Blake when I asked for the day off. Hedging the truth didn't seem as likely to blast me with bad karma, so I told her that I was sorry to cancel at the last minute, but I *really* wanted to go on a date.

I just conveniently forgot to mention the name of the guy taking me out.

And then I tried to get off the phone as quickly as humanely possible to prevent her from doing any serious prying. I only felt a small twinge of guilt as Mrs. Blake assured me that she could manage perfectly well without me and then insisted I take Sunday off as well. Not that I fought her on it. I needed those extra hours for studying. The newspaper story had already taken up way too much of my time, and I couldn't afford to let anything fall through the cracks.

Even for my first date with Miles Kent.

So after confirming with Mrs. Blake that I'd see her on Wednesday, I instantly called Kenzie. I knew she wouldn't solve the whole "What should I wear?" dilemma, but none of it would feel real until she knew all the details. We had promised years ago to tell each other first if we developed any kind of love life. And it still mattered to me, even after Kenzie had failed to keep her side of the deal. It still bothered me that I had found out about her relationship with Logan the same way everyone else did: via Facebook notification.

That had sucked a lot of the fun out of her big news for me.

Which was why I refused to tell her about it by voice mail. Instead, I left a cryptic message for her to call me back right away. And then, since I was stuck waiting in the school parking lot for my dad to pick me up post-audition, I tried her home phone number too. Kenzie's little brother, Dylan, picked up.

"Hullo?" I heard the unmistakable sound of chewing.

"Hey, Dylan. Is Kenzie around?"

"Sorry, she's in Portland shopping with Melanie." Dylan's tone brightened. "I could call them for you. Pass on your message to Melanie."

He definitely had it *bad* for the freshman girl, but I wasn't sure if the feeling was mutual. I doubted she had noticed him as anything beyond Mackenzie's little brother. She was only one year older than him, but since that year currently placed him in middle school, I had trouble picturing them together.

Then again, I was also having a hard time picturing Kenzie shopping of her own free will. She doesn't *like* shopping—an oddity the two of us have always shared.

"What could Kenzie possibly need to buy?" I demanded. "Isn't she still drowning in free designer handouts?"

"Don't ask me. Girl stuff for the big party next weekend?"

That stopped me cold.

I garbled a quick good-bye into the phone and hung up. Kenzie was planning outfits *over a week in advance* for some party I hadn't even heard about, and it had never occurred to her that I might want to know. I shouldn't have been surprised, but no matter how many times it happened, it hurt.

And I had no idea how to make it stop hurting.

It was strange because the girl who chatted with Notables

earlier hadn't felt entirely like me. Now that it was over, the whole thing seemed like an out-of-body experience with the *real* Jane Smith observing a fake body double whose only job was to keep smiling until she fled the auditorium. Then I should have returned to my normal self.

Except *that* Jane had landed herself a really attractive date. *That* Jane had scored a lunch invite to the Notable table. *That* Jane wasn't pathetically hoping for a scrap of her best friend's attention.

Maybe it was time to consider making the change permanent.

My phone beeped that I had a new text message, and I instantly felt ridiculous. Of course, Kenzie wanted to talk to me. She had probably gotten roped into the whole shopping thing and wanted to call me later tonight when she could concentrate on my update.

Maybe she would even extend an invite to this mysterious party then.

I felt better already.

Or at least I *did* until I noticed that Corey was the one sending the message.

Can't talk. Got 2 tix. Later.

Disappointment battled with nervous anticipation. The terse message wasn't exactly what I had hoped to read, but it did confirm that I was going to the Wilco/ReadySet concert . . . right after my very first date.

My stomach lurched, and I fought the urge to call Corey. His text had made it pretty clear that he couldn't talk, but this time the advice I needed went way beyond fashion advice. I wouldn't stop panicking until he assured the normal me—who had chosen a spectacularly poor time to return—that going on a date with a guy in tights I had lusted after wasn't a disaster in the making.

That normal people did stuff like this all the time.

I scrolled through my cell phone call history, hit call, and was relieved when the ringing was replaced by Isobel's cheerful greeting. "Hey, Jane. What's going on?"

"Oh, I, uh, just wanted to chat. How was the baking club?"

"It was so much fun, Jane! We made chocolate chip cookies, and Claire, do you know Claire? Claire Ip . . . ling. Ipston, maybe? Anyway, she's hilarious."

"Yeah?" I said, because it felt like I should say something.

"She was supposed to be in charge of reading the directions . . . and then she got distracted. We ended up *tripling* half of the ingredients so then we had to triple everything else. It was a total free-for-all, but somehow the dough turned out okay. I think. I might let someone else taste them first."

I laughed. "That might be for the best."

"Yeah, but I haven't told you the funny part. Sam suggested that we freeze half of the dough. That way we can make cookies next week or the week after—or maybe both. Only she turned it into a sculpture and now it looks *exactly* like Principal Taylor. It's creepy how well she captured his look of disapproval. She even molded a little football whistle that sort of dangles around his neck."

"Wow." I had never heard Isobel talk so much. "Sounds like you had fun."

"I wish you could have made it, Jane! Sam . . . uh, well, she's not quite as scary as I first thought."

I grinned. "Sam still intimidates me, but I'm pretty sure she's all bark and no bite."

"I wouldn't go quite *that* far, considering that she offered to mace Alex Thompson for me. She also told me not to buy into his bullshit and that"—Isobel's voice dropped to a whisper—"there is nothing wrong with my body."

"She's right. I should have told you that myself. I got caught up in the journalism stuff and . . . I still should have told you."

"It's fine," Isobel said quickly. "Not a big deal."

But it was a big deal.

"Sam wanted to know if you were interested in joining us for lunch tomorrow."

I wanted to comment on the "us," but decided against it. Isobel had somehow found her place within Sam's social scene, and I was determined to be happy for her.

Even if I was a little jealous at how easily it had worked for her.

"I really need to talk with Kenzie and Corey. . . ." I let my words dribble out. "Rain check?"

"Oh, okay. Sure." There was a long pause. "Well, I'll see you on the bus tomorrow."

"Right. Tomorrow," I repeated. Somehow, I was drifting away from the people who meant the most to me, and I didn't know whom to blame. Myself probably.

"Jane?"

"Yeah?"

"I'm glad you called."

"Me too." My dad pulled into the lot. "Listen, I have to go. Just—thanks, Isobel. For everything." Then, shutting the phone, I opened the door and jumped in.

"Hey, kiddo. How was your day?"

Way too complicated to explain . . . not that he really wanted the details. My dad definitely didn't want to listen to me obsess over which outfit I should wear on my first date.

The whole thing felt so out of character for me. Elle was the one who complained about having *nothing* to wear, while I waited for my sweatshirts to disintegrate before I would even consider replacing them. But this time I wanted to look nice . . . and comfortable . . . and maybe a little sexy.

Something that would subconsciously tell Miles that I liked him but that we should probably take it slow, since dating was new territory for me.

And since obviously that wasn't asking too much from an outfit, I might as well demand that my shoes somehow solve world hunger.

* * *

I was half buried in piles of clothing when Elle barged into my room without even bothering to knock.

"It's almost dinnertime and—what are you *doing?*" she demanded.

I refused to let her disturb my concentration. "Elle, I'm a little busy here."

"Wait, are you seriously trying to become fashionable?" I glanced over and saw the surprise written all over her face. "I thought it was just a phase."

"I have a date tomorrow."

I'm not sure why I said it. My original plan was to keep my mouth shut around my sister. It was just a simple safety precaution in case the whole thing was a disaster. As long as Elle never heard about it, I could pretend it never happened.

Date? Me? Nope.

I still hadn't told my best friends, and yet my older sister— the bane of my existence—somehow got the truth out of me in under thirty seconds.

Elle flopped down on my bed as if I had invited her in for a little heart-to-heart chat. "I know you don't have a boyfriend. Yesterday, you were doing the head-tilt thing that only happens when you're lying."

I tried to look unfazed by this discovery as I stared her down.

"I have a date tomorrow that is making me really nervous. So *please* don't mess with me right now."

She sat up straight. "Overreact much? I was just trying to be *nice,* dork."

My sister is great when it comes to her friends and her sorority sisters, but with me? Not so much. Still, it was possible this was her attempt at sisterly bonding.

And that I was killing the moment.

"Sorry," I said. "Just . . . stressed right now."

"Well—" Elle eyeballed the shirt in my hands. "You'll look like a washed-out cream puff in that one."

"Thanks, I feel *so* much better now!"

"I'm being honest. You should go for that one." She pointed to a forest-green blouse Mackenzie had brought over. "Combine it with that gray skirt and those textured tights. And don't even think about wearing sneakers. Heels only."

Usually I get annoyed when Elle starts bulldozing. But I could picture the outfit coming together, and even though the whole thing screamed, "I'm a preppy Notable!" I found myself oddly drawn to the image. Maybe if I looked the part, I would feel the confidence that always appeared to go along with it. That might be something worth asking Chelsea about over lunch.

Or not.

"Oh, and to cover the bruise you should use a yellow-based concealer before applying eye shadow." She snorted. "That should help you avoid caking on makeup like you've been doing these past few days."

I thought "caking" was a gross exaggeration. I'd done a pretty good job of hiding my black eye. No one at school had criticized my makeup . . . to my face.

"Did it ever cross your mind to be, I don't know, *worried* about me?" Anger began churning through me.

Elle looked taken aback, and then she laughed. "You? No! You fell down, didn't you? That's what Mom said. God, the biggest danger in your life is getting a paper cut from one of your textbooks."

"You couldn't be more wrong."

"Oh yeah?" Elle fisted her hands on her waist. "Look, Jane, you don't need to invent drama to make yourself seem more exciting. Just deal with it, already."

"Well, thanks for that." I yanked open my bedroom door. "You can leave now."

"Fine. Enjoy your date." She put air quotes around "date"

just to make it clear that she still thought I was lying. Except it was completely true. Miles Kent would be picking me up and taking me . . . somewhere. I really hoped he didn't have any hiking in mind, because the outfit Elle had picked out would not hold up if we went anywhere off the beaten path.

"Thanks. I will."

And for the first time I had no trouble believing that I would enjoy myself. I might not know Miles that well, but I doubted he would suddenly transform into a jerk when we left school property.

It would be great.

I kept telling myself that every time my upcoming date distracted me from my homework. Everything was going to work out. I'd take advantage of my Friend of Celebrity status to write a story about the concert that would impress my journalism teacher *and* my brand-new boyfriend. Just as soon as I finished all my AP Calculus problems.

That lasted well into the early hours of the morning.

Which meant that when my alarm clock rang a few scant hours later, I smacked the snooze button. I rationalized that, thanks to Elle, I already knew exactly what I would be wearing. Something I instantly regretted when I remembered that the second part of the evening included a concert with Corey. And *that* meant I needed to pack a spare change of clothes, just in case Corey vetoed Elle's selection.

I barely resisted tossing in my most comfortable sweatshirt, just to annoy him.

Then I left a note on the kitchen counter saying that I had made some late-night plans with Kenzie and Corey. I didn't even have to ask for permission or mention what time I would be returning home. One of the benefits of a life of complete geekdom is that my parents never worry that I'm out making poor life decisions. Not when my idea of a crazy night is a *Firefly* marathon *and* a showing of *Dr. Horrible's Sing-Along Blog* to complete the Whedon-fest.

Which also might explain why, unlike Elle, I don't get invited to things.

So I omitted all mention of the concert and my date with a relatively clean conscience, because *technically* I hadn't lied. I just hoped my parents never found out what this particular "late night" with Corey and Kenzie entailed, since I doubted they would accept my technicality.

There was no harm in letting them assume that my life was as boring as ever. It even felt like the truth when I sat on the bus with Isobel and discussed how best to entertain Sam at a sleepover. Somehow I didn't think the musical episode from *Buffy* was going to cut it. We agreed that sometime next week might work, and Isobel began searching for Sam to check with her.

Which was when Chelsea noticed me from her place on the crescent-shaped cement platform on the quad outside that separates the Notables from the Invisibles. I pulled up short. The Crescent is considered sacred territory by Notables and Not-ables alike. Completely off-limits to all geeks . . . or at least it *was* until Kenzie started dating Logan.

Except now I had Chelsea Halloway crooking one perfectly painted fingernail, beckoning me over.

Ignoring her wasn't an option. That would be kind of like pretending not to see an alligator munching away on a clown; it's terrifying, but trying to wish the situation away won't work. Not if you plan on getting out of there with all your limbs intact. Frankly, I still thought Chelsea was a lot more dangerous than any reptile—regardless of the fact that she lacked the requisite number of teeth. She had acted nice to me yesterday, but that didn't mean I could trust her.

Especially since I knew she was gunning for my best friend.

Then again, maybe it was possible for this particular alligator to change. After all, her lunch invitation was practically unheard-of Notable behavior. So instead of freezing, like I would have done yesterday, I casually waved as if I greeted the Queen of the Notables all the time and then pointed in front of me to the English building with a look I hoped she'd interpret as: *Sorry, I can't stop. I have class. See you later!*

Her nod and expressive eye roll was all the response I needed.

Fine, geek. I'll see you later then.

It was bizarre to find myself carrying on a nonverbal conversation with *Chelsea,* but I didn't have time to obsess over it. Instead, I walked right into my journalism class with a goofy grin plastered all over my face. I was slowly getting the hang of this social stuff. Outfits. Concerts. Dating.

Compared to all of that, this article should be a simple procedure.

That's when I spotted Scott fiddling on Photoshop with a picture of my panic-stricken face that he had clearly snapped during the audition.

Too bad nothing was ever simple when Scott Fraser was around.

Chapter 20

"So we've got tickets."

That's all I could come up with to say to Scott. Not *Good morning.* Not *How's it going.* Those would imply that I might actually enjoy spending time in his company.

Which I didn't.

Well, okay, he could be pretty entertaining around Mrs. Blake. But when it was just the two of us . . . not so much.

Given that he inevitably insulted me.

Still, I guess *We've got tickets* was a nicer greeting than *Congratulations, jerkwad, you talked your way into going somewhere else with me.*

Although I definitely had been tempted to go with the second option.

Scott didn't even look up as he adjusted the color on the photo. "Great. You can give it to me later. Right before your date with Romeo."

"You weren't serious about joining us." I made it a statement, not a question, simply because I knew he had to be messing with me. No guy in his right mind would volunteer to shadow a nerdy girl on her first date. Not even the one currently tinkering with his computer in front of me.

"Yeah."

"Yeah, you weren't serious about tagging along?" I specified.

"Yeah, I'll be coming." He smiled distractedly as the sequence of commands he entered sharpened the image. "Wouldn't miss it."

"I mean this as nicely as possible," I lied. "But you are not wanted."

"And I mean this as nicely as possible—you don't have a choice."

I was fed up with hearing that I was all out of options, or maybe I was just sick of saying it to myself. Either way, I couldn't refrain from snapping, "Oh, really? Since when?"

"Since Mr. Elliot promoted me or since Lisa Anne gave me free rein to use you for my portfolio. I'll let you decide."

"I told you that portfolio wasn't going to happen."

His grin only widened. "What do you think the chances are of you stopping me?"

One in a billion.

I balled my hands in frustration. "*Why?* Why would you want to observe my date? I honestly don't see the appeal for you."

"Taking photos of Jane Smith and her Romeo? Priceless."

"Gee, thanks."

"You're welcome."

There had to be an alternative.

"What would it take to convince you not to join us?"

He paused as if to give the question some serious thought. "A nude shot. Very tasteful."

"You'll never make it as a stand-up comic."

He smirked but looked completely at ease with our back-and-forth, like it was some kind of twisted game we were playing. Weirdly enough, *I* had become accustomed to it, and with the one Notable exception of Alex Thompson, I don't fight people. I aim for appeasement or invisibility; either way, I *never* look forward to a face-off.

Except neither of those approaches ever seemed like real possibilities with Scott.

"Eh, I've decided to use my talents elsewhere."

"Well, don't give up your day job."

"I don't plan to, which is exactly why I will be seeing you and your Romeo after school."

And that was all I got out of him. He went right back to his photography with a single-minded intensity that was impressive albeit annoying. The last time I had been that focused on my writing, I died in a tragic tuna incident.

That had been a good one.

Although, I couldn't help wondering how Mr. Elliot would react if he stumbled upon the contents of my notebook. Most likely he would yell, "This isn't how you step up your game, *Smith!*" before shipping me off to spend quality time with Mr. Shelder in the Guidance Office. Not that I had to worry about my teacher reading it, or anyone else for that matter. There weren't a lot of people dying to sneak a peek at the inner workings of my life. My friends didn't even care enough to return my calls.

Okay, that wasn't exactly true. They cared. *Of course,* they cared. They just hadn't asked for an update . . . yet. Not necessarily a bad thing considering I no longer knew how much I wanted to tell them. If they had called me right back I would have felt obligated to share everything.

Now I could keep some of it to myself without guilt.

I would still have to tell Kenzie *something,* because . . . regardless of her shopping spree with her new best friend, I couldn't keep her in the dark. At least, I wouldn't have if I had been able to get a word in edgewise over lunch. Corey chattered away incessantly, pausing only intermittently to breathe and to thrust two tickets into my hand.

"I can't drive Jane. I know I'm usually the carpool direc-
tor, but I'm going into Portland in a few hours, which *I know*
is early and maybe a little needy, but I don't care. I am just
one physics test away from more alone time with Tim." He
sighed hugely. "So close! Anyhow, I'm getting there way before any of you. And I also don't know when I'm going to
leave. The concert will probably end around midnight, but I
really want to be with him as much as possible, you know?"

Yeah, we knew. Corey was not the type to nobly suffer in
silence about the pain of a long-distance relationship. Not
that I could blame him. If Logan were a rock star and Kenzie
couldn't see him on a regular basis, she'd probably be acting
the same way. That didn't stop me from finding it annoying.

"Sure, we can take her," Logan said, like I was a sack of
potatoes that needed transporting. "No problem."

Except with Scott shadowing my every move, it made more
sense for me to carpool with him.

"I don't think I need a ride, guys."

No one paid me any attention.

"Great! I really appreciate it, Logan." Corey's broad smile
included everyone in the cafeteria. "Have I mentioned that
today is a *very* good day?"

Only fifteen hundred times already.

If I *ever* became that nauseating in a relationship, I hoped
my friends would have the decency to tell me. Or at the very
least, I wanted them to have to sit there, nodding support-
ively for hours.

Payback.

I frowned. Not payback exactly, because it wasn't like I
wanted to *punish* my friends. I just needed them to understand that sometimes it would be nice to share the spotlight.

Not in front of the entire school or anything. But every
now and then . . .

I glanced over at Chelsea Halloway, who was simultaneously ruling over the Notable table and looking like every geeky girl's worst nightmare. It defied all logic, but our brief conversation after the audition hadn't felt one-sided to me.

Maybe Scott had a point about doing stuff unsanctioned by my friends, because there was no way Kenzie would get behind a Notable-related hangout session. Especially one that revolved around her boyfriend's ex. It just wasn't going to happen. But that didn't mean *I* couldn't extend my social boundaries.

I could march right over to the Notable table . . . or I could find my date.

Throughout lunch, I kept scanning the cafeteria to catch even a glimpse of Miles. I didn't see him once, which left me with absolutely no idea what to expect for our date. I might be a late arrival to the flirting scene, but I thought a pre-date casual run-in could effectively set the tone. If Miles strode across the cafeteria looking all hot and purposeful and *intense*, just because he wanted to talk to me, that would be a *very* good sign. If he studiously ignored me around his friends—not such a good sign.

It also meant I couldn't ask him about the level of outdoorsy stuff we might be doing.

I nearly changed back into my jeans anyway. My sister may have great fashion sense, but I'm still not big on skirts—especially in Forest Grove, Oregon, where the weather is generally cold with a 90 percent chance of wet. Even wearing Kenzie's textured tights, I wasn't exactly feeling warm and relaxed. More like chilled and icy.

I fought the urge to warm up with some jumping jacks while I waited in the parking lot to see if Miles had stood me up. The place was an absolute mob scene with everyone jostling one another in their rush to put as much distance between themselves and Smith High School as they could manage. Impatient drivers stuck their heads out of their windows and yelled, *Yo, douche bag! Move!*

Classy.

All the people scurrying around made it hard to spot any-one, and I was tempted to hide in the background.

"Hey, Jane. Ready for your lesson?"

I jerked my head up and smiled at Miles, who looked every bit as cute as I remembered from the audition. It was a relief to know that even with my performance jitters, I hadn't over-exaggerated his appeal. I might not be fond of Scott's nickname for me, but I had to admit that Romeo fit perfectly for Miles. His dark-blond hair looked effortlessly wind-swept.

"Hey," I said, unsure how to continue. All this dating stuff was freaking me out, and suddenly flirting sounded like the hardest thing in the world. My newfound confidence evapo-rated as I stared at him.

"So . . . uh, two things before we go."

He smiled. "Okay. What's up?"

"The first is that, erm, Scott really wants to come along." Some of my words slurred together as I forced myself to spit them out. "He's taking photos of me for this project, and he's insisting on following us. I know it's annoying, and ordinar-ily I would tell him to buzz off . . . but there's this girl in my journalism class, Lisa Anne, who would happily stick me back on Grammar Patrol if I so much as blink funny, so . . ."—I sucked in some air—"do you mind?"

"That's fine."

"Really?"

"Sure. He'll snap a few pictures and leave us alone." Miles shrugged. "No big deal. What's the other thing?"

"The other—oh, right. I don't know if you had any plans, but I was sort of hoping we could go into Portland. Again, feel free to say no. Really. I will not be offended."

"Portland sounds great."

I couldn't believe my own luck. Although, I don't know why I'd been expecting Miles to scowl and say something like *Portland would've been fine if* someone *had given me advance notice.* My Romeo wasn't a jerk. I smiled up at him as a warm feeling tingled inside me, and I wondered if this was what it felt like to fall in . . . something or other. Love sounded way too intense—not to mention cheesy. But maybe something a bit more comfortable like . . . affection. I could handle that.

Unfortunately, that's when Scott showed up.

"Hey, Miles." Scott greeted him casually, as if it were totally normal for him to crash a first date. "I'll be tagging along today with my camera. I hope you don't mind."

He almost sounded sincere.

"Yeah, man. It's fine. No problem."

"Cool. So where are we headed?"

Miles simply shrugged and slung his arm over my shoulder. "Anywhere milady wants."

Okay, so I had no idea how to respond to *that,* because being called "milady" was a new one for me. Pet names of any kind sounded strange to me, unless "Grammar Girl" somehow counted. Considering the way everyone in my journalism class used it . . . not exactly a term of endearment.

"Uh." I felt incredibly awkward. "Portland. That's the plan."

Scott was clearly amused by my discomfort, but he restrained himself from commenting on it.

"I'll follow you guys then," he called over his shoulder as he opened the dented driver's side door of his car.

"Shall we?" Miles looked so gentlemanly and *nice* that I felt ridiculous for freaking out about the date. It was hard to believe that I had spent hours obsessing over my outfit. No wonder my mom and sister acted like my body had been taken over by a cyborg. I never should have panicked over something so insignificant—Miles wasn't the type to lose interest because of some ratty jeans. Nice guys who shield awk-

ward girls during theater auditions have way too much substance to only date on a superficial level.

Which meant that while I had been stressing and over-
thinking everything, I had somehow managed to overlook
the fact that I was going out with one of the good guys.

One of the *best* guys.

Now if I could only bring myself to ignore one persistent
photographer, everything would be perfect.

Chapter 21

The drive into Portland was great.

Perfect, actually. Miles turned on the radio so that when we weren't chatting about the audition, we lapsed into a comfortable silence. And, okay, we don't share the same musical taste. Not a big deal. It was only a little awkward when he started singing to Taylor Swift's "Love Song."

It was a *lot* awkward when he suggested I chime in at the part when Taylor starts begging for Romeo to take her away. He even jokingly said the Shakespeare reference made it *our* song.

At least, I hope he was joking.

Either way, he kept insisting that I sing, probably because he thought it was nerves that had tripped me up in the theater. I tried my best to warn him that my voice wouldn't magically improve in a car, but I didn't want him to think of me as boring. Bland. Predictable. So I braced myself for some good-natured teasing and began caterwauling along with the radio. Miles winced, but he didn't laugh it off. Instead, he hurriedly asked for my opinion of the auditions.

And somehow we never ran out of things to say during the whole car ride.

Which definitely surprised me, because with the exception of Corey (gay) and Logan (dating my best friend), I've never been good at talking to guys. Well . . . okay, and Scott. Although, since his main goal in life was to irritate me, I wasn't sure if our bickering should count.

It wasn't like he took any pleasure in hanging out with me.

In fact, Scott looked downright sullen as he dumped change into his parking meter. It wasn't residual road rage, either. Not when both cars had somehow managed to find an open space only a few blocks away from Pioneer Courthouse Square, in downtown Portland. By all rights he should have been thanking the patron saint of parking.

"You hungry?" Miles asked, probably because he noticed where my attention had strayed.

I didn't hesitate. "Yes."

He grinned. "How does Thai food sound?"

"Just lead the way."

Miles took my hand and began moving faster than anyone else on the sidewalk—the geeky type of cardio speed walking my mom recommends at the gym when people refuse to run. I suspected that Miles probably only kept his speed in check because he didn't want me to trip in my stupid kitten-heeled shoes. Still, it felt like we were stealing away for a private romantic moment—photographer not included. I had to make a considerable effort to stifle a laugh when I looked over my shoulder and caught Scott's irritated expression as he increased his own speed.

About time he didn't get his way.

Not that he gave up on his photography. I could hear him snapping away behind us, although when I glanced at him again I saw that I wasn't the focus of every shot. Instead, he looked intent on capturing everything about the food carts; the supercolorful trailers and signs, the steam issuing from the takeout containers, the blissful expressions of people munching on everything from Mexican to Mongolian cuisine—all of it. The backdrop of Portland's overcast skies only made the carts feel even more cheerful and welcoming. As far as I was concerned, they only had one downside: the complete lack of indoor seating. Eating takeout on park benches wasn't exactly romantic, given the way the clouds inevitably led to drizzle. Not unless you wanted the seat of your pants to be wet for the rest of the day.

Usually, I was game to stand around the carts with Corey and Kenzie while we happily stuffed our faces.

Although in the past, I was standing—not shivering—in jeans and a sweatshirt.

Quickly scanning the I Like Thai menu, while I felt uncomfortably aware of Scott's approach, I ordered some Pad Thai and pulled out my wallet.

Miles shook his head. "Oh, don't worry about it, Jane. I've got it."

Elle probably would have leveled him with her most sultry look and purred something like, *Why, thank you, Miles. How thoughtful of you!* Then she would graciously accept the food and move on.

I just stared at him in confusion.

"Are you sure?" I started pulling out a ten-dollar bill. "It's fine. Really. I can—"

Miles looked at me in amused disbelief. "It's Thai food from a cart, Jane. Not lobster and caviar. Relax."

But I couldn't.

Having someone else pay for me just felt . . . weird. And having Scott documenting the whole exchange through his photography didn't exactly help put me at ease. At this rate, Scott's portfolio entitled *Jane Smith: A Study in Failure* would be complete in no time. I mentally began flipping through the past few days in his photographs. Alex Thompson's fist hurtling toward my face . . . my terrified expression at the audition . . . my obvious confusion with dating protocol.

Scott's camera needed to meet with some kind of freak, memory-erasing accident.

I grinned. One bolt of lightning and *game over*. Or maybe if Scott accidentally snapped a picture of a crime, his camera would be temporarily confiscated by the police as evidence. Anything could happen from there. A coffee spill, an evidence-locker mix-up, and Scott would be left with nothing.

Theoretically, at least.

"What's the joke?" Miles asked, and I turned my attention back to my date.

Date. That term still felt strange when it was connected to *me*.

"Nothing. Want to sit on the bench?" It sounded better to me than standing foolishly with our takeout. As long as Scott didn't take close-up photos of me chewing, while I perched on one of the scarred armrests.

I wouldn't put it past him to make me look like an idiot.

"Sure. But what do you want to do about—" Miles didn't have to finish his sentence to make it clear that he was referring to our hovering third wheel.

"Hey, Scott, we'd like some space here." I pointed at a middle-aged couple who were ordering sandwiches. "They look accustomed to privacy. Go get 'em!"

Scott narrowed his eyes, probably because I was using the tone of voice I usually reserve for dogs. I barely refrained from clapping my hands and saying, *Go fetch!* But instead of putting up a fight, he shrugged and left to talk with the brunette at a nearby Greek cart.

The twinge I felt in my stomach was pity for her. Really.

Miles laughed. "I guess there isn't anything between the two of you."

It wasn't a question, but I didn't know what I was supposed to say. Something reassuring? *Nope, I only have eyes for you.*

I couldn't say anything like that with a straight face. Which left . . . something pithy? *Oh, there's something between us—if mutual aggravation counts.*

Except, that wasn't entirely true. Sure, I'd wanted to strangle Scott half of the time we were in Fiction Addiction—but occasionally I caught myself enjoying his company. Or maybe it was that I enjoyed the person I became when I was around him. I never knew if *that* Jane Smith would do something daring, reckless . . . bold. The flirty things I had said to Scott in the bookstore I could never repeat to anyone. Not even Miles, my perfect Romeo, could get me mad enough to let my guard down.

I couldn't shake the feeling that the undercurrent of attraction between us wasn't there. It was just my luck that *finally* someone wanted to go out with me, and our wattage could barely power a solar flashlight. Surely, I should have felt an extra sizzle around Miles, but even eating Thai food together was rather like hanging out with my gay best friend. Unless my romance novels had been seriously misleading, I didn't think that was a good sign.

Although it was possible that kind of electricity needed more time to develop.

Maybe.

"Jane?"

I snapped back to attention. What had he just said? Oh, right. Nothing going on between Scott and me.

Nothing at all.

Miles and I roamed around Portland aimlessly, while we pretended Scott wasn't tagging along behind us. He wasn't easy to ignore, partly because a flurry of flashes constantly barraged the pair of us. It actually could've been fun watching him adjust the settings until he found his perfect shot, if the three of us were hanging out. And if the image he wanted to capture hadn't been mine.

On a first date . . . not so much.

Miles didn't appear to mind Scott's photography or our lack of a formal plan. He was so easygoing, I suspected he was rarely bothered by anything. Instead of trying to move the date in any particular direction, he kept pausing to check out cool shop displays and flyers for upcoming concerts.

"So do you see a lot of plays in Portland?" he asked after memorizing the performance dates of *Mary Poppins*.

"Um, rarely," I admitted. "That's more my sister's thing."

"If your sister likes something, that automatically disqualifies you?"

I shrugged. "We sort of split things up. She gets theater; I get World of Warcraft. She gets ballet; I get the local used bookstore. She gets to be a Notable, and I get . . ."

My voice trailed off. I didn't want to come out and say, *I get to be Invisible. Fair deal, right?* Especially not with Scott shamelessly eavesdropping.

"Well, you seem to have made it work for you."

Totally nice of Miles to say, even though Scott's skeptically raised eyebrow took something away from the moment.

"Thanks."

The conversation drifted into a companionable silence, and I tried to imagine my life if I hadn't been saddled with a perfect Notable sister who made it impossible for me to measure up. Maybe I would have taken ballet lessons and become a Notable myself. Maybe this wouldn't be my first date, because guys would've been clamoring to go out with me since middle school. Maybe Chelsea would have become my best friend instead of Kenzie.

I debated telling Miles about the whole alternate-universe-without-Elle scenario, when his cell phone started vibrating and *MOM* flashed across his caller ID. He cringed before answering.

"Hey, Mom."

The following indignant squawk did not bode well.

"I thought Alicia's audition wasn't until tomorrow."

More squawking.

"Okay. Okay. I get it. You don't want to leave Felicity alone. I'm heading home now, okay?"

So I guess our date was officially over.

Miles and I might not have much in the way of chemistry, but I wasn't ready to call it quits. It was nice wandering around Portland with someone who didn't see me as Grammar Girl or little Jane Smith.

Part of me didn't want to give that up quite yet.

Not that I had a choice.

Miles disconnected and turned to me with a grimace. "That would be my mom. She's something of a stage parent."

I couldn't help smiling, even as we began walking back toward his car. "So is she the reason you got into acting?"

"Oh yeah. Acting, ballet, ice-skating. Anything that appealed to my three sisters became mandatory for me."

"Ballet?"

"All of it."

"And acting stuck."

He looked very nonchalant about the whole thing. "Well, yeah. Not to overplay the three sisters thing, but I'm around drama on a regular basis. The difference is that what happens onstage is scripted so I don't have to worry about saying the wrong thing." Miles shook his head dolefully. "Unlike at my house where I'm guaranteed to say the wrong thing at least once a month."

I laughed as our long strides ate up the distance to his car. "So I guess I'll see you around."

"Right."

Wait. Was that it? *See you around* suddenly felt every bit as vague as *I'll call* you. When? Where? Why? I had no idea if he wanted to go on another date or to slot me into the friend zone. Not that I could blame him for noticing the lack of fireworks between us too. Then again, maybe if we spent more time together—alone—it would be different. Maybe I was like a bomb with a really long fuse: I needed time before I exploded in a big bang of lust.

It could happen.

"So how does next weekend look for you?"

I barely stopped myself from sighing in relief. Maybe I hadn't screwed up our date irreparably. "I don't have any plans."

"Good."

He didn't rush me.

Even when we reached his car, he didn't try to manipulate his way into a kiss. He merely pulled me in for a hug.

"Do you want me to take you home?" Miles glanced pointedly at Scott. "I can swing by your house on my way home. It's really not a problem."

"I'm supposed to meet Kenzie and Corey here anyway," I admitted, while I reclaimed my backpack and extra bag of clothes from his car. "So . . . this is probably for the best."

He paused as if expecting me to reconsider, but when I just smiled reassuringly, he climbed in his car and drove away without another word.

Leaving me alone in downtown Portland with Scott.

Chapter 22

"Well, you and Romeo seemed to hit it off."

I glared at Scott, flinching only when he captured the expression on camera to add to his collection of my unattractive looks.

"Too soon? I guess I shouldn't start calling you Juliet yet."

"I am not discussing this with you." I didn't care if I sounded snooty. I wasn't the one commenting on *his* love life. Of course, that made me wonder if he had one. Maybe there was a girl in LA with a picture of him in her locker, pining over his absence at that very moment. Maybe there was a companion photo in Scott's room at home.

The idea of Scott longing for some strange girl made me feel uncomfortable in my own skin. Of course, the only reason I felt queasy—well, besides from eating Thai food too quickly—was because Scott probably had a thing for girls like Lisa Anne: smart, efficient, hardworking . . . overcontrolling and generally bitchy. Either that or she was a total wimp who just said, *Yes, Scott. That sounds wonderful, Scott. You're a genius, Scott,* no matter what he did. Actually, that made even more sense. He probably loved empty-headed Notable types like Fake.

Gross.

"I got some good pictures."

"I can't tell you how relieved I am to hear it."

Okay, maybe that was a bit more sarcastic than was necessary. But given the way he had effectively chaperoned my date, I felt entitled.

"What's wrong with you?" Scott raised an eyebrow. "Did Miles try to cop a feel at the end of that hug?"

I glared at him again. "Gee, I wonder why I could possibly be annoyed. It's not like you crashed my date by following me around and playing paparazzi. Oh wait, *that's exactly what you did!*"

Scott didn't appear even remotely embarrassed by it either.

"I gave you guys some privacy."

I rolled my eyes. "For all of three minutes!"

"I didn't mess up anything for you. It's not like you would've initiated a massive orgy if I hadn't been there."

"Oh, I don't know. Maybe I would've ripped off my clothes and jumped him while we were waiting for the Thai food."

I'm not sure why I came up with such a ridiculous lie, considering that there was a zero-percent likelihood I would ever do anything *that* crazy.

Scott stared at me, momentarily stunned, and then burst out laughing.

I crossed my arms, but I couldn't help grinning as I watched humor replace his most condescending expression.

"Yeah, that'll be the day that Lisa Anne chooses community college over Harvard."

"Actually, out of the two, the community college thing is far more likely."

His grin widened. "Probably."

"So . . . what do you want to do until the concert begins, approximately"—I glanced down at my watch—"two hours from now?"

"Let's go to Powell's."

I nearly did a double take in my excitement, just to make

sure he wasn't kidding. The world's largest independent used and new bookstore, Powell's is akin to a holy site for geeks like me. The only reason I hadn't mentioned it earlier was because it didn't seem like first-date material.

Hi, Miles! I'm glad you asked me out. Mind if we go somewhere so distractingly awesome that I will inevitably ignore you?

Not the best way to make a good impression.

"Yes!" I tugged once on Scott's shirtsleeve until my body registered his proximity and I dropped my hand as if I had just been singed. Staring up into Scott's green eyes, I thought I caught a glimmer of surprise and awareness that matched my own.

I panicked and bolted. The cold wind slapped at my face, but I didn't have any intention of stopping until I reached Powell's. And maybe not even then.

Scott didn't yell for me to slow down. He didn't say a word. Instead, he began running right next to me, as if it were perfectly normal for him to race a girl in heels.

That's when the run morphed into a competition.

Scott's sneakers and jeans definitely gave him an unfair advantage—plus, he wasn't carrying a bag of clothing *and* a backpack. All he had to deal with was his camera. Yet I doubted Scott even considered slowing his speed to even up the odds. I found myself surprisingly pleased that he didn't, especially since I was holding my own. Just two more blocks. Just one. I was going to win . . . until the DON'T WALK signal started flashing. Instinctively halting at the corner, I watched in disgust while Scott calmly jaywalked over to the store.

His leisurely stroll only rubbed in my defeat while I waited for the stupid signal to change.

"No fair!"

He flashed his smuggest smile. "You're just saying that because you lost."

Probably, but I wasn't about to admit it.

"You broke the basic rules of traffic. I think that means you forfeit your win."

"Not going to happen, Grammar Girl. You're just too slow."

The light changed, and I called upon every last drop of dignity I possessed to meet him on the other side of the street without trying to strangle him.

"Take it back."

"Or what? You'll fight me?" His grin made it clear he was remembering how easily he'd immobilized me in our last skirmish. "We both know how that would end."

"On second thought, I'd rather humble you where it really hurts."

"Oh yeah? Where do you think *that* is?"

"With your photography." I held out my hand for his camera. "Pass it to me."

Scott made no move to do as I directed. "I don't trust you with it."

I rolled my eyes. "Right, because a girl who can't defy a *crosswalk* is really going to get involved with the destruction of personal property."

He considered that for a moment before warily placing it in my hands. "If you so much as scratch the lens cap—"

"Relax!" I cut him off as I strode over to the nearest tree. "I know what I'm doing."

Then I raised the camera above my head and—without looking at the screen—I took a series of rapid shots. It felt good to march right over to him and thrust the camera in his face. "Now see for yourself."

He clicked on the display button so that we could both check out my photos on the small screen, as long as we stood close enough together for our shoulders to brush. "What am I supposed to be seeing?"

"A novice photographer who knows absolutely *nothing* about composition just took photos every bit as artistic as the ones you would've spent hours agonizing over."

He raised the camera closer to examine my work. "Not even close. Still, they're not bad."

This time it was my turn to grin smugly. "I think what you meant to say was, *Jane, these are fantastic! What an interesting technique you have.*"

"Your whole point is that you don't have a technique."

"No, my whole point is that you don't have to be a pompous jerk to get a good photo. You can just have fun with it."

He raised an eyebrow skeptically. "Since when does Smith High School's biggest pushover give lectures on how to have fun?"

"Hey! I stand up for myself just fine!" I protested.

"Right, you've sure told Lisa Anne where she can shove all her threats."

"I've got the Lisa Anne situation under control without a confrontation, *thank you very much*. How do you know she's been threatening me, anyway?"

His *you have got to be kidding* expression spoke volumes. "This is Lisa Anne we're talking about. If you don't nail this story, she'll keep you trapped fixing grammar. And she doesn't care who knows it."

"And you never even considered helping me out? Gee, thanks!"

He shrugged. "You're good with grammar, and I'm not interested in playing the knight in shining armor. They tend to end up casualties in other people's wars."

The rough quality to his voice made me suspect that he was no longer referring to Lisa Anne.

"Know any fallen heroes personally?"

He looked as if I'd sucker punched him in the stomach, before he began scrutinizing my photographs without meeting my eyes.

"Not yet."

He had once mentioned having friends in the military. I racked my brain trying to remember the details.

"Afghanistan?" I blurted out loud.

"Yeah, among other places."

"Friends?"

He kept right on scrolling. "Family."

"Your dad?" I guessed.

"What? No." He finally looked up from his Nikon. "He's a foreign correspondent so he travels a lot, sometimes with the troops, but he's not in the military."

"Then who—"

"My older brother."

"I thought you were an only child."

"You thought wrong."

"You never mentioned him."

"You never asked."

He had a point. I hadn't asked him anything about his past. At first because it seemed rude to bombard the new kid with personal questions and later because after the whole "She doesn't have what it takes to be a reporter" crack, I honestly didn't care.

"So, your brother . . . Navy SEAL, right? He's okay?"

"Yes."

I nodded. "Good."

Then I pulled back and punched him in the arm.

"Ow! What the *hell?*"

"That's for calling me a pushover."

Before he could retaliate or regroup, I bolted into Powell's. It had been so much easier to think of Scott as a camera-wielding jerk, incapable of human emotions. I didn't know what to think anymore. The guy jumped from insulting to entertaining to mildly flirtatious every time I thought I had a handle on his mood.

That's why I was dating Miles. My Romeo was undoubtedly a good guy I could trust not to hurt me. If Scott was cast in a Shakespeare play, he would probably land the role of Hamlet—stewing in his issues, completely unaware of all the pain he caused in his wake.

No girl in her right mind would choose Hamlet over Romeo.

Right?

Chapter 23

I love Powell's.

So spending two hours there with Scott wasn't exactly a hardship. Then again, I could go into the bookstore with *anyone* and leave smiling. Even two noxious Notables like Fake and Bake. Still, I was surprised to find myself relaxing as we discussed the merits of movie adaptations of our favorite books, especially when I accidentally told him about my love of romance novels.

I hadn't intended to mention it, but once my little secret was out, there was no taking it back. Scott wouldn't let it go. He kept prodding at me until I confessed that I'd been hooked ever since Elle handed one to me in the Portland airport. She hadn't exactly done it selflessly—I think her exact words were, "Read this and shut up already!" but she definitely succeeded in distracting me. Unfortunately, I became so paranoid that all my fellow travelers knew what I was reading, I couldn't handle even skimming the sexy parts in public.

That's when Scott laughed and asked if I still skipped over them.

I declined to answer.

I also completely forgot about the concert until Scott reminded me, by which time the threat of rain had materialized into a reality with fat droplets splattering against the sidewalk.

"Um, yeah. Give me a second to change and then we'll—"

Scott didn't even give me a chance to finish my sentence. He just grinned and started walking toward his car, leaving me torn between changing in the Powell's bathroom and getting a ride to the concert. Not much of a choice, since I seriously doubted Scott would stick around waiting for me and I couldn't afford a cab. So I scurried right behind him, shivering in my stupid little skirt while the rain plastered my hair against my face. Elle would probably say that I looked like a drowned rat.

Not quite what I was aiming for when I woke up that morning.

The instant Scott unlocked his car doors, I crawled inside and began pawing through my bag of spare clothes. "Close your eyes."

He narrowed them instead. "Why?"

I toed off my shoes, hoping that tugging on jeans over the tights would help me warm up.

"Most people prefer to pull on more layers in private. Strange, isn't it? It's a total mystery to me why some people don't want to be caught with their pants around their ankles."

"It's a little late for you to start worrying about your image." Scott appeared utterly unfazed by my sarcasm, but at least he shut his eyes. "Especially after your audition for the musical."

"I'm trying to forget that ever happened." I yanked and wiggled until my jeans slid up past my nonexistent boyish hips, where I should've been able to button them if my skirt stopped flopping in the way. "But thanks for that reminder."

He began to drum impatiently against the steering wheel.

"You know, in Powell's they have these remarkable things called bathrooms. Completely private areas. It's amazing how far society has come."

"I didn't realize it would be this wet outside."

"It's Portland."

"Thanks for the geography lesson. I also don't ever wear tights." My unbuttoned skirt pooled on the floor as I swapped out my shirt in two fluid movements. I only did it because I thought that the layer of steam from the warm air now filling the car provided sufficient privacy from the outside world . . . and because even if Scott peeked, my bra was far less scandalous than most bikini tops. "Done."

Scott wasn't in any hurry to start the car now. "You look more like the girl I first met."

I shrugged. "That's because this was the only outfit in my closet preapproved by Corey before Kenzie's YouTube video changed everything."

"Yeah, that's pretty obvious."

I glared at him. "Meaning what, *exactly?* That I need my friends to dress me?"

The pathetic part was that I did need Corey, or Elle, or *someone* telling me what not to wear; otherwise I would settle for my favorite sweatshirt and a baseball cap. But everyone really needed to stop giving me a hard time about it.

It's not like I was incapable of dressing myself. . . . I just couldn't do so fashionably.

"Wow. I guess I struck a nerve."

"Shut up, Scott."

"Since you've got body-image issues, you probably shouldn't continue modeling professionally."

I rolled my eyes. "And I had my heart set on a modeling career. I guess this means I'll never walk a runway with two million dollars' worth of diamonds on my bra. Such a shame."

Scott pulled out into the line of traffic. "Every now and then you can be pretty entertaining, Grammar Girl."

I decided to take that as a compliment.

But even at my most outrageous, no way could I compete with the sheer chaos of being backstage at a concert. Lighting technicians and assistants sprinted around double-checking things before waving their arms and yelling about the placement of the amps.

Madness.

By the time we navigated the craziness and found the ReadySet room we were fifteen minutes late. Not that anyone had worried. Corey and Tim both looked deliriously happy on the couch where they were snuggling, so they must have figured out a way to make the whole long-distance thing work. The other guys in the band, Dominic and Chris, were laughing with Kenzie and Logan as if the four of them had been best friends for years. I instantly felt like a total third wheel. Fifth wheel, really, since both of my best friends looked so . . . couple-y. But I just stood there while Scott snapped pictures of my obvious discomfort.

Great.

"Scott," I muttered. "I'm begging here. Photograph someone else."

He snapped one last shot of me before taking stock of the scene.

"They really seem like a unit."

I had wondered how long it would take for him to comment on Corey and Tim as a couple. The way that Corey was resting his head on the rock star's shoulder was something of a giveaway. Still, I didn't intend to make that line of questioning easy for him.

"Who do you mean?" I asked innocently.

"Kenzie and Logan."

"Mackenzie." My instinctive correction surprised even

me, but I couldn't let it go without comment. "Kenzie's my private nickname for her."

"Oh yeah? Why is that?"

"It's just . . . we've been best friends since elementary school. It's our thing."

That's when Kenzie spotted us.

"You made it, Jane!" She smiled gratefully at Scott. "Thanks for giving her a lift. I completely forgot to confirm with you about the ride situation."

Scott smiled back at Kenzie, without a hint of the smugness I always saw when he looked at me, but he didn't say a word. Probably because he expected me to start filling Kenzie in on all the details of my date. I would've confessed everything if I knew how to do it with even a modicum of subtlety.

Hey, I would've mentioned it earlier, but none of you were listening. . . . I just had a date with a superhot guy! And he honestly seems to like me, even though our chemistry was a little bit off.

Okay, truthfully, it was kind of like dating your little brother, Dylan.

Yeah, that would have been *real* subtle.

Even when Logan walked over and slung an arm around my shoulder, I kept my mouth shut.

"Let's get you a drink, Jane."

Then he steered me over to the selection of soda cans on the table. Clearly, Smith High School's hockey captain didn't plan on letting me anywhere near the hard stuff.

Not that I actually wanted any alcohol . . . just the option.

"I don't trust that guy," Logan muttered, when we were safely out of earshot. "He watches you too much."

There was no point in explaining that was Scott's job as school photographer, since no excuse was going to satisfy Logan. Not when he clearly thought of me as a geeky little sister in need of defending.

So instead of patiently trying to make him come around to the situation, I grinned. "Are you trying to protect me?"

Logan's expression became panic-stricken when he realized there was no right answer. Either he lied or he implied I couldn't take care of myself; either way he was treading in dangerous waters. "Er . . . maybe? Yes."

"Yes, you want to protect me?"

He squared his shoulders as if bracing for the full-blown rant that Kenzie would've delivered. I figured the guy already knew he was being a bit on the overprotective side, but I decided to let it slide. This time.

"That's right."

"Looks like Kenzie snagged the last decent guy at our high school," I mock sighed. "Are you sure I can't convince you to run away with me instead?"

He ruffled my hair like we'd been hanging out for years instead of weeks. That's just part of Logan's charm. The guy can defuse tension in any social encounter—a good skill to have when your girlfriend is famous for being America's Most Awkward Girl.

I couldn't resist messing with him, though. Just a little bit.

"Maybe you should set me up with one of your friends. Is . . . I dunno, Spencer seeing anyone?"

Somehow Logan managed to pale even faster than my dad had over the condom in my backpack. "Oh *hell* no. That's never going to happen."

"Why not?" I teased. "Am I not his type?"

"Spencer's type is female," Logan said, confirming all my suspicions about his best friend. "You, however, are off-limits."

"And why is that?"

Logan stared at me in disbelief. "Because he's not looking for anything even remotely serious, and you're . . . uh . . . you?"

I laughed even though I no longer found the situation funny.

Other people could look for something fleeting and fun, but not me. I was automatically disqualified before I could even decide if I wanted to play. It didn't matter that I didn't actually want to date Spencer. . . . It was the principle of the thing.

I wanted *somebody* to tell me what they thought I couldn't handle.

And then I wanted to prove them wrong.

Chapter 24

The ReadySet band manager simultaneously hustled the boys onstage and hassled Kenzie.

Would she be willing to perform a few numbers with the band? Just one?

Maybe she could just dance around the stage for a while?

The guy obviously didn't know my best friend. Kenzie politely insisted that she would enjoy the show a whole lot more from the wings. It wasn't a false show of modesty either; Kenzie knew exactly what she was giving up—and gaining—every time she decided not to capitalize on her YouTube fame.

The cons simply outweighed the pros for her.

Which was really lucky for me, because without my best friend around, Smith High School would quickly go from annoying to intolerable. Then again, if she was traveling on rock tours and attending movie premieres, at least she wouldn't be able to make as many assumptions about my life.

She might even call me from the road so we could catch up.

That would be nice.

Thankfully, the manager's phone rang not long after the guys took the stage, and he left to go pester someone else. Which meant that the rest of us could enjoy watching ReadySet prove that it didn't matter if they were opening for a concert or headlining one—all they needed was a stage.

I forgot about the stupid journalism article while they performed.

Instead, I simply enjoyed the intensity of the crowd, the crackle of excitement in the air, and the pounding beat of the music in the floorboards. I wanted to suspend that moment forever, but when Wilco took over the stage, our small group in the wings became significantly bigger. Corey instantly glued himself to Tim while the other band members, Dominic and Chris, went right back to hanging out with Kenzie. A clique must have formed when I wasn't looking.

Making me officially invisible even around my best friends.

I pretended not to find Wilco's hit song "I Am Trying to Break Your Heart" extra poignant, given the circumstances. Instead, I stood there with a big smile plastered on my face, trying to fight off the urge to start running again. Sprinting all the way to Powell's in my annoying little heels probably shouldn't have sounded so appealing, especially since I was literally surrounded by rock stars . . . but I wanted out. Even before Wilco finished their encore I felt like if I had to fake it any longer I might combust.

I don't think you guys care that I'm here. That hurts too much for me to stay. Can I get a ride home now?

I couldn't actually say that to any of them, so I tugged on Scott's sleeve while everyone else was still clapping, cheering, and wolf whistling.

"Mind getting out of here a little early?"

"Fine by me." He raised his voice to be heard over the chaos. "Jane and I are heading out. Nice to meet you all."

Logan's head jerked up. "Mack and I can take you home later, Jane. It's no problem."

Except I couldn't maintain the pretense that I was fine with remaining Invisible.

"No, it's fine. You guys have fun. I've got homework wait-ing."

"On a Friday night?" Logan asked skeptically.

I nodded and then swallowed past the lump of emotion forming in my throat as Kenzie pulled me into a brief hug. "Okay. Well, I'll see you later."

In this case, I assumed "later" meant lunch on Monday, because between homework and tutoring Logan, Kenzie wasn't going to be hanging out at my house anytime soon. Not any-more.

"Right."

That's when I would fill her in on my date with Miles too. Later.

Except it was only fifteen minutes into the drive home from Portland that Scott asked me the one question I needed to hear from Kenzie. The one I wasn't sure I could even an-swer honestly to myself.

"Are you okay?"

"Sure. The concert was great." I tried to bump up my level of enthusiasm, but it wasn't working.

I was running on empty.

"You look like a Hummer just ran over your dog."

"I don't have a dog."

"So what's the problem?"

I stared out the window at all the lights twinkling above the Willamette River.

"I don't have a problem, okay! Nothing life-threatening or—"

"Just spit it out already, Grammar Girl. I don't want to deal with this crap all the way home. You have ten seconds to stop sulking."

"I'm not sulking!"

"Could've fooled me."

I glared at him. "It's simple: My friends have moved on. They don't need me. They have boyfriends and concerts and this whole other world that doesn't include me. And it has never *once* occurred to them that I might feel left behind!"

I don't know where all of that came from. It was the truth . . . but I hadn't meant to share it with Scott. He nodded slowly and kept right on driving.

"Not belonging sucks."

I leaned back, feeling drained from my outburst. "Yeah. It does."

"It's kind of like moving. Suddenly, everyone who matters isn't there, and you have to build a sense of history from nothing. Half the time you're stuck waiting to understand the inside jokes."

I fiddled uncomfortably with a damp strand of my hair. "Are you trying to make me feel guilty right now? Because if this is your idea of a pep talk—"

He laughed. "I'm just pointing out that you're not alone in feeling . . . alone."

"Yeah, you looked superlonely in journalism when Lisa Anne and Mr. Elliot promoted you. Admit it: You fit in better than I do now."

"I could still make room for another friend."

"And you think we could pull that off?" I had a hard time believing it. We spent most of our time insulting each other—not exactly a firm foundation for friendship. Especially not after he'd shot me down with Lisa Anne. "Funny. It didn't seem like you were interested in that when we met."

He stiffened, and I instantly regretted even remotely referencing the whole using-me-to-get-access-to-Kenzie thing. The last thing I wanted to deal with was a big confrontation.

"Yeah, I guess you're right."

I stared at him, absolutely speechless. When I'd imagined Scott admitting that our friendship had been a ruse, I'd thought he would say something more like: *It only started as a way to photograph your famous best friend. Then it became real to me!*

Then I kind of liked to imagine he would cry and beg for my forgiveness.

Still, at no point did I ever expect to hear Scott Fraser say that I was right.

"Any reason we can't be friends now?" All traces of his customary cocky grin were gone.

"You mean it?"

"Yeah, why not," he replied flippantly. "It's always useful to befriend the copy editor. If Mr. Elliot makes me write a story, you'll check my grammar, right?"

I laughed. "Nope. I'm retiring from the scintillating world of commas. Thanks for sticking me with that nickname, by the way."

"Oh, it was no trouble."

I rolled my eyes, but I couldn't help hoping the whole being-friends thing would work. Partly because I could use all the journalism support I could get, but mostly because of his speech. It did suck being alone, but it wasn't like I had no control over that situation. I chose to pine after my friends and wait for them to come around.

As far as plans go, that one hadn't been working out too well for me.

Maybe instead of feeling sorry for myself because my best friends were moving on without me . . . I needed to do some branching out of my own.

I wasn't about to start joining in trust exercises until after I finished catching up with my homework and writing my article, however. It turned out that those two tasks sucked up my entire weekend. Still, I thought my lack of a normal social life completely paid off when I strolled into the journalism classroom on Monday, story in hand.

Success.

Even watching Lisa Anne prowl around the classroom didn't

scare me—I was *that* confident my piece was onto something good.

"Your time is up, Grammar Girl." She smirked. "What have you got for me?"

I opened my notebook and handed Lisa Anne a single loose page. Maybe it's stupid and old-fashioned of me, but I enjoy writing first drafts by hand. It makes the words feel more personal to me.

And until my writing had the Lisa Anne seal of approval, I was choosing to consider it a first draft.

Lisa Anne barely scanned the page. "You're kidding me with this, right?"

"Um . . . no."

She laughed but not an amused, *that's funny* laugh. "*ReadySet Is Ready to Rock with Wilco.* This is all you've got?"

"Well . . . yeah? Wilco is a huge name in the indie rock world, and teaming up with a more mainstream rock group like ReadySet could mean lots of cross-genre enthusiasm and sales revenue. It's all there in the article—"

"What part of *Get me a great cover story* did you not understand, Grammar Girl? Scott says you got a *backstage pass,* and this is the best you could do? Pathetic."

"But I thought—"

"No. See, that's the problem: You didn't think. You wrote a fluff piece. And now you get to continue your career in commas. Congratulations."

"But it wasn't . . . I mean, I didn't. That's not—"

"Hey, Grammar Girl! Mind looking this over for me?" Brad Crenshaw thrust his article at me. "Thanks."

"Uh, sure." I was *not* going to cry in front of the whole class. "Fine."

I sat down and began focusing on basic sentence-structure stuff. Comma here. Apostrophe there. All the while I tried to block out my sense of utter stupidity for believing that Lisa Anne would ever like my story.

Scott had sat silently in his chair the whole time I was publicly reamed. Sure, we could be friends . . . if he understood the meaning of the word. It didn't help knowing that he had pegged me as a failure from day one of the assignment, and that in the end, I proved him right.

"Just don't say anything, okay?" I kept my eyes glued on the sheet riddled with grammatical errors even as I felt Scott hovering behind me.

"What happened? You *crumbled*."

Apparently, even that one simple request was beyond him. "I did not!"

"One second you were fine, and the next, you disintegrated."

"What do you want, Scott?" I ran a frustrated hand through my hair. "To gloat? You were right, okay? Is that what you want to hear? I can't hack it. You were right."

I handed Brad his stupid football article on my way out the door.

Scott was the only one who even noticed me leave.

Chapter 25

I still had my invitation to eat lunch with Chelsea. But after the way my story had just been skewered by Lisa Anne, I wasn't ready to navigate the Notables. Maybe my first impression of Chelsea had been horribly off base, but that didn't mean I'd misjudged everyone.

I didn't even feel up to seeing Miles.

Sure, I smiled back when he waved to me in the cafeteria, but then I dumped the remnants of my lunch in the trash and hid in the library until the bell rang.

If I hadn't accidentally left my trusty notebook behind in journalism, I probably would have spent most of lunch writing fictional deaths. Although I was definitely starting to see the appeal in murder mysteries, starting with the mysterious disappearance of Lisa Anne Montgomery. Except after only a few minutes spent trying to imagine all the awful things that could befall her, I felt guilty, petty, and rather heartless.

Maybe instead she could watch *The Devil Wears Prada* and have some huge epiphany about not needing to make other people feel like crap to prove her own worth.

Yeah, and maybe she would hand me back my notebook with the suggestion that I write stories for a fiction page in The Smithsonian.

I wasn't going to start placing bets on that happening either.

My concentration wasn't exactly at the normal level of intensity the rest of the day. When I should have been paying attention to problems where f is continuous on (a, b) and F is any antiderivative of . . . I couldn't muster up the energy to care. It blurred together while I wondered whether I was really going to finish high school stressing over college, complete my four years at the University of Something-or-Other freaking out over grad school, then join the real world only to be woefully unprepared since I had spent all my time with my head in a textbook.

All that line of thinking got me was a killer headache. So I took a deep breath and told myself that it was one stupid newspaper story. One failure for a *school* newspaper—not the final nail in my coffin or whatever. I could make a comeback. At the very least, someday I could reminisce about how something so insignificant ever seemed important.

Although since I wanted to live it down, I decided *not* to mention my recent failure to my parents or Elle. Instead, that evening I locked myself in my bedroom and tried to rewrite my ReadySet story.

Only five hundred more failures now lined my trash can.

"Janie!" my mom hollered at me through the door. "You need to come out now."

Sometimes I really wish she would just call me Jane like everyone else.

"Um . . . just a minute?"

"Your boyfriend is here."

I sat bolt upright. "My *what?*"

"Your boyfriend. Scott. I invited him over to dinner, remember? I thought you were getting ready!" I guess she expected me to be fussing over my appearance, which wasn't a crazy assumption given the way I'd primped for Miles a few days ago. Not that my mom knew about my date with Romeo. But with Scott that effort struck me as an incredible waste of time. Who cared if I showed up in a color-coordinated outfit or in my loosest jeans?

Either way, I wouldn't be writing fiction for the paper.

But while I didn't rush to comb my disheveled hair, I definitely cared enough about what he might spill to my family members to rush downstairs.

"Um, hey," I said self-consciously. "What are you doing— I mean, *how* are you doing?"

His lightning-quick grin made it clear he'd caught my slip. "I'm good. Lisa Anne wanted me to return this to you."

Scott raised my notebook, and I nearly sagged with relief. At least I wouldn't have to go searching for it now. Or asking Lisa Anne if she had seen it.

"Th—"

"He's stopping by with her schoolwork. That's so sweet!" Mom gushed. "Isn't that right, Henry?"

Dad winced, probably because my mom had elbowed him. "Yeah. Real nice."

Elle pulled out her most charming smile, in case it wasn't already obvious why she was considered the popular one. "So how long have you two been dating?"

"No grilling," I intervened, grabbing Scott's arm. "I've got something I need to show Scott in my room. We'll just go now."

"The door stays open!" my dad hollered after us, even though there was no reason for him to worry.

Nothing was going to stop him from panicking over his little girl.

It probably didn't help that in order to prevent Elle from "accidentally" overhearing us, I had to shut the door.

"You weren't kidding about your family." Scott's smile made me feel incredibly gawky standing in my own bedroom. The dark green button-down shirt he wore brought out the color of his eyes, and I absentmindedly wondered why he'd changed since school. "They're . . . intense."

"Yeah, I know."

There was an awkward conversational lull as Scott appeared to soak in the messy state of my room. The four-poster bed with a tangle of blankets, the underwear draped on my laundry hamper, the trash can literally overflowing with poorly written newspaper article attempts.

I forced myself not to make excuses.

"Nice room."

"Thanks."

Yet another long pause.

"I should leave. I can tell your parents that something came up, if you want."

"No!" I blurted. "You can't!"

Scott looked skeptically at me. "You seriously want me to stay?"

"Well . . . yeah. You can't cancel on my mom now. She's way too excited about it." I rolled my eyes. "Trust me, it's important that we, uh, stick to the story."

"You're sure you don't want to introduce them to your real boyfriend instead? I'm betting Romeo would make a brilliant first impression."

I folded my arms. "He's *not* my boyfriend . . . yet. One date doesn't merit that label."

He shrugged and leaned back against my desk. "I thought you were mad at me earlier."

"I usually am," I said flippantly. "You know, most people don't enjoy being told that they disintegrate under pressure. But I'm over it now."

Scott didn't look like he believed a word of it. "You sure?"

It was my turn to shrug. "It's only a high school paper. So what if I can't write my way out of a paper bag. Doesn't matter."

My voice sounded too rough for my own liking.

"It's not that you can't write." Scott ignored my snort of derision while he gestured at my overfull trash can. "Your passion for it comes across on the page too."

"How would *you* know?"

"I read your article after Lisa Anne. It would make an excellent thesis project, but it's not the right material for the front page of *The Smithsonian*. It's just ... not the right tone."

"You can come out and say what you think, Scott. It's pretty obvious that 'thesis project' is your diplomatic way of calling it boring. Message received."

Scott glared at me. "That's not what I meant."

"Really?" All my earlier frustration bubbled back to the surface. "That's interesting. Then why did you tell Lisa Anne a month ago that, what was it? Oh yeah, that *I couldn't hack it as a reporter*. What's the story behind *that*, Scott?"

His green eyes narrowed. "So that's why you stopped speaking to me. You overheard one conversation and ran to your friends instead of asking me about it. That explains a lot." He pushed off from the desk, tension radiating from his body. "For the record: I still don't see you as a journalist. My dad taught me that it takes a certain kind of drive to get at the heart of a story. That can't be faked. No matter how hard you try, it's going to sound off-key—rather like the gargling noises from your singing audition."

"Hey!"

"That first day in class I thought you were shy and ... funny. But you never pried. You didn't look for an angle. If you had a natural instinct for journalism, you would've searched for a story. So, yeah, when Lisa Anne asked for my opinion, I told her the truth. I also mentioned that Brad and Kyle have yet to grasp the basics of the English language. But if you can't handle my honesty, I'll leave right now."

It had never occurred to me that he was anything but a

jerk when he criticized my journalistic abilities to Lisa Anne. Probably because the classroom is the only place where Elle doesn't perpetually outshine me.

So maybe when the new guy began undermining my self-confidence there, I jumped to some conclusions.

All I knew was that I didn't want to explain why my "boy-friend" needed to make a hasty pre-dinner departure.

"No. Stay." I choked out the words. "I'm sorry, I shouldn't have brought it up."

Scott shook his head in disbelief. "You're not sorry. You meant every word of it. I bet that if your family wasn't wait-ing downstairs for us, you would've already kicked me out."

"I apologized. Can we drop it?"

"For what, though? Apologized for making assumptions? For whining to your friends without bothering to get the story straight? Or are you just sorry that I'm calling you on it now? Which one is it, Jane? You tell me."

When he put it that way, I was almost ready to plead guilty to all charges. But . . .

"Did I have it wrong?" I blurted out. "I mean, all of it? Be-cause right after you spoke to Lisa Anne, you set your sights on taking photos of my best friend. Admit it: You were using me to get to Kenzie."

"Let's be clear: I didn't use you to get a shot of Mackenzie, primarily because I don't need any help in that area. I man-age just fine on my own."

I folded my arms. "Logan would stop you if you tried to get in her face."

"Hockey Boy could certainly try to glower me to death. But when I want something, I get it."

I couldn't help wondering if one of those things he might want was Kenzie. It definitely sounded like he might be inter-ested in my best friend. I couldn't even fault his taste, if that was the case, because Kenzie has always been so . . . nice. But I also couldn't help gritting my teeth.

"You do know she's not going to break up with Logan, right?"

Scott glanced disdainfully at me. "Yeah, I think that's pretty obvious to everyone. Although I still think she can do better."

I forced myself not to say, *Oh yeah? Because she could be dating you instead, right? Is that what you mean?*

The last thing I wanted was to sound jealous.

"Okay." I struggled to find the right words. "Well, then—"

"Dinner's ready!" Elle hollered from downstairs. I eyed Scott nervously, unsure how to respond to our summons.

"So . . . are you staying?"

I held my breath, knowing that the way my entire family treated me for at least the next four months depended on his answer.

Scott shrugged noncommittally. "Fine. Let's get it over with, already."

With enthusiasm like *that*, what could possibly go wrong?

Chapter 26

The dinner could have been worse.

My dad never demanded that Scott reveal his intentions toward his youngest daughter, and my mom sniffled about my transition into womanhood through only half of the meal. Elle even passed on a few opportunities to make me look like a total geek. Much to my relief, they all appeared to be on their best behavior. And if Scott felt any residual annoyance with me, he didn't let it show as he fielded their questions.

Even when my dad asked hundreds of follow-up questions about his brother's military service, Scott never appeared rattled. Without so much as missing a beat, Scott said he was grateful modern technology made it possible for them to keep in touch . . . then changed the subject.

I couldn't imagine anyone being a bigger hit with my parents, including Miles. Scott had exceeded their expectations. They weren't going to take it well when I announced our fake breakup, especially if I tried to introduce them to someone else the next week. Not even Elle at her peak of Notable popularity ever moved through boyfriends that quickly. Maybe it would be best for me to hold off on that particular introduction until Miles and I became official—if we ever did.

I didn't want to give my dad an aneurism.

Although I probably should've been more concerned about his eyesight, since I doubted the optometrist would recommend that my entire family press their noses against the kitchen window and peer outside while I escorted Scott back to his car.

That wasn't uncomfortable in the slightest.

Oh wait . . . yes, it really was.

Scott's eyes gleamed wickedly in the light of a streetlamp. "Want to put on a show for our audience? A quick goodnight kiss to sell the act."

I almost considered saying yes. Except did I really want my first kiss to be a performance for my *parents* with a guy who wished he could substitute my best friend for me?

Not so much.

Especially since I still had something-or-other going on with the most wonderful guy at my high school. Miles would never take advantage of the weirdness of the situation to push his own agenda. So even if my parents hadn't been watching, I wouldn't have agreed.

Also, it was Scott. *Scott Fraser.* Never going to happen.

"Not going to happen," I informed him, just so we would definitely be on the same page.

"Not even a hug? That would look suspicious to me."

He had a point. I tentatively wrapped my arms around him while I did my best not to notice how good my body felt pressed against his. The way my every nerve snapped to attention. Then I tried not to shriek in surprise when his hands traveled, effectively transforming our hug into a very different kind of embrace.

"Hey there!"

"Yes?" Scott replied innocently.

"What was *that?*"

The glint in his eyes belied his casual shrug. "My hands slipped."

Yeah, right.

But confronting him about it while my family watched from the kitchen seemed like a spectacularly bad idea, right up there with reconsidering my anti-kissing policy while I was still within a ten-mile radius of Scott. Horrible timing. Terrible plan.

And yet so very tempting.

"Um, okay. See you later!" I bolted straight back to my bedroom so that I wouldn't have to hear my mom's play-by-play account of the evening. That way I could analyze every detail of our hug until the memory was burned into my skin. Some of which I would have to immediately relay to Corey, excluding the part about Scott's crush on Kenzie.

That particular suspicion I definitely planned on keeping to myself.

The following day, every minute that separated me from the cafeteria seemed to last much longer than sixty seconds. I kept trying to imagine Corey's reaction to the whole "accidental" groping part of the story. Laughter, probably. Maybe some excited clapping before he got himself back under control. Even then, I pictured a wide grin spreading across his face as he demanded to hear details.

But when I finally made my way to our usual table, Corey didn't exactly appear to be in the mood to joke around with me . . . or with anyone else for that matter. His face was ashen, his fists were clenched, and Kenzie sat at his side, murmuring something like *It's going to be okay.*

I picked up my pace. "Corey? Are you all right?"

He lit up when he saw me, but not in the normal way. Not because he was so happy to see me. My best friend practically radiated unadulterated loathing.

And it was directed at me.

"Get the hell away from me."

I stared at him in shock, while his words reverberated

around the now-silent cafeteria. I half expected him to burst out laughing at my gullibility.

Of course, I'm acting, Jane. Tim thinks he may have a potential role for me in a music video. So . . . what did you think of my performance? Were the clenched fists too much?

Except he didn't say any of that, and Kenzie and Logan looked incapable of speech. They continued gaping at me.

"Um . . . what?"

I couldn't make sense out of any of it.

"It's one thing to be jealous of my boyfriend, but what you did is *unforgivable,* Jane."

I turned, wide-eyed, from Corey to Kenzie. "What did I do? What's unforgivable? I don't know what you're talking about!"

Kenzie wordlessly handed me a copy of *The Smithsonian* and tapped one finger on the screaming headline: GAY ROCK STAR RELATIONSHIP ON THE ROCKS?

Followed by the byline . . . *Jane Smith.*

My stomach lurched. Lisa Anne must have stumbled across the article I'd written in my notebook about Corey and Tim's long-distance relationship and printed it—with a few alterations to add some extra drama.

I looked up from the article to Corey's indignant face. "I didn't—I mean, I never wanted to—I wrote it, but I didn't—"

"*Right.* You 'accidentally' outed me and my boyfriend in print. Go to hell, Jane. And take your pathetic excuses with you."

I stared at him in horror. "But it was an accident! You have to believe me, Corey—you're my best friend."

But the damage was done.

"Get away from me, Jane," Corey repeated as his clenched fists began turning white. "Get away and stay gone."

I was too stunned to move. I stood there—speechless—holding the school paper, while I waited for Kenzie and Logan to help me fix this. To defend me. To explain to Corey that I would do my best to rectify the mistake after I groveled for his forgiveness.

But they didn't say anything. Not even a quiet suggestion that maybe Corey should give me the benefit of the doubt. I couldn't even hide the tears streaming down my cheeks as I realized that none of them believed in me anymore. That betrayal made me ache in a way I never would've believed possible.

I officially had nobody.

"I—I'm so sorry, Corey."

That's as far as I got before Alex Thompson interrupted loudly. "Nice article, loser. I always knew that ReadySet sucked, I just didn't realize what they were sucking."

Logan and Kenzie simultaneously lurched to their feet, but before any of us could throw a punch, a clear voice rang out through the cafeteria.

"I heard you were having trouble moving your ass on the field, Alex. Now we know why. It must be pretty hard to run with your head shoved that far up it."

Chelsea Halloway, the Queen of the Notables, universally admired for her beauty and grace, was insulting a fellow Notable.

I never saw that one coming.

"You know you look pathetic, right?" she continued, tossing her long blond hair back over her shoulder. "Really pathetic. That's what everyone is thinking right now."

Actually, I had a feeling everyone was thinking: *Since when does Chelsea Halloway defend geeks?* As an unspoken rule, Chelsea's moments of bitchiness were exclusively reserved for keeping the social order in place. I doubted she had ever considered defending anyone before, since all her cohorts were exclusively Notables.

Until now.

"This doesn't concern you, Chelsea," Alex fumed.

"Let me make myself clear. You mess with Jane or . . . whatshisname again, and I'll destroy you. Got it?"

Alex straightened. "A slut like you doesn't scare me."

Chelsea glanced quickly at Logan, but he was a little too preoccupied with keeping Kenzie from clawing Alex to notice. Then Chelsea mock yawned with her eyelids sexily at half-mast.

"You bore me, Alex. Go spread your filth somewhere else. Come on, Jane."

She led me away from where my best friends (now ex–best friends) were sitting, unable to even meet my eyes, right to the Notable table. Chelsea spared Fake and Bake only the briefest of glances.

"Scoot, please. We need to make room."

Only it wasn't a request but a royal command.

I half expected Kenzie to jump up from her seat and yell, *I object!* like we were in some kind of courtroom drama before dragging me away from all those prying eyes. But she didn't so much as twitch as I sat down right next to Chelsea Halloway at the Notable table and made it official.

I was in.

Chapter 27

"Well . . . thanks."

I didn't know what else to say to Chelsea.

I'm completely stunned that you used your powers for good rather than evil. Why did you do it?

That sounded more like a backhanded insult, actually. Probably not the way I should treat somebody who had just done me a favor.

Chelsea waved it off. "It was nothing."

"Loaning me a pencil, that's nothing. Facing down Alex Thompson for me . . . that's *huge!*"

She rolled her eyes, but a self-satisfied smile began to spread across her face. "Alex just doesn't always think with the right part of his anatomy. That's all."

"The guy is certifiably evil."

Chelsea pointed at my eye, which thankfully had pretty much returned to normal. "You're not exactly unbiased."

A watery smile was the best I could manage. "Maybe. Thanks for stepping in. I didn't expect it and, uh . . . it was really nice."

She laughed darkly. "You didn't expect it because I'm such a bitch, right?"

I didn't want to go anywhere near that question, but I knew that if I evaded it, Chelsea would think less of me.

I didn't want to disappoint the one person still speaking to me.

"Uh . . . you have your moments," I said hesitantly. "Just like everyone—"

"I know exactly what other people think of me," Chelsea interrupted. "I terrify them and they hate me for it. But the more they hate me, the more they want to be me. Why fold when you've got a winning hand?"

It didn't sound like a winning hand to me, but I could see the appeal of controlling the masses at Smith High School. The power, the sense of belonging—being a Notable clearly came with perks. Although, I couldn't picture ever trading in my friends for popularity-chasers who would rush to do my bidding.

Then again, I never imagined that my friends would despise me after I accidentally outed America's hottest rock star and his boyfriend to the world.

And that had happened.

My stomach twisted painfully. That stupid article would probably be quoted and plastered all over the Internet within hours. Tim's rock-star status, the gay factor, the backstage introduction by YouTube sensation Mackenzie Wellesley; the press was going to be all over it.

I had hurt my closest friend, and I doubted he would even let me try to make it better.

"Jane? Are you okay? You look like you're going to be sick."

I looked straight into Chelsea's clear blue eyes, forcing down a sudden wave of panic. I couldn't sit at the Notable table, chatting away with the most popular girl at school, *while my life disintegrated into a million pieces.* One play audition and suddenly she was acting like our friendship spanned years.

I couldn't even begin to handle my life.

"Did you read the article?" I blurted out.

Chelsea gave me a cool, measuring look before she answered. "I saw it. So why did you shove your friend out of the closet?"

"It was an accident!"

"How do you *accidentally* out someone? Trip, hit your head, and fall on your laptop?"

I didn't appreciate her sarcasm.

"Look, I *never* meant for the story to be released. Lisa Anne must have seen it and . . ." The rest seemed pretty obvious to me.

"So you never meant for any of this to happen?"

"Of course not!"

She nodded in approval. "Good."

Then she turned to Fake and Bake—er, Steffani and Ashley—and shot them a look that made it clear she didn't appreciate their eavesdropping. The two girls suddenly felt a pressing need to compare the rumors they'd heard about ReadySet drummer Dominic Wyatt's new girlfriend, Holly.

At least my mistake wasn't the only public relations nightmare the band had weathered recently, though I wasn't sure if that helped my case or only made it worse.

"So what are you going to do now that your loser friends want nothing to do with you?"

Okay, that was blunt . . . and harsh . . . and not entirely true. I mean, *Corey* was mad at me, but I wasn't ready to give up on him. I *couldn't* give up on him. He'd eventually accept that it was an accident—I hoped.

And none of them were losers.

"They need time," I said hesitantly. "I'll lay low until Corey is ready to hear me out."

"America's hottest male rock star was just shoved out of the closet, and he's taking your best friend with him. That's going to dominate newsstands for weeks. One apology isn't going to cut it."

"So, what do you suggest?" My voice cracked in desperation. "I should hang out with you until I graduate?"

I didn't mean to say that out loud, especially since our newfound friendship was exactly that: *new*. But blunt honesty seemed like one of the few things Chelsea and I had in common.

"I'm leaving, Jane."

I did a double take. "Wait, what?"

"My parents are getting a divorce. They don't want me to see it turn nasty." She rolled her eyes. "*Nastier,* so I'm being shipped off on a study abroad program to Cambodia."

"Why are you telling me all of this? Isn't it . . . personal?"

Chelsea laughed. "Jane, I'm leaving for *Cambodia* in a few weeks. No offense, but there is nothing you can do to make my life worse. Plus, it looks like we both might be desperate enough to become pen pals or something."

If the one person at Smith High School willing to stand up for me left . . . I'd be alone.

My panic rose a notch, and I didn't even think that was possible.

"You leave in a few *weeks?*"

Chelsea shrugged. "Once my parents make a decision, they move fast. And since what *I* want isn't a factor, the process goes pretty smoothly."

"You sound, uh, really calm about the whole thing."

She shot me her best Notable look of derision. "What am I supposed to do? Ugly cry in front of everyone? Not likely."

"I think I'm going to miss you."

Shocking but true. I had never expected to bond with *Chelsea Halloway,* let alone spill my guts to her. Then again, I never thought she'd have the nerve to stare down Alex Thompson.

Nothing was working out the way I'd planned.

She grinned. "You say that now. But if you land the role of Juliet, you'll be singing—or screeching—a different tune."

"Yeah, I'm sure they will hand over the leading role to the triple non-threat. I don't envy Ms. Helsenberg, though. You're going to be nearly impossible to replace, Chelsea."

Her smile looked pained, probably because being forced to abdicate the throne and Juliet in the high school musical . . . it had to hurt like hell. But she regained her composure so quickly it made me wonder if I had only imagined a temporary slip.

"You're really easy to talk to, you know that?"

"Yeah, I get that a lot."

Mainly because I tend to let other people talk, which is all they really want in the first place.

Chelsea met my gaze squarely. "I still hate your best friend."

"Mackenzie?"

Her lip curled. "That's the one."

"She's really nice."

"She thinks she's smarter than everyone else."

I considered that for a moment. "She is smarter than most of the kids here."

"With a textbook maybe. But not socially."

I noticed that Chelsea's eyes strayed to Logan as she said it. I had a feeling the ex-factor was the real reason Chelsea disliked her. Kenzie's a very hard person to hate.

Even when she becomes too preoccupied with her own life to notice her best friend spiraling out of control.

"You, um—" I faltered. "You don't happen to know who posted that video of her on YouTube, do you? Because we never found out and I was just wondering . . ."

"If it was me? I didn't post it, and I never asked who did." Her smile widened Cheshire-like. "I did watch it a few . . . hundred times."

I laughed hoarsely, and almost every head in the cafeteria swiveled to observe us.

"Hanging out with me for a few weeks at this table won't

make a difference, Jane. Not in the long run. I'm leaving for Cambodia. And *you* still need a plan."

Chelsea was absolutely right—I just didn't know what to do.

The massive knot in my stomach only tightened when Miles halfheartedly waved my way. It didn't help that all of his friends were glaring at me.

Jane Smith, you are slime for outing your best friend.

They weren't completely wrong either.

I hadn't intentionally leaked the story . . . but when I abandoned my notebook in the classroom, I left myself open for attack.

And I wasn't proud of my story.

Corey and Tim made such a great couple. They genuinely cared about each other and were doing everything possible to make the long-distance thing work. And instead of focusing on *that,* I made them sound insecure and dysfunctional.

It was painfully ironic. I'd delivered the story Lisa Anne wanted—one that might make me a journalism all-star—and immediately I wished I'd never even considered writing for *The Smithsonian.* I didn't care if I was stuck correcting grammar for the rest of high school, as long as I could call my friends at the end of the day.

But it didn't look like Corey would answer his phone if he saw my name on his caller ID.

Great.

I had absolutely no idea what to do, especially when I spotted news crews pulling up to the school. Any second the story was probably going to break on *TMZ,* and millions of people would be dogging Corey for the full story. And if they couldn't contact him, they would probably take a pass at me.

I sprinted over to the Guidance Office. Not that Mr. Shelder had been all that helpful after the whole Alex fistfight thing . . . but desperate times call for desperate measures. I could have sworn Mr. Shelder scanned my face for new bruises before he greeted me.

"Jennifer! Good to see you again. No more trouble with football players, I hope."

So he did remember me. Sort of.

"It's Jane."

"Ah, I see. Do you want to tell me about your conflict with her?"

"Er, no. *I'm* Jane."

"Right. Of course. And I'm here to listen. Is there anything in particular you want to discuss?"

I glanced around the office, soaking in a few details that had escaped my attention last time, like the framed family photos and an inspirational poster of an open road. He cleared his throat, and I officially broke down.

"I did something horrible, and I don't know how to fix it."

I told him everything. Well, I tried to anyway. Bawling my eyes out kind of made it difficult to speak. Still, it felt good to have someone listen, hand me tissues, and nod understandingly. When the bell rang I didn't so much as twitch, intentionally skipping class for the first time. Under different circumstances, Corey probably would've told me that he was proud of my miniature act of rebellion.

Only now he wouldn't care.

Still, my heart lurched when Mr. Shelder slipped out and I heard: *Corey O'Neal, please come to the Guidance Office. Corey O'Neal to the Guidance Office* over the school loudspeakers. Maybe Mr. Shelder could convince him that it was all a big misunderstanding. But when Corey showed up, his face pale and his slim body rigid and stiff . . . it was clear that wouldn't be happening any time soon.

"Uh, hey," I said nervously, swiping at my cheeks with a crumpled Kleenex.

He ignored me entirely. "I'm not speaking to her. If that's why you paged me, you can forget about it."

"I'm not here to force a reconciliation, Corey. Now why don't you take a seat? Jane was about to leave."

That was news to me. I didn't think he could send me away without guiding me first. That's what he was there for, right? And what I needed were some very specific instructions. When my parents told me to get a job, I got one. When my teachers assigned homework, I turned it in on time, double-spaced, and with impeccable grammar. That's just the way I work.

But now there were no guidelines, and the one person I thought was *required* to provide them was booting me out of his office.

I remained frozen by the door.

"The reason I brought you here, Corey," Mr. Shelder continued, "is to discuss your, er, new situation. I thought we might go over some coping strategies. Do you have any planned?"

Corey looked at Mr. Shelder as if he had lost his mind— sort of the way the secretary was looking at all three of us through the open office door.

"No, I don't have any *coping strategies planned out!* I never expected my best friend to stab me in the back right before my boyfriend dumped me via *text.*"

"Ah . . . and how are you handling this?"

Corey's eyes were glazed with a mixture of pain and fury. "How do you think I'm handling it?"

Horribly. He looked like he was going through hell . . . and I was mostly to blame.

I wanted to tell Corey not to worry; Tim had obviously panicked, but it was only a temporary relationship setback. What they had was too good to throw away.

But if I said any of that, he might try to add some color to my fading black eye.

"I see," Mr. Shelder said slowly.

"No, I don't think you do. You know what I'm going to be now? A national gay *icon*. A freaking symbol! And people are going to expect me to represent the community. If word gets out that I actually *enjoy* helping Mackenzie primp for her dates, I'm going to be blasted by activists for falling into all the gay male stereotypes!" He raked his hands through his hair. "I'm going to be reduced to one freaking label: gay. *So don't you dare tell me that you see!*"

The room lapsed into a tense silence.

"Corey, I don't think this is the best environment for you right now. I already had Mrs. Morgan call your parents. I believe your dad is on his way. Would you like to sit in my office until he arrives?"

"Now you're kicking me out of school?" he demanded. "She destroys my life, but do you send *her* home? No. Only the gay boy gets a one-way ticket to social Siberia. Well, thanks, but you can take all of your well-intentioned advice and you can shove it up your—"

"Corey!" His dad burst into the room right on cue, his face contorted in concern. "What's going on? I heard it was urgent."

Corey went limp at the first sight of his dad. It was strange to see since Corey's always been the one to keep his composure in the face of adversity, but I guess even he could hit emotional bottom and require someone else to step in and save the day.

I'd just never witnessed it before.

"What's going on?" Corey's dad repeated as he pulled his son into a one-armed hug. "Is it that Thompson kid again? Damn it, Rob! If that monster's parents aren't going to do anything, I swear I'm pressing harassment charges."

"No, it's . . . more complicated. I think you should take Corey home, but your son appears to be a little, er, resistant to the idea."

He turned to Corey, concern evident in his warm brown eyes. "Up to you, sport. How do you want to play this?"

Corey could go three rounds in a ring with Alex Thompson and still claim that he was ready for more, but his dad's quiet support was his undoing. Maybe because his dad would back him up no matter what he decided. Corey shook his head, as if trying to rouse himself from a nightmare.

"Just . . . take me home."

"Okay, then." They were almost out the door when Corey's dad finally noticed me. His face split into a broad grin. "I should've known you'd be here, Jane. I assume Mackenzie will be dropping by soon enough. Would you like to come with us? I can call your parents and explain."

"Dad, no. Let's go."

Mr. O'Neal looked from me to his son in confusion, but the edge to Corey's voice prevented him from asking any questions. "Okay, sport."

Neither of them glanced back at me once.

Chapter 28

M r. Shelder assumed—wrongly—that I would leave the Guidance Office.

But I refused to move until I had a little more clarity on my life. Somehow I had gone from the role of the supportive best friend to the villain in under a day. Except . . . I refused to be the only one to pay for a mistake that was only partially mine.

It was time for me to live up to my new reputation for recklessness.

"Mr. Shelder needs you to page Lisa Anne Montgomery," I lied to his secretary without feeling even a shred of guilt.

She nodded, and I had the satisfaction of hearing, *"Lisa Anne Montgomery, please come to the Guidance Office. Lisa Anne Montgomery to the Guidance Office."*

Excellent.

I mentally began rehearsing my speech so that I'd be prepared to blast her the moment she arrived.

How dare you print this story without checking with me first!

Lisa Anne didn't give me a chance to say any of it. She strolled into the Guidance Office wearing another one of her annoyingly perfect interview outfits, took one look at me, and rolled her eyes.

"I should've known. You're not going to start *whining,* are you, Grammar Girl? You should be thanking me for helping you."

I stared at her in disbelief. "For *helping* me?"

"Yeah!" she said as if it were obvious. "If it weren't for me, you would still be a complete nobody, quivering in the cesspool of your own ineptitude."

I glared at her. "That's not true."

"Oh sure it is, Grammar Girl. I saved you from obscurity. Now maybe people will have something to remember you by when they flip through the high school yearbook. You know that inserting commas isn't a real talent, right?"

She sauntered forward with every word, and as my anger built I couldn't stop myself from shoving her backward hard enough to slam her into the wall, dislodging some pamphlets about dealing with depression. "What's your talent, Lisa Anne? Destroying lives?"

I probably should have known by the way the secretary kept clearing her throat and saying stuff like, "*Really,* girls! Inside voices!" that we were going to be busted by Mr. Shelder.

Correction: that *I* was going to be busted by Mr. Shelder.

Still, not even hearing him snap "Into my office, Jean!" could make me want to back down from this particular fight.

Not when Lisa Anne had it coming.

"He doesn't even know your name!" she crowed triumphantly, even as she darted out of range of my fists. "Don't worry, I'm sure the nice reporters at *People* magazine will cite their source correctly."

One good blow was all I wanted. A single punch right to her snobby, stuck-up nose so that she would bleed all over her stupid, preppy argyle sweater—but Mr. Shelder dragged me into his office before I could try. Then he just sat there watching me while I struggled to get my breathing under control and my fists to unclench.

"Er, Jane, right?"

I nodded, not trusting myself to say anything even remotely civil.

"Look, in light of recent events, I'm concerned that your fight with Alex Thompson was not an isolated incident. I'm seeing a pattern of violence. I want you to go home for a few days. Cool down a little bit. Do you want me to call your parents and have them pick you up?"

"No!" I took a deep breath. "They're at work right now and . . . I'll call someone else, okay?"

I pulled out my cell phone and began scrolling through my contacts before he even had the chance to nod in agreement. Although maybe having my parents show up would have been less painful, since I wasn't sure if any of my contacts were still speaking to me.

Corey: No.

Kenzie: Maybe.

Logan: Less likely.

Isobel?

I paused for a moment on the name, feeling guilty for nearly forgetting her. After the Alex Thompson cafeteria incident, if there was one person who should believe I only had good intentions, it was her. But Isobel couldn't drive.

There was really only one person I could call for a ride, albeit with a great deal of groveling.

"I'm working on important forms right now, so unless you are *bleeding*—"

"I need you to pick me up from school, Elle."

Long pause.

"Are you bleeding?"

"No, but I think I've been suspended."

I glanced at Mr. Shelder for confirmation, and he nodded. Well, that was going to look *great* on my permanent record, right next to my time in detention.

"Jane, this isn't funny. Stop wasting my time."

"It's not a joke, Elle. Please pick me up. I'll wait outside on the steps, okay?"

"Fine. But you'll owe me, and don't think I won't collect!"

She disconnected, and I left the Guidance Office, relieved to discover that Lisa Anne hadn't stuck around. I was less excited to see Scott leaning against the lockers outside the room, almost exactly where he'd waited after my fight with Alex.

Except that time I was surrounded by my friends.

Now it was just him.

Scott scrutinized me, his eyes lingering on the blotchy evidence of tears on my face. "Jesus, Jane. You look like hell."

I managed a feeble grin. "You mean you don't want to take a photo? That's a first."

"I'd rather not remember you looking this way."

"What way?"

"Like you've lost every ounce of fight in you."

"Did I have any fight in me to begin with?" I doubted it. Sam had the courage to fight for what she believed in by taping up condoms in bathrooms, regardless of the punishments Principal Taylor devised.

I had a tendency to screw things up—not the same thing.

"Yeah, you've got fight, Jane. You just don't always know how to use it."

"Well, I think I used the last bit of it getting myself suspended."

His eyes darkened with concern. "What happened?"

"I confronted Lisa Anne." I shrugged and started walking toward the parking lot. "Apparently, I'm starting to demonstrate a pattern of aggression."

Scott grinned. "Really? I'm having a hard time picturing that. Actually, girl-on-girl fighting . . . got it. Any hair pulling?"

I laughed. "Almost. Mr. Shelder blocked me before I got the chance."

"Oh, that's a shame." His smirk said otherwise. "So . . . you're suspended."

"Looks like it."

"Do you need a ride home?"

"My sister is picking me up." I was both surprised that he had offered and . . . not. Scott could be a really great guy— when he felt like it. He could've easily backed out of playing the role of the respectful new boyfriend for my parents, but he hadn't. Scott nearly made *me* believe there was something between us. Which there wasn't. Because he was interested in Kenzie.

I just had to keep reminding myself of that fact.

"Thanks for the offer, Scott."

On impulse, I raised my arms so that they linked around his neck and pulled him into a quick hug. The familiar warmth radiating from his body made me feel safe while I pretended that my world hadn't just imploded and started spraying nearby planets with shrapnel.

It felt dangerously nice.

Until we were interrupted by the most intrusive people on the face of the earth: celebrity reporters. Given my interest in high school journalism, I probably should have found them fascinating. It was a great opportunity for me to tap someone on the shoulder and politely ask how they got into journalism.

Except I had seen reporters like them in action before Kenzie's fame peaked. The kind who follow teenagers home from school, snapping photos the whole way. The kind who would willingly jostle my best friend for an excuse to use TRIPPING OVER FAME! THE MACKENZIE WELLESLEY STORY as their headline. After Kenzie told Ellen DeGeneres that she had no intention of pursuing a life in the spotlight, it looked like they might leave us alone.

But they were back, determined to dig up as much dirt as possible on the romance between rock sensation Timothy Goff and high school student Corey O'Neal.

I never wanted to be the target of this kind of media insanity, and I hoped that Corey and his dad were able to safely make it home before the newshounds picked up their scent.

"Do either of you know Corey O'Neal?"

"Do you think he is dating Timothy Goff?"

"What's it like having the boyfriend of a celebrity at your school?"

We weren't even their intended targets and they were already hounding us . . . probably because everyone else was in class, whereas we were ditching our responsibilities. Actually, Scott was the only one ditching. I had been suspended.

He casually slung an arm over my shoulder and repeated, "No comment" until we were in the parking lot next to his beat-up car. "Are you sure you still want to stick around here waiting for your sister?"

I almost took him up on the offer, but before I could even pull out my cell phone to let Elle know I had found an alternative method of transportation, she pulled up to the school, rolled down her window . . . and promptly began shouting at me.

"Are you *kidding me!* You think you can ditch class with your boyfriend and I'll pick you up? Well, screw that! And don't think for a second that I'll cover for you with Mom and Dad!"

Without giving me a chance to explain, she gunned out of the lot as quickly as she'd entered it. So much for sisterly support.

"Well"—Scott broke my stupefied silence—"I guess jumping to conclusions runs in the family."

"Um, about that ride you offered . . ."

"I don't know what you're talking about."

I stared up at him in horror. "But—but you *just* said that—"

He laughed. "I'm kidding, Jane. Get in."

He didn't have to tell me twice.

Chapter 29

"Where are we going?"

I've always been a backseat driver. Luckily, I have a really good sense of direction and I'm excellent with maps, so my parents usually use me as their navigation system, especially on road trips. Still, it didn't exactly take a genius to know that we were headed in the opposite direction from my house.

"I don't know."

I stared at Scott in surprise. "You don't know? But you drove to my house last night."

"Yeah."

I gritted my teeth at his non-answer. "And yet you don't know where we're going?"

"That's what I said."

"But—"

Scott shot me a piercing look. "Do you honestly want to go home right now, Jane?"

I didn't. At least not until Elle had calmed down.

"Well, no . . ."

"Then what difference does it make?"

The guy had a point. As far as I could tell, suspension came with only a few perks: I didn't have to be anywhere, see anyone, or do anything. I might as well take advantage of them before I had to explain everything to my family, a conversation that probably wasn't going to end well. So I decided not to squander a golden opportunity to relax, even if it was only temporary and included Scott.

I leaned back in my seat. "Okay. Sounds good to me."

Scott reached out to turn on his music, then hesitated. "Promise you won't sing? I don't think I could take it."

"I won't sing!"

"Excellent."

I didn't break my promise, even though his mix included some of my favorite Wilco and ReadySet songs. Still, I couldn't let the subject drop.

"You know I *can* sing on occasion."

"One of those occasions *not* being in my car."

I rolled my eyes. "I get it. But *on occasion* . . . like the last time I was sick, I could do a *really* good version of 'I Try' by Macy Gray."

He didn't look impressed. "Isn't she the one who always sounds raspy?"

"Right. I nailed it."

He grinned. "Yeah? So when else can you sing?"

"Hmm . . . well, *I* think I sound pretty good in the shower, but Elle always bangs on the door and tells me to shut up."

"Sounds like what you need is an impartial third-party judge. I'm ready to volunteer my services."

"That's, um . . . generous of you."

"I aim to please."

I laughed. "I don't think that'd go over too well with my dad. He already thinks we're planning on spending a few hours at the nearest motel."

Scott's grin widened. "Which motel might that be? It's not too late for me to turn around."

"Not telling."

"And where did he get this idea?"

"Um . . . from me."

Scott's hands seemed to tighten reflexively on the steering wheel. "Seriously? What did you tell him?"

"I may have mentioned that I had a condom and that I wasn't afraid to use it."

I expected Scott to laugh, maybe make a snarky comment about things heating up with my Romeo, but he didn't. That's when I realized that Mr. Shelder was right to send me home. I wasn't myself, or at least not the version I've always been up until a week ago. That Jane Smith never could've casually mentioned condoms, especially while riding in a car with *Scott Fraser*.

"Well, that's . . . uh, okay." Scott fumbled for words. "That's . . . fine."

"Scott?"

"Yeah?"

"I'm kidding. I mean, I did mention condoms, but it was just to make them stop treating me like a preschooler."

Much to my relief, Scott's grin returned in full force. "Did it work?"

"Well, my mom keeps saying that her little girl is all grown up." I shrugged. "I wonder if she'll feel that way when she hears about my suspension."

I stared sightlessly out at the green foliage whizzing past the window.

"She'll probably find it hard to believe I've been kicked out, even temporarily." I couldn't bring myself to look at Scott. I wasn't sure I wanted to see his reaction.

"You're not feeling guilty about it?"

I paused to consider. "Not really. I don't want to tell my parents, but no real guilt. Then again, I still can't believe Lisa Anne printed that piece, so maybe the guilt will sink in later too."

"You didn't know?"

"Of course not! I *never* would have signed off on that story."

Except Lisa Anne couldn't have been the only one involved, the way I had assumed. Maybe she was the primary force behind the article, but Scott's photos from the concert were featured on the front page. I tried to remember what Scott had said the night before when he'd returned my notebook: *Lisa Anne wanted me to return this to you.* At the time, I'd thought he was doing me a favor.

And all along he was playing me for the front page of *The Smithsonian.*

"Pull over, Scott. Now."

He drove onto the shoulder of the road, unclicked his seat belt, and turned to face me. "What?"

"You worked with Lisa Anne on this, didn't you?"

I saw the truth flash across his face before he even said a word.

"Yes."

"But I—I thought we were friends!"

He didn't even have the nerve to look ashamed. "What does that have to do with the newspaper?"

"You helped Lisa Anne publicly out my best friend!"

"Actually, I submitted some photos for the paper."

I stared at him in disbelief. "How can you be so nonchalant about this? Do you have any idea what you've done to Corey? To *me?* This is just . . ." I flapped my hands when no adjectives strong enough came to mind.

"Jane?"

"What?" I snapped. "What can you possibly say to make it better?"

That's when he leaned in and . . . kissed me.

I never saw it coming, and everything I felt—my anger, my guilt, my confusion, my sense of betrayal, and okay, even a *really* stupid jolt of physical reaction as Scott's hand tangled in my hair and his lips pressed against mine—it was more than I could handle.

"No!"

Scott instantly pulled back. "What's wrong?"

"You. Me. This. I thought . . . I don't . . . you can't do this, because it's just . . . it's all wrong! *You outed my best friend!*"

Scott looked out the windshield. "I don't get you, Jane. One moment we're getting along great and I think you're interested in me, and the next you come up with these insane accusations. So either you aren't aware of the mixed messages, in which case you're stupid, or you know exactly what you're doing, and you're a tease. Or you are straight-up crazy. Which one is it, Jane?"

"I have *not* been coming on to you!"

"Stupid. Got it."

I ignored him. "I'm *not* stupid, and I wasn't coming on to you. I may have tried flirting, but . . . that's not the point! You thought . . . what? That you could just kiss me and make everything better?"

Scott rubbed his forehead as if our conversation was giving him a migraine. "No, I didn't."

But I was on a roll.

"Did you think I'd be glad to find out that you helped *destroy my friend's life?*"

"This is bullshit! You want to blame everyone else? Fine. Lisa Anne ran your story, and I supplied the photos. I guess it doesn't make a difference that I wouldn't have worked on it unless I goddamn well thought you had cleared it with your friend first!" He released an exasperated breath and then continued more calmly. "I didn't mean to yell. That was . . . out of line. I thought Corey and Tim wanted the article to show how hard it was to maintain a relationship under the scrutiny of the American public. Then again, I also thought . . . doesn't matter, you're not worth it."

"What the hell does that mean?" I asked, stung.

"It means that you're waiting for Prince Charming to sweep you off into a stunning life of mediocrity."

"That's not tr—"

"I'm not finished. Now you have your Romeo and that's *great*. I thought when you said that the two of you weren't dating . . . doesn't matter. You seem happier playing the victim and being ignored by your own friends than you are standing up for yourself. That's why you never confronted them about the concert, right? Why you never asked to join them? It's so much easier to put on a good face in public and sulk in private. Less risk that way. But it's sad how little you're willing to settle for in your life, Jane. And if you really want people to treat you like an adult, demand it of them. Carrying around a whole box of Trojans isn't going to fix it for you."

Each word felt like a sucker punch to the gut.

"Take me home, please. Now."

"My pleasure."

We didn't say another word to each other the whole ride back.

Chapter 30

I set a new personal crying record in my bedroom.

Not exactly a goal of mine. In fact, I spent the first ten minutes ordering myself to snap out of my pity-fest and pull myself together. But I wasn't physically capable of stopping, not when five seconds after my first kiss the boy openly admitted to regretting the impulse. I figured that, on top of everything else, warranted some time sobbing into my pillows.

I kept torturing myself with replaying snippets from the car ride.

The resigned look on Scott's face when he said, "You're not worth it" had me curled in the fetal position under the covers for hours. Maybe Kenzie was right to call me a hopeless romantic, but I always thought my first kiss would be sweet and tender and make me go all mushy inside.

I thought it would feel like forever and that afterward I'd call up Kenzie and Corey and the three of us would analyze every detail.

Not that he would turn around and call me pathetic.

Actually, to be fair, the word he used was "sad," not pathetic, but I didn't consider that much of an improvement. Especially since he also implied that I was a calculating tease. I found that part patently ridiculous.

So he was wrong about everything.

Except . . . I had definitely jumped to some conclusions about his interest in Kenzie. And his comment about settling for a life of mediocrity struck painfully close to home. Even after the kiss it was hard for me to fathom anyone choosing me over my best friend—for anything. I was too used to thinking of myself as second-rate, because life was safer for me once I accepted that status. Nobody could disappoint me if I went into most social situations with low expectations.

But it was a really crappy way to spend my life.

My cell phone wouldn't stop beeping, so I sat up, instinctively wiping my cheeks, before I began scrolling through my four new texts.

Isobel: **How are you, Jane? I'm worried about you!**

Chelsea: **Lunch again tomorrow?**

Sam: **Heard you took on Alex T again. Badass! See you in detention?**

Miles: **Hey, hope you are ok.**

My lips curved into a watery smile—it was nice to know I hadn't managed to alienate *everyone* at Smith High School. I planned on using the same response for everyone:

Hey! I'm fine, but suspended. I don't know when I'll be back. See you then!

After briefly debating the exclamation points, which I decided might sound chipper enough to fool people into thinking that I hadn't been bawling my eyes out for hours, I pressed send.

Then I composed a special text for Corey: **I'm sorry. It was an accident. Anything I can do?**

His response was equally fast and straightforward: **Leave me alone.**

Okay . . . that sucked.

Things only got worse when my parents came home and heard the third message on our answering machine.

Hi, Mr. and Mrs. Smith, this is Rob Shelder from the Smith

High School counseling office calling in regards to Jane Smith's current academic suspension. We believe that her recent problematic behavior requires parental attention and hope that spending two days at home contemplating the consequences of her actions will help. Don't hesitate to call if you have any questions.

He rattled off his school extension number before hanging up.

"Jane Elizabeth Smith. Get down here right this instant!" My dad didn't look even remotely moved by my red-rimmed eyes. "Explain. Now."

I didn't even know where to begin, but I instinctively skirted the whole Alex Thompson debacle. No need for me to dig myself even more deeply into trouble. So I kept things as simple as possible.

"I accidentally outed Corey's relationship with a rock star when Lisa Anne printed something I wrote in *The Smithsonian*. Then I, uh, yelled at her about it. In the guidance counselor's office."

My mom sighed. "We never had to deal with anything like *this* with your sister."

I bit down on my tongue to prevent myself from pointing out that Elle's friends also weren't YouTube sensations. That wouldn't help matters.

"This isn't like you at all, Janie."

My dad shook his head. "I'm not so sure, honey. Remember the time you forgot to pack her favorite blanket? She wouldn't calm down until we retrieved the damn thing."

I stared at him. "Really? Are you seriously bringing up Binky *now*?"

Elle couldn't resist hollering her opinion from the kitchen, where she was shamelessly eavesdropping. "Well, you still act like you're five, so . . ."

I forced myself to stay calm as I concentrated on my dad. "Look, I'm sorry. I never meant for any of this to happen."

" 'Sorry' isn't going to cut it this time, Jane."

"And where's *my* apology? I'm the one who drove all the way over there just to find you plastered against your new boyfriend!"

Thanks, Elle. Thanks a whole lot.

My dad's face darkened, if that was even possible. "You found her doing *what?*"

"It wasn't like that! Scott walked me to the parking lot and then gave me a ride home after Elle freaked out. Nothing happened."

It didn't seem like a good time to mention that he'd pulled off to the shoulder of the road and kissed me.

"You never got into trouble before this boy." My dad turned to my mom for confirmation. "I don't think he's a good influence."

My mom chewed on her lip thoughtfully. "He has a point, sweetie."

"This has nothing to do with Scott! I make my own decisions, and some of those landed me in trouble. But you know what? You don't need to worry because he dumped me. *Dumped me.* Right before he dropped me off. Happy now?"

My parents traded looks, but my dad did a poor job of disguising his relief.

"Of course we're not happy about it, Jane. But your mother and I also can't just ignore the gravity of the situation. Consider yourself grounded for—" He turned to my mom. "Two weeks?"

She nodded.

"Two weeks. Got it?"

I nodded, but I couldn't help wondering if they realized they weren't dealing with Elle. I didn't have an active social life for them to interrupt, especially now that two of my friends were no longer speaking to me. In fact, I doubted that my grounding would have even the slightest impact on my daily routine.

But I certainly wasn't going to suggest more creative ideas for punishment.

I ate dinner in silence before retreating back to my room . . . only to have Elle barge in.

"Hey! Seriously, Elle. Try *knocking!* Everyone's doing it."

Elle just ignored me and concentrated on twirling one of her rings around her finger instead. "I'm . . . uh, sorry."

I would've choked if I had still been eating. "You're *what?*"

Her eyes narrowed into a glare. "I said, I'm sorry."

"Okay. Um, for the knocking thing or what?"

"I, uh, probably shouldn't have ditched you in the parking lot earlier."

There was no *probably* about it, in my opinion, but by Elle's standards even that small admission of imperfection was huge. And judging by the way she continued twirling the band of silver on her index finger, she wasn't done.

"And I'm sorry to hear about your breakup. You guys made a cute couple."

"Yeah, well." I shrugged, because I didn't know what else to do. Thankfully, I was all out of tears. "I'm sure he'll find someone else better. It's a miracle it ever happened in the first place, right?"

She didn't smile at my joke. Maybe because it wasn't funny.

Elle took a deep breath. "I should have been more supportive about your first date. I'm sorry I was . . . jealous."

I stared at my sister in disbelief. "You? Jealous? Of Scott and me?"

"I just—look, I'm not proud of it, okay? I didn't want to be overshadowed by my little sister. Seeing you wrapped around your perfect little boyfriend rubbed me the wrong way."

It was surreal hearing Elle describe any aspect of my life as "perfect," let alone my relationship with Scott.

She couldn't have been any farther from the truth.

"Well, it's over now," I said bitterly. "You're still the perfect daughter and the popular one and . . . everything else, okay? So you can relax."

Elle shook her head in disbelief. "I'm not the perfect daughter."

I snorted. "Right. Sure you're not."

"Seriously. I'm not. I put Mom and Dad through hell." She grinned wryly. "The drinking, the parties—they hated it. Why do you think they are so worried about you now? It's because they don't want you spending high school the way I did."

"Captain of the dance team, lead in the school plays, admit it: You were the most popular girl in school, Elle."

She shrugged. "For a while, yeah. Then again, I was also the girl most likely to get hammered at a party too. I'm not exactly proud of that."

"But everyone wanted to be just like you." I pitched my voice higher to really nail my imitation of Fake. "*You're* Elle Smith's *sister? No. Freaking. Way.*"

"Most people just liked the gloss, Jane. Hell, I didn't want to be myself for most of it." She glanced at the clock on my wall, obviously looking for an excuse to leave. "I have to get back to my forms."

"Elle?"

She paused at the door. "Yeah?"

"I love you."

"Love you too, punk."

I fell asleep thinking that maybe the day hadn't been a complete bust.

Chapter 31

ReadySet dominated the media all the next day.

They dominated pop culture Web sites, trended on Twitter, and even made it as a breaking news story on the entertainment channel, where an "expert" examined pictures of Tim's facial structure to speculate on his sexual identity. And everyone kept referencing my article as if it were undisputed fact, because the truth didn't matter as long as the lies captured attention.

Everyone wanted to know all the details on the dirt, including me.

Not that I had anything more important to do than watch the news cycle I'd accidentally created spin out of control, especially since I was both suspended *and* grounded. At least I could wear whatever I wanted again. Flipping through channels looking for good ReadySet coverage in my rattiest sweatpants and my dad's college sweatshirt felt more like a vacation than a punishment. Although it was kind of weird having Elle nearby filling out her paperwork, especially after our talk last night. Technically, I could have hidden in my bedroom, but I didn't want to look like I was making too much out of our brief bonding moment.

I forgot all about my sister when new headlines started popping up everywhere.

"I'M OFFENDED!" GOFF STRIKES BACK!

Timothy Goff, the eighteen-year-old lead singer for rock band ReadySet, just released a statement to squash the rumors about his sexual orientation. Goff denied ever dating high school student Corey O'Neal, and has gone on record saying, "I'm offended by the way people have jumped to conclusions about my personal life." The person responsible for these rumors? Mr. O'Neal's fellow high school classmate Jane Smith, whom Goff described as "a lonely girl using my love life as a cry for professional help." Smith is currently under school suspension due to her history of violent behavior. "I wish her the best," Goff offered magnanimously. "Hopefully, she will realize that spreading rumors isn't a good way to get attention. Maybe she'll get her medication straightened out."

I stared at the screen in horror as I processed the jabs embedded in the story.

Jane Smith needs professional help. Jane Smith is a liar. Jane Smith is a pathetic, spotlight-grabbing psychopath who should mind her own business.

Those were the comments right under the article.

Jane Smith needs to get a life.

"I've got to see Corey."

Elle looked up from her mountain of paperwork and eyed me warily. "What's going on?"

"I have to set the record straight, whether he wants to hear it or not." My legs trembled as I stood. "Right now. And if this doesn't work, I'm done."

"Jane, that's not a good idea," Elle warned. "You're grounded *and* suspended. Not exactly the time to visit someone who hates your guts. Just wait it out, and I'm sure the whole thing will blow over."

I nearly laughed. "That's exactly how I got into this mess in the first place! I waited for things to get better, and I didn't speak up because I *hate* confrontations. But I'm not going to keep doing this. I can't."

"Yes, you can. It's easy. Sit down, turn on the TV, and wallow while some overly tanned people scream."

"I'm going to Corey's. If Mom and Dad ask..." I shrugged. "I don't know, tell them I took a walk to clear my head."

Elle's look was one of pure disgust. "I'm not your jailer. You're old enough to make your own stupid decisions."

Not quite the way I would've liked her to phrase it, but at least my sister wasn't treating me like a kindergartener.

That counted as a slight improvement.

"Okay then," I said, opening the door. "If you drive, you can get a good up-close look at this disaster in progress."

"You're baiting me for a ride."

I didn't so much as blink. "Yes."

"Will it make a difference if I say no?"

"Nope. It just means it'll take me a little longer to get to his house."

Elle sauntered over to the door, looking every inch the Notable queen, as she snatched her keys from the hook. "Fine. But if anything happens to my car, you're paying for the damages."

Not that she was willing to risk it as soon as she saw the paparazzi swarming Corey's house.

"You're on your own, punk. Try not to do anything I wouldn't."

"Too late."

I didn't give her a chance to issue any other warnings and began shoving my way toward the house. Nobody gave me so much as a second glance. At most all I earned was a few glares, probably because in my dad's ugly gray sweatshirt I didn't exactly look newsworthy . . . at least until I started pounding on the front door.

That's when some of the cameras started flashing at me.

"Corey!" I yelled out. "Let me in!"

Nothing happened. Well, except that a whole bunch of the reporters started hounding me.

Do you believe he's still dating Timothy Goff?

Why all the secrecy?

Can you comment on O'Neal's state of mind?

So I did what any irate teenage girl would do after she has been besmirched by the press, alienated by her friends, and generally treated like crap: I whipped out my cell phone.

All I had to say on the O'Neal family answering machine was, "It's Jane. I'm at your house, and unless you let me in, I'm telling the press everything" to get Corey's dad to open the door and allow me inside.

The reception I received once the door slammed behind me was less than friendly. Both of Corey's parents must have taken the day off work, just in case he needed their support. I always liked that protective streak in them, although it was harder to appreciate it now that I was on the other side of the barrier.

"Hello, Mr. and Mrs. O'Neal," I said politely.

"Jane." Coming from Corey's dad it was more of a statement than a welcome.

"I need to talk to Corey."

I thought they might refuse me until Corey's mom spoke up. "He's in his room, but let's make this clear: If you do anything to hurt my son, I will sue you for harassment. Do you understand?"

I nodded.

"Okay then."

And on that note I went to confront my ex–best friend—only to find him hanging out with Kenzie and Logan, as if it were a normal day after school. As if they hadn't recently cut me out of their lives.

"We need to talk."

Their heads swiveled at the sound of my voice, and all three of them looked appalled to see me standing in the doorway.

"Get the hell out of here!" Corey yelled. "Mackenzie, please make her leave."

I stepped farther into the room and shut the door behind me. "Hear me out. Give me five minutes. After that, I'm gone. I won't bother you again either."

There was a long, painful silence before he finally nodded. "Fine. Five minutes."

"Okay, here it is: I'm sorry, Corey. Something I wrote in my notebook, which I never intended to publish in a million years, was *stolen* and printed without my permission—and that landed you here. I'm so sorry, Corey. I never intended to hurt you. . . . I hope someday you will believe me that it was an accident."

Corey's expression never altered. I took a deep breath and braced myself.

"That said: All of you suck."

Shock and disbelief flashed across their faces.

"Hey!"

"I'm *not* finished! I still have four minutes to explain." I rounded on Kenzie. "Let's start with you. Makes sense, right?" I concentrated on forcing the right words past the lump in my throat, which was trying to choke me. "We've been best friends since elementary school, but it never occurred to you that I was hurting. None of you gave me the benefit of the doubt. No phone calls. You couldn't even be bothered to *text* me. Guess who did, Kenzie?"

She shook her head mutely.

"Chelsea Halloway. Your nemesis. The Queen of the Notables. *She* has been a better friend to me than any of you!"

Kenzie's mouth fell open, but I wasn't ready to hear any of her protests.

"Ever since you started dating Logan, our friendship hasn't been a priority. You guys never invite me to do things. You don't call me. You just go off and have your little shopping sprees with your *new best friend, Melanie,* and then conveniently forget to mention them to me."

Kenzie reddened, and I knew that I was right. She hadn't been planning on inviting me to go with her to whatever party she'd been shopping for with Melanie. The invitation hadn't just slipped her mind the way I'd wanted so desperately to believe. I dug my nails into my palm and forced myself to continue instead of bawling my eyes out as I ran as fast as I could away from them.

"You act like you're ashamed of me now. Now that you have your precious boyfriend and more glamorous friends, you don't want me tagging along."

Kenzie shook her head violently "Jane, that's not—"

"That's how it feels! That's how it feels every single time you guys blow me off. And I can't keep waiting on the sidelines for you to notice that maybe I don't want to be treated as *Invisible* by my *best friends!*"

I raked back my hair, knowing that I probably sounded every bit as mentally unhinged as Tim had described me in his interview. The ache wouldn't go away. No matter what I said, my heart continued breaking farther apart until I started to believe that soon I'd be left with nothing more than bloody goop.

Death by best friends' betrayal. I wondered why it had never occurred to me sooner.

"Let's look at the facts: When Kenzie became the laughingstock of YouTube, everyone supported her. *I* have an accident, and suddenly our friendship is terminated," I croaked hoarsely. "Did any of you consider that this media attention is destroying *my* life too? My academic suspension is going to be discussed on the news tonight, along with a whole bunch of insinuations that I'm off medication that I never took in the first place! Universities might like Kenzie's essay about becoming an overnight Internet sensation, but I doubt they will feel the same way about admitting students who have been publicly condemned as attention-seeking liars."

I glanced down at my watch. "Thirty seconds left. I'll leave you with this then: I can't seem to stop caring about you guys. Even after all of this . . . *crap,* I can't erase what we've been through together. Trust me, it would hurt a hell of a lot less right now if I could. But apparently there is something even worse than losing the three of you. And that's losing myself."

On that final note, I finally gave in to my instinctive flight response and made a mad dash out of the house, ducking my head until I cleared the paparazzi, as an emotional numbness began to sink in. I didn't even realize hot, angry tears kept spilling down my face until I tasted the bitterness on my lips. The sting was nothing compared to realizing the people who had once been the very best parts of my life were gone.

But it was a cold comfort knowing that at least I had finally told the truth.

Elle didn't say a word when I climbed back into her car. She drove me straight home in silence, while I contemplated my options. I wanted to fight this new media image of myself as a violent, publicity-obsessed psychopath-in-training. To set the record straight publicly, even if that meant writing an insider's look into Timothy Goff and Corey O'Neal's relationship. Now that our friendship had been terminated, there should have been nothing holding me back. It wasn't like I had anything to lose by telling my side of the story for a boatload of cash . . . except my own self-respect. That was one trade-off I wasn't willing to make.

The truth might set me free, but in this case it wasn't my truth to tell.

It looked like Scott's assessment of me was right: I wasn't reporter material, certainly not by Lisa Anne's standards. A true journalist was someone determined to give people the latest news with his or her name attached to the byline.

But there are some things the public just doesn't need to know, because it is none of their business.

Still, I did know one person who might be able to help me fix what I had accidentally broken. Someone with the power to change the news cycle. Once again I pulled out my cell phone.

Only this time it was to call a rock star.

Chapter 32

The ringing of my cell phone woke me up.

"Hello?" I croaked, without bothering to check my caller ID.

"Did you put him up to it?"

Corey.

I sat bolt upright, wondering dimly whether this could be a supervivid dream, until I glanced over at my alarm clock. Not even in my worst nightmares would anyone be sadistic enough to call me at six in the morning when I was suspended from school and could theoretically sleep as late as I wanted.

The distinct tone of wariness in Corey's voice had me struggling to keep up.

"What are you talking about?"

"Tim mentioned that you called him."

I rubbed my eyes, which felt like sandpaper after all my crying the day before, and fought the urge to close them again. "Uh-huh."

"So did you put him up to this?" Corey's obvious impatience was so familiar that it was comforting to hear.

"Uh, what *exactly* did he do?"

"Only the sweetest, most romantic gesture known to mankind. He painted a billboard in LA—well, I think he painted it. . . . It could have been done some other way, I'm not sure—"

"Let's stay on point, Corey. What did it say?"

"He painted 'I love Corey O'Neal' and signed it clearly to eliminate any doubt over who did it."

Smooth. The rock star definitely had moves.

"Then he texted a picture of himself standing in front of it to me. And he—" Corey's voice broke with emotion. "He wrote, 'I'm not hiding anymore. Sorry I panicked. Forgive me?' "

"Uh . . ." I was almost at a loss for words. "Yeah, that's pretty romantic."

"*Right!* What should I do?"

I slowly shook my head in an attempt to clear it. "Why are you asking me? I thought you wanted my head on a platter."

There was a long pause while I instantly regretted my words. For this one brief moment, I had my best friend back—if that was a dream, I didn't want to wake up; if it was a random accident, I didn't want to be the one to kill it.

"There was no one I wanted to talk to more."

I felt my throat close. "Really?"

"Yeah. That doesn't mean everything is fine between us," Corey added quickly. "Maybe it was an accident—"

"It was!"

"But it still hurt."

I nodded, forgetting that he couldn't see it over the phone.

"But you were right: Even at my angriest I couldn't erase our years of friendship either. So . . . I called you. And if you want to get back in my good graces, you better start dishing out some brilliant advice right now. What should I do?"

I laughed, and the chokehold of tension around my heart eased. "Okay, well, advice is not really my strong suit. The idea to declare his love on a *billboard* didn't come from me, so you might want to lower your expectations. But . . . the guy spent an hour grilling me for information about how you were handling the split."

"And you said that I was doing fine, so he'd have to work *really* hard to get me back?"

"Nope. I told him that you were a mess." Corey made indignant choking noises, but I ignored them. "He sounded devastated."

"He did?"

"*Of course* he did! The guy is completely in love with you, Corey!" I thought back to Tim's romantic gesture. "Obviously, he wants to fix things."

"But he dumped me and then publicly *lied* about us!"

"True. So here is my advice: You have to decide if you want to throw away your relationship because he panicked. I'm not saying what he did was right: It wasn't. I'm saying that the decision is yours."

"You really do suck at giving advice!" he groused. "You sound like a freaking fortune cookie."

I grinned and leaned back against the headboard of my bed. "Yep. So what did you tell him after you saw the text?"

"I—I haven't called him yet."

"*What!*" I squawked. "I'm hanging up now so that you can call him. Then I'd love to hear how it goes."

There was a slight pause before he said hesitantly, "Okay. I'll let you know how it goes."

My smile widened. "Sounds perfect to me."

Maybe I hadn't lost *all* my friends by taking a stand, especially since Corey definitely had the best reason to hate me. Then again, he was also probably the most forgiving person at Smith High School. And it had been an accident.

Yelling at Kenzie in his bedroom hadn't happened by mistake though.

Since I was already fully awake, I went downstairs and began rummaging around for omelet-making supplies—

cheese, onions, tomatoes, the works—in the hope that maybe some culinary groveling would lessen my grounding sentence.

I was in the midst of a chopping frenzy when my parents entered the kitchen.

"This is a nice surprise!" My mom eyed the items sprawled across the counter. "Any particular reason for it?"

"Corey called me this morning, and I think we're going to be okay."

"Oh, Janie! That's wonderful!"

My dad nodded less effusively. "That's great, Jane. I know how much his friendship means to you."

"Yep. Now I hope you're both hungry. Maybe later we could discuss the terms of my punishment?"

No such luck.

My dad was insisting that parents don't negotiate with teenagers, when Elle wandered into the kitchen.

"Jane, there's a guy at the door for you."

I rushed out of the room, only to pull up short when I saw Miles waiting on my porch. Leaning against the side of my house, he still looked perfectly suited to play Romeo. I half expected him to quote some verse and hand me a single perfect rose . . . but I couldn't help feeling oddly disappointed that it wasn't Scott.

"Hey, Jane. Sorry just to drop by unannounced, but Ms. Helsenberg mentioned having homework to give you during play rehearsal . . . and I figured you could use a friend right now."

I stared at him in confusion as I tried to figure out if he meant *Hey, let's take our relationship slow* or *You've been dumped.*

"Right. A friend."

"And I'd really like to be one to you."

"A friend," I repeated stupidly.

"Right."

I rubbed my temples and tried not to jump to conclusions. "As your friend, I think I should give you a heads-up. . . . Your 'it's not you, it's me' speech . . . it could use a little work."

He grinned wryly and then slung an arm around my shoulder. No sparks. Not even a tingle of awareness. "Oh no. It's definitely you."

I couldn't help laughing at the blunt way he put it, especially since I felt oddly relieved at the ease with which we had moved out of dating territory. *This* I could handle. "Fair enough. I still had a good time hanging out with you in Portland."

"Yeah, it was fun. We should do it again sometime—as friends. Catch a play or something."

"Sounds good to me."

We stood there for a moment as I tried to wrap my head around the fact that Miles inspired absolutely no desire in me to have his tongue in my mouth. The guy might be perfect, but he would never be my Romeo. And yeah, it stung to have him lose interest, although that was definitely preferable to him showing up and expecting another date.

"So . . . I'll see you around?"

He handed me the assignments with a wink. "See you later, Jane."

Leaving me stuck explaining to my parents that Miles was a friend (true) who had auditioned with me for the school musical (true) and only stopped by to be helpful (true, considering the way he brought over my assignments before he helpfully dumped me). I didn't get a break from the interrogation until my parents left for work and Elle finally accepted that I wouldn't be revealing any juicy gossip. She rolled her eyes, but left me alone to call Mrs. Blake and ask for another day off from Fiction Addiction. Which is why she missed out on hearing my excellent imitation of static when Mrs. Blake started asking questions about how my date went with Scott, before I tried to distract myself with my new assignments.

As far as diversions go, it was seriously lacking.

But I was still buried beneath a pile of handouts when I heard a tentative knock on my door.

Definitely not Elle and, since everyone else I knew was still in school, it left me without a list of likely candidates.

"Um . . . come in?"

A painfully familiar face peered into my room but entered no farther, as if too uncertain about her reception to cross the threshold.

Kenzie.

"Hey, Jane."

"What are you doing here?" I blurted out in disbelief. I hadn't expected to see Miles earlier that day, but even *that* was less bizarre than the notion that Kenzie would skip class for any reason. Let alone for me. "Shouldn't you be at school?"

"I snuck away during lunch. Logan dropped me off, but we don't really have that long to talk before I have to leave. I—I just wanted to see you."

"Really?" I couldn't prevent the sarcasm from leaking out even as every corpuscle in my body began screaming at me to patch things up. To apologize, if necessary. To accept any small crumb of affection if it could get us back to how we once were. "That's interesting. Since when? Because you sure as hell haven't made an effort in a long time."

Kenzie pushed the door open wider but didn't approach me. "Look, I get that you're mad at me. You made that really clear yesterday. And I should've been more supportive when the article came out, okay? I knew you would never intentionally hurt Corey, but his life was falling apart, and he needed me and . . . I'm sorry, Jane. I didn't know what to do."

I nodded slowly, but stopped when I realized that she wasn't finished.

"But the way you blasted us yesterday wasn't right either.

You can't emotionally dive-bomb somebody and then run away before they get a chance to defend themselves."

My stomach plummeted, and I braced myself for the worst.

"Okay, fine. What did you want to say?"

"I wanted to tell you that I know that I've been busy lately, and it *sucks*—for both of us—but I'm doing the best I can!"

I forced myself to remain sitting. "Kenzie, I get it. Trust me, I've been repeating the excuses for a long time now. AP History classes, tutoring, a boyfriend . . . that's a lot even before you add the sudden Internet fame. But we both know that you don't see me anymore. That's why somehow the invitations never extend to me!"

"That's ridiculous. I didn't invite you to Spencer's stupid party because *you wouldn't want to go!*"

Her words hung in the air, but before the uncomfortable silence could fully settle upon us, Kenzie continued in a softer tone.

"I only agreed to go because I thought Melanie might hit it off with Spencer, okay? And I feel guilty about how much time Logan spends with me instead of his best friend. But I haven't forgotten about you, Jane. You're my best friend."

I nodded weakly as her words settled warmly around me, easing the sharp ache that had taken up residence inside me for far too long. Maybe it was nerdy of me, but hearing her call me her best friend in the *present* tense . . . it made all the difference.

"I'm sorry if I've been dropping the ball lately. I can do better." She grinned, and suddenly everything seemed just a little bit brighter because she looked like herself once more. "Somehow, I'll work on it, okay? But if you ever feel unseen again, don't make up stupid excuses for me and then get mad when nothing changes. I'm not a mind reader, you know. You have to actually use those words you're so good at writing, and let me know when something is wrong. Preferably without blowing up in my face."

Somehow it hadn't occurred to me that she would want to know when we had a problem. I just assumed she would want me to handle stuff like party invitation–related insecurities on my own.

Maybe she had forgotten how to be a best friend, but it looked like I had too.

I pretended that required some deep consideration. "I think I can manage that."

"Good." Kenzie confidently entered the room and sprawled out next to me on the bed. "Now, we've got a limited amount of time and a lot of catching up to do. Want to fill me in on what I've missed?"

I laughed. "Remember the photographer Logan wanted to punch? Yeah, well, he kissed me. How's that for news?"

Kenzie very nearly skipped class by demanding all the details. As it was, she sprinted out to Logan's car only after he'd already honked twice.

And for the first time since Kenzie's YouTube video was posted, it felt like things were back to normal between us. That even if I never truly emerged from my sister's Notable shadow or Kenzie's own celebrity status, I wasn't Invisible— not to her.

Oddly enough, that was all the validation I really needed.

Especially when my cell phone started ringing.

"Are you back together or what?" I demanded after nearly dropping the phone in my excitement. "What did he say, Corey?"

"*Well*, he really did sound miserable without me."

"That is not news. Get to the good stuff, already!"

"He apologized for panicking and promised that it would never happen again. I guess his manager told him this could destroy his music career, and . . . well, he apologized."

"So are you together again?"

"We came to an understanding."

I groaned while he laughed at my obvious impatience. "Now you're just torturing me."

"You can take it. I told him that we need to have regularly scheduled Skype dates—not just random text messages—to make this relationship work long distance."

"That sounds like an excellent plan."

"And I said I couldn't hide with him. Full disclosure: Facebook profile included. He wants to officially come out during the interview Ellen's scheduled with the band."

"Wow, that's . . . huge."

"I know." Corey's voice lost some of its excitement. "It scares me. Not the interview, but the public reaction to it. At this point, I'm just praying that his manager isn't right about it destroying his career. About *me* destroying his career."

"What did Tim say about it?"

"That he talked it over with the guys, and they're behind the decision. No matter what happens."

"Then at least he's going into it knowing the risks."

"Yeah. He's incredible. My boyfriend is coming out on national television, and I'm worried about dealing with one football player. Pretty stupid, right?"

My voice took on an edge of steel. "No, it's not stupid. It's dangerous. You should have told me earlier that Alex wasn't leaving you alone. You always smile and pretend nothing affects you, and I honestly started believing you were impervious to his bullshit."

Corey laughed. "Yeah, not so much."

"Well, you have a whole support network behind you. Given my suspension, I'd rather not be the one to punch Alex next time, but I'm sure Logan would happily do the honors."

"No fighting necessary. Not when my parents can simply file their lawsuit. I didn't want one at first, but . . . well, if it continues, then I will."

"Good."

"I asked Tim to do me a favor."

"Yeah?"

"He's going to tell Ellen that he was outed when my good friend made a mistake. No medication involved. Although I still think we should make the guilty party pay."

"I really appreciate the public name-clearing, but that's enough. Let's forget the payback."

"*What?* Are you serious?"

"Nothing good can come from it. Best-case scenario, we screw up someone's life. I don't know about you, but I'm hoping we can just let karma do the zapping."

"Hmm." Corey didn't sound convinced. "Well, my parents think I should wait for the story to die down a little more before going back to school."

"That sounds smart."

"Yeah, too bad I'm already getting cabin fever. They keep checking up on me. It was nice at first, but now I'm getting sick of the interruptions."

"Dinner, Jane!" Elle hollered from downstairs.

I laughed. "I know exactly how you feel. And on that note, I'll talk to you later, okay?"

"Sure, but first . . . you know how I've told you to stand up for yourself?"

"Yeah, I remember hearing something about that a time or two *thousand*."

"I'm proud of you for doing it, even if it was to me. I guess we needed to clear the air. And judging by that ensemble you wore to my house, you definitely need me in your life."

"There was nothing wrong with my sweatpants/sweatshirt combination."

"Never wear anything with the word 'sweat' in public, Jane. Promise me."

"What about *sweat*er?" I challenged.

"The one exception."

Elle started hollering again.

"I have to go, Corey. Although, for the record, I need you in my life for a whole host of reasons that don't include fashion. I think I can handle that myself now. I'll see you later!"

Then I hurried downstairs to appease my family.

Chapter 33

I refused to let my two-day suspension scare me back into being a pushover.

And I saw no reason to hide that fact from everyone at Smith High School, starting with my outfit. Opening my closet, I barely glanced at the options before I grabbed my most comfortable jeans and a silky designer shirt from Kenzie.

Problem solved.

I pulled them on, and for the first time since I had been assigned to write an article for *The Smithsonian*, I didn't stress about it afterward. No second-guessing myself on something as insignificant as the selection of a freaking *shirt*. Leaving me free to obsess over questions that actually deserved my attention, like figuring out how to act on my feelings for Scott.

I had a thing for a cranky photographer.

It didn't even seem to matter that he was the anti-Romeo who was every bit as likely to dare me as he was to kiss me. That he was more likely to smirk than he was to smile. It didn't matter if he was annoying my friends, charming my nemesis, cringing at my singing, crashing my date, or meeting my family—he made me feel alive.

And I thought it was quite possible that I did the same for him.

Not Elle's geeky little sister. Not Mackenzie's best friend. Not Grammar Girl.

Me.

It was time for me to finish what I'd started, which was why I walked past Scott, who didn't even bother giving me a nod of recognition, straight up to Mr. Elliot's desk and stood there patiently until I had his full attention.

Of course, by that time I had everyone else's attention too. Well, except for Scott. He was staring at the computer screen in front of him as if he found it endlessly fascinating. But all of my other classmates were eyeing me appraisingly.

"Can I write fiction for the paper, Mr. Elliot?"

"You mean you don't already?" Brad sniggered. "That's what Timothy Goff is saying. Did you forget to take your meds today, Grammar Girl?"

I forced myself to ignore the jerk and concentrate solely on my teacher.

"Of course you can't, Smith. This is a *newspaper*."

I nodded. "So there is no way I could convince you to approve adding a page for short stories and poems?"

Mr. Elliot shook his head. "Not going to happen, Smith."

I paused for a moment, letting that sink in. "Well, okay then."

And surprisingly, it was okay. I had believed enough in my project to fight for it. To demand that he really consider what I had in mind. Sure, I wanted him to get onboard and tell me that it would breathe new life into *The Smithsonian,* but that just wasn't going to happen.

Which didn't mean I couldn't pursue my fiction writing anyway.

"I'm ready to step up," I informed Mr. Elliot, who looked rather confused by the sudden turn in the conversation.

"Ahem, that's good. I mean, *it's about time you did, Smith!*"

"I totally agree. Past time, actually. But for me to step up, you've got to do it too."

There was a collective gasp as everyone in the journalism classroom eyed Mr. Elliot warily.

"*How* dare *you*—" he began to bluster.

"We have some problems that only you can fix." I forced myself to continue looking him squarely in the eyes. "And I'm not going to continue copyediting if certain conditions aren't met. You've got to require everyone to learn at least the basics of grammar."

Brad crossed his arms smugly. "Isn't that your only contribution?"

"Subject-verb agreement, Brad. *They* don't *runs,* okay? *They run!*" I turned back to Mr. Elliot. "I don't care who gives the tutorial, but it's not going to be me."

"That's a tremendous waste of valuable class time," Mr. Elliot grumbled.

"No, it's not. Because when I refuse to edit—and I promise you, I'm not going to crack—then you'll have no one doing the grunt work. Unless *you* want to be stuck making all those corrections?"

We both knew the answer to that was a resounding *hell no.*

"I want a place at staff meetings and a voice in deciding which stories we pursue."

He nodded his consent, and Lisa Anne couldn't restrain herself any longer.

"She can't just *waltz* into a senior staff position! She—she's *Grammar Girl,* for crying out loud!"

"I *was* Grammar Girl," I corrected politely. "Now I'm chief editor. Deal with it."

The satisfaction I got from saying those simple words was so much better than the shove that had landed me with a suspension.

Apparently Mr. Shelder had a point with nonviolent conflict resolution. It could be quite gratifying on its own.

"But, Mr. Elliot, you can't possibly want her after what she did to—"

"You don't want to go there, Lisa Anne. Believe it or not, there are now several newspapers that might find my story rather interesting. Especially the part about how my article landed on the front page."

I had her and she knew it. Ms. Perfect wouldn't want anything to mess up her shot at Harvard or Yale. If I came forward accusing her of cruelly outing America's favorite rock star . . . that wouldn't impress the people in admissions. Especially if I had Timothy Goff and the rest of ReadySet backing me up.

She stared at me mutely before flouncing over to a computer and pounding on the keyboard as she typed.

She was probably writing a little death fiction of her own, but I suspected I was the one gasping for my last breath.

"One more thing." I paused, relishing the moment. For the first time I wished Scott was taking photos of me with his camera, because I wanted all the details of this perfectly preserved forever. "Since you refuse to allow fiction into the paper, I'm going to start a school publication of my own. And you're going to agree to be my advisor or I walk right now."

He stared at me in disbelief. "I don't really have the, uh, time for another project right now, Smith."

"You don't have the time to handle this paper without me. And trust me, I'm ready to take full responsibility for this project." I grinned. "I'm thinking of calling it *The Wordsmith*. But we can figure out those details later. Do we have a deal, Mr. Elliot?"

He sputtered momentarily, probably hoping that Lisa Anne would somehow throw him a lifeline out of this mess. But when no rescue appeared, his massive shoulders straightened, and he began speaking in his regular booming voice as if being blackmailed by his most timid student was a regular occurrence.

"Of course, Smith! You know I've always encouraged this kind of initiative in my students." He whistled for everyone's attention, not that he didn't already have it. "Everyone, *this* is what I'm talking about when I tell you to step up!"

I smiled, but being the focus of so many appraising stares only increased my need to make a quick escape. "On that note, I'm going to borrow your photographer. Temporarily."

Reaching out, I snagged Scott's camera off the table and didn't stop walking until I reached my hiding alcove in the school library. The place I always went when I needed to disappear. Except this time I had one seriously pissed-off photographer trailing behind me.

His unreadable green eyes studied me. "Give me back my camera."

My throat felt parched, and my stomach lurched. Talking to Mr. Elliot was nothing compared to dealing with Scott, but I held my ground.

"I fixed things with Corey," I blurted out.

"Great. I don't care. Give me my camera, Jane."

I continued as if he hadn't spoken. "Things are fine with Kenzie too. You know why?"

"Give. Me. The. Camera."

"I went to Corey's house yesterday and yelled at them because of you."

Scott crossed his arms. "Of course, so that's all my fault now too, right?"

"Hear me out, Scott. You're dead wrong about the whole tease thing, but you did say something in the car that rang true to me."

"Get to the point, or give me back my camera, Jane."

I took a deep breath. "You pointed out that my willingness to settle for so little was sad."

He didn't exactly look impressed. "Your point?"

"Shut up, Scott. This is hard enough already. I want you to know that I broke up with Miles."

He raised an eyebrow but didn't say anything.

"Well, okay, *technically* he broke up with me. Although I don't even know if the word 'breakup' applies, because we only went out once, and it's not like we were ever official."

I caught myself mid-ramble and forced myself back on topic before he could comment on it.

"Anyhow, Miles and I are just friends now. And I don't expect that you and I can have that because"—I gestured between us—"of all the, uh, tension. The article is finished, and I understand if you don't want to spend time with me, but . . . I'm not ready for this thing between us to end."

He shifted, and I knew he was going to say, *Sorry, not interested. I prefer girls who aren't neurotic kissing disasters.*

So I panicked.

"I jump to conclusions and love romance novels and compare myself with Elle and . . . you met her, she's the popular one. But I just thought—"

"Hand me the camera, Jane."

So that was it. No second chance for me.

At least I now had terrific material if I ever wanted to write a death by rejection.

I straightened my spine and told myself that it was his loss. If he couldn't look beyond a few of my flaws, then I deserved better anyway. That's what Kenzie, Corey, and Isobel would tell me. Chelsea would probably toss her blond hair and give me flirting advice while Sam handed me yet another condom. No matter how much his words hurt, I wasn't pathetically going to try persuading him to like me back.

Not when he obviously never felt that strongly about me in the first place.

So I handed him his camera and watched in silence as he

unscrewed the lens cap, briefly adjusted the settings, and then snapped a photo of me.

"What was that for?" I demanded.

"I wanted a photo of Jane Smith asking me out on a date."

"I didn't—"

"Yeah, you did."

It was mortifying enough that I had been rejected. I didn't need him rubbing it in.

"Okay, I did. But don't worry about it. I don't want things to be awkward in journalism class or—"

But I never finished my sentence because his lips connected with mine. This time I felt the sizzle in every part of my body, as I wrapped my arms around his neck and rose up on tiptoes. Only when the heroines on the covers of my romance novels did stuff like that, they never appeared to be struggling to maintain their balance.

Unlike me.

Then again, they also weren't able to use their wobbling as an excuse to press against their heroes even more tightly.

Not that I needed an excuse.

"So when is this date going to happen?" Scott asked, when we came up for air.

"Um—" I struggled to remember how to speak. It seemed so unimportant when his lips were within kissing distance. "I, uh, I'm grounded."

"You're grounded, huh?" He paused to consider this new development. "How long are you going to be under house arrest?"

"Just the next two weeks."

"That's too bad."

I stiffened momentarily, in case he said, *I'm not waiting that long for you, but this was fun. Let's do it again sometime;* then I ordered the stupid, insecure voice in my head to shut up and relaxed again. I trusted Scott. Even more importantly, I trusted my instincts too much to sabotage us over a few nerves.

"You know, I promised Mrs. Blake that I would bring in those photos of the two of you."

A grin spread across my face. "That's right. You did."

"So I might drop by while you're working."

"It's a bookstore. Everyone's welcome."

"Of course, I'd just be there to hand over the photos." The wicked glint in his eyes said otherwise.

"Of course."

"But I distinctly remember some parts of the bookstore being pretty secluded."

I laughed. "I'll have to reacquaint you with the memoir section."

"Great, I'd love to read all about the lives of—"

"Scott?" I interrupted.

"Yeah?"

"Can we go back to the part where you were kissing me?"

"Definitely."

And that's exactly what we did.

Wonder what's on ReadySet's Timothy Goff's playlist?

OK Go: "Maybe, This Time"
I love the line about the art of a good excuse. I tend to find myself repeating that when I catch myself stalling instead of doing some songwriting of my own.

Just Jack: "Starz in Their Eyes"
This song captures the very real pressures of a music career brilliantly. Don't get me wrong: This is still my dream job. But being tailed everywhere by tabloid reporters who are hoping to watch us crash and burn . . . yeah, that never becomes easier.

The Kooks: "She Moves in Her Own Way"
This song reminds me of Corey O'Neal. Because he would totally come to one of our shows just to hear about my day.

She & Him: "Black Hole"
Okay, this is how I usually feel after spending too much time on the road. Luckily, the guys make me take a break every time I start approaching a burnout.

Sleepercar: "Stumble In"
Whenever I hear this song I want to stare out the window of our tour bus and watch the landscape change until I fall asleep.

Badly Drawn Boy: "The Shining"
There is something about this song that makes me feel wonderfully insignificant. For me, it's the musical equivalent of looking at the Grand Canyon.

Ben Folds featuring Regina Spektor: "You Don't Know Me"
As much as I love my fans, there are times when I find myself wanting to point out that memorizing a few facts about my life doesn't mean they know me. At all.

Neon Trees: "Everybody Talks"
Great beat. Excellent pacing. It's a good time. Need I say more?

Foster the People: "Pumped Up Kicks"
I really like the contrast between the dark threat of violence in the lyrics and the cheerful beat that underlies the song. It's both disconcerting and engrossing.

Ingrid Michaelson: "The Way I Am"
I think this song is incredibly romantic. At the end of the day, all that anyone can hope for is to find someone who will accept and love them for who they are—imperfections included.

Chelsea Halloway is Smith High's queen bee, but all that's about to change in *Notable,* available this November.

Chapter 1

It was complete and total bullshit.

Oh sure, in the movies, the geeky girl gets the guy, but let's all get real for a second: High school doesn't actually work like that. No way. The absurdly sweet (yet popular) guy might continue being tutored by the geek, but he also keeps making out with his beautiful ex-girlfriend until they decide to give their relationship another shot.

That's how it *should* have worked, but apparently my good luck had run out a long time ago.

Because not only did my perfect hockey-captain ex-boyfriend Logan Beckett *reject me*, Chelsea Halloway, but he then started dating the most awkward girl at our high school. Actually, thanks to an embarrassing YouTube video, the geek accidentally raised her profile beyond the hallways of Smith High School until she became best known as America's Most Awkward Girl.

Yet he still chose *her* over *me*.

Did I mention that all of this was after I had poured my heart out to him? After I had groveled for breaking up with him the first time? After I had put everything—including my self-respect—on the line?

And what did I get for all my trouble? A big, fat rejection.

Maybe I had miscalculated by asking him to reconsider

our relationship at his best friend Spencer's party, considering that it was also the location of our breakup. But part of me thought that if we stood together in the gazebo, overlooking the fountain, and kissed one more time, he would realize that we were meant to be together.

I thought he would see that losing him was still hurting me. That regardless of the rumors that had circulated our middle school in the wake of our breakup (mainly that I was ecstatic to have traded Logan in for a more popular high school boy), I'd been a wreck over our split.

I hoped confessing everything would bring us back together.

But now I was finding out firsthand that it hurt even more to be dumped than it does to do the dumping.

Still, I forced myself to keep it together. Even when I saw Logan gently leading geeky Mackenzie Wellesley to his car, smiling at her with transparent affection in a way I didn't think he ever once did with me, I pretended I was fine.

I did just what everyone expected of me.

I tossed my long, shiny, blond hair over my shoulder, sauntered over to the nearest, hottest, available guy, and flirted shamelessly. All the while fighting to keep my voice even and my eyes dry. A girl has to keep up appearances, especially if she wants to maintain her status as the most popular girl at school. So I batted my baby blues at some guy whose name I didn't bother to learn before making my getaway.

My mom always instructed me that it was best to leave them wanting more.

Of course, she had said that in the context of my dance recitals, but it applied to flirting too. In both cases, it takes a lot of practice to hide sweat, nerves, and performance anxiety, but if you let any of it show, it kills the magic. It was a sad testament to my life that I had spent enough time faking happiness that I could flirt while replaying exactly how it felt to have Logan's lips pressed against mine when I rose up on tiptoes and kissed him—a soaring hope that was dashed when he looked at me with nothing more than pity.

But fleeing the party in tears wasn't an option for me.

I couldn't cry over the fact that my perfect ex-boyfriend had shut me down for some loser brainiac. I couldn't spend hours staring at the photos of us drinking hot chocolate at the ice-skating rink and smiling at the camera. I couldn't even rant about the cosmic unfairness of realizing that I had never gotten over my first love only to find out that he had *definitely* gotten over me.

Oh no.

I couldn't do any of that at home.

Because when I pulled into my driveway, I had something much worse waiting for me by the door. My dad's suitcase. I have his teaching schedule memorized, and I knew for a fact that there were no upcoming academic conferences scribbled on the kitchen calendar for *months*. There was no logical reason for his luggage to be slumped against one of our enormous ceramic flowerpots.

That's how I knew exactly what I was about to walk in on: The divorce exit walk of blame.

Not just a trial separation. Not a temporary experiment. Not something that would blow over eventually, like it always did.

And I was right: He was leaving.

I just didn't realize when I stood in the driveway, numbly staring at my dad's suitcase, that I was going to be forced into relocating too.

You would think that losing both Logan and my father in one night would forever earn it the dubious honor of being the very worst evening of my life. It should have been my all-time low. Rock-freaking-bottom.

But it wasn't.

It's funny how being hunted down by a group of certifiable bad guys in a third-world country can change a girl's perspective on what constitutes a tragedy. Not *ha ha* funny, *obviously*. It's more of a *laughing is my only alternative to disintegrating into a million pieces* type of funny. When your every decision is a matter of life or death, even truly ridiculous amounts of personal drama fade into insignificance.

Eat or be eaten.

Hunt or be hunted.

Hide or . . . wind up with a gun aimed at your head.

I found that out the hard way.